MONEY, BLOOD

and

CONSCIENCE

DAVID STEINMAN

FREE PLANET
PUBLISHING

With the exception of Meles Zenawi and other public figures, all
characters appearing in this work are fictitious. Any resemblance to
other real persons, living or dead, is purely coincidental. Some historic
events and their dates have been altered for dramatic purposes.
The depiction of the terror and torture inflicted on Ethiopia's people by
their dictatorship is, unfortunately, all too real.

Free Planet Publishing
New York, NY

First Edition, Hardcover

ISBN-13: 978-0692854174

MoneyBloodAndConscience.com

This book was produced and published with the guidance of Social
Motion Publishing, a benefit corporation that specializes in social-
impact books. For more information, check out their website at
SocialMotionPublishing.com.

*To the brave Ethiopian men and women
who stood up for freedom. And to my inspiring parents.*

Buddy Schwartz's Ethiopia

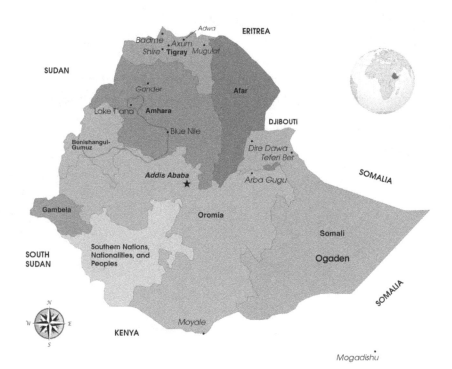

BOOK 1

THE BLACK SEDAN drove slowly up a palm-lined Beverly Hills street, its funereal appearance out of place in the bright sunshine. It was August 20, 2012.

Few people were outside on the broiling afternoon. The great homes' histories and ghosts of dead movie stars didn't interest the car's driver, a middle-aged Ethiopian man in a suit. Their shrubbery and lawns did. How did these rich Americans keep them green despite the drought afflicting Los Angeles? When he was a boy, he had to walk six kilometers for water.

The car turned onto Crestview Drive and stopped in front of a large, Tudor-style mansion. With its gables and bay windows, it might have been plucked from the sixteenth century if not for the clean bricks.

The driver looked for a number on the house to make sure he had the right address. There it was, 216, on a bronze plaque beside the front door. He lowered all the windows so the car wouldn't be too hot when he returned to it. Unlike his own neighborhood on the other side of Los Angeles, there was no need to worry about a break-in here.

The Ethiopian got out of the car and checked his reflection in its window to see if his tie was straight. His fine, Semitic features and tawny complexion suggested the northern part of his country.

It was too hot to linger. Deciding he looked pretty fit for a man in his forties, and proud he had wound up in a job that required a suit—in America, no less—he strolled up the front walk.

The well-tended roses reminded him of his last posting in India. He tried to figure out the association and recalled the rosewater they put in the milk there. He had a good memory, a faculty that served him well as an intelligence agent. There were so many names, faces and numbers to remember. Few Ethiopians lived in India—that government had too many poor of its own to be generous with visas. But there were lots of Ethiopians in America, and most of them hated his employer. It was hard to keep track of them, his memory notwithstanding. It was a good thing the files were computerized now.

He pushed the doorbell and heard a deep chime. *Hadish*, he thought in his native Tigrinya—strange—how the Indians had come to his country and dominated the world rose market with their gigantic plantations. He'd been assigned overseas by then, but he imagined the rose farms were very beautiful. He hoped to see one someday.

It was the maid's day off. In the kitchen, Hanna Schwartz, an attractive Ethiopian woman of nearly fifty, seasoned two steaks herself. On hers went the ground mixture of red chili peppers, garlic, ginger and basil her people called *berbere*. Her American husband's was graced with butter and garlic. Despite the pleasant chore, her large, expressive eyes hinted at a painful past.

A countertop TV played *Oprah*. Next to it sat an expensive, copper espresso machine, a birthday gift from her husband.

The kitchen was already furnished when she had arrived six years earlier, but she liked its cozy, Dutch country decor. The appliances were big, more suited for a hotel kitchen than a home. Her husband used to do a lot of entertaining. It had taken her a long time to feel comfortable buying the delicacies that filled the cabinets.

She heard the doorbell and peered out the window. The black car in the driveway puzzled her. It wouldn't belong to her husband's friends or business associates. They drove Jaguars, Mercedes and Porsches.

Then she saw the diplomatic license plate.

"Buddy!" she called in a soft, slightly lisping accent.

Across the hall, in an oak-paneled study lined with bookshelves and adorned with entertainment industry awards, her husband looked up from his computer. Buddy Schwartz was a Jewish, highly successful television producer in his early sixties. Soft-spoken and accustomed to power, he was a sensitive man who was still a writer at heart. He didn't like to be disturbed when he worked, and the financial report he read was irritatingly difficult to understand. But he could tell from her voice something was amiss.

They met in the front hall. She hesitated at the door. He opened it himself.

"Mr. Schwartz?"

"Yes?"

"I am Colonel Kabede. From the Ethiopian consulate."

"Please come in. This is my wife, Hanna."

The colonel gave her a practiced smile and greeted her in the Arabic-sounding Tigrinya they both spoke.

"He's gone?" Buddy asked.

Colonel Kabede nodded.

"I will bring coffee," Hanna said. She returned to the kitchen to prepare it.

Buddy led the colonel into the living room. Museum-quality paintings hung on the walls. Open curtains presented a view of a tennis court bordered by peach and red hibiscus. He offered Kebede an armchair and sat on a sofa.

"I am very sorry," he said. "I hope he didn't suffer."

"He had the highest regard for you."

"Thank you."

"We are trying to make sense of the situation," the colonel explained. "And since you were one of his last visitors, we wanted to get your impression."

"He looked perfectly healthy to me. What did the doctors say?"

"A blood infection. Leading to multiple organ failure."

Following the Ethiopian tradition of serving coffee in threes, Hanna entered with a trio of steaming cups that scented the room with their rich aroma. The colonel's was salted according to their country's custom. She gave Buddy his sugared one.

"Thank you, sweetie." The intimate term warned Kabede she was under his protection.

Buddy took a sip and placed his cup on a coaster on an antique coffee table. Colonel Kabede did likewise.

Hanna curled up beside her husband on the sofa. He put his arm around her. There was a silver-framed photo on the coffee table of him with former President Clinton. Both men grinned big, American smiles.

"A blood infection..." Buddy mused in a dismayed tone.

Glancing sideways, she could still, after all these years, admire his broad, almost-handsome face with its high, intelligent forehead, strong jaw and soulful, brown eyes. It was his eyes she'd especially noticed the first time they'd met. He must be kind, she had thought.

"It seems like only yesterday." Buddy kicked back on the couch. He stretched his long legs, his self-assurance helping her relax. "God, it had to be how many years ago?"

Twenty-six years earlier, when the Southern California entertainment industry was still awash with drugs, fearless sex and easy money, before the HIV virus and rescission of the film tax credit humbled it, the house was newly built and the roses not yet planted. With the earnings from his first hit series, Buddy had purchased a smaller home on the site, torn it down and built his own. It was a lot of house for someone still in his thirties.

The downstairs was furnished in Traditional style. Nearly everything on the upper floor, including his bedroom, was white except for the Impressionist paintings he had bought at Sotheby's after his second series also proved successful.

He used his bedroom as a second office. And in this bedroom, on a lovely Southern California day in 1986, he sat, recently divorced, on the edge of a king-sized bed that had already hosted a parade of sexual partners. Absentmindedly, he gazed out the window to the familiar sound of his childhood friend and producing partner, Alan Goldstein, sniffing cocaine off a glass end table.

"TV Producers of the Year," Alan said reverently. He was a brassy, well-dressed, thirty-six-year-old man—the same age as Buddy. They'd been in grade school together. Alan handled the numbers and the nuts-and-bolts production details while Buddy focused on the creative side.

His partner had another useful talent. Television production took a lot of saying "no" to people. Buddy disliked confrontation. Alan seemed to thrive on it.

On the glass table, surrounded by a circle of cocaine, stood a crystal "People's Choice Awards" statuette. Alan loudly sniffed part of the circle with a rolled-up one-hundred-dollar bill.

"We did it," he proclaimed. He fell back in his chair with a satisfied air and contemplated the award.

Buddy, unimpressed, watched a bird on a branch outside his bedroom window. What was it was thinking? Food, he supposed. Temperature? Territory? It was smarter than anyone realized, he decided.

Alan offered the rolled-up bill. Buddy shook his head.

"We should celebrate," Alan insisted, disappointed his good mood was unshared. "We're the biggest in Hollywood now."

"One of the biggest."

Alan ticked the titles off on his fingers. "*Texas Lovin'*. *Cheerleader Express*. *Surf Squad*. Three out of the top ten by revenue. Nobody's bigger." He offered the rolled-up bill again. "You sure?"

Buddy waved it away.

"What?" Alan asked with genuine concern.

"When I was a kid, I wanted to be somebody who helped people," Buddy mused. His swimming pool glittered in the sun. "A scientist. An explorer. Maybe a senator. Instead, I'm making junk."

"You're pulling in eighteen million a year." Alan's coke-numbed lips slurred the Bronx accent he shared with Buddy. "You give three hundred and seven people a paycheck every Friday. You're practically bankrolling the California Democratic Party. You give a ton of money to charity. That's helping people."

A palm frond drifted in the pool. "If I died tomorrow, what would my epitaph be?" Buddy asked moodily. "Executive Producer of *Surf Squad*?"

"*Surf Squad's* a great show."

Bored, Buddy picked up the remote control and turned on the television. A game show was on.

"People are out there curing cancer," he said ruefully. On the show, a couple had won a Caribbean holiday. "Running for president. Even being a cop or a fireman, you're helping people. Saving lives." The couple on television hugged with exaggerated joy at the direction of some off-stage assistant director. Buddy gave the television a baleful look. "And I've helped create this shitty culture."

"Why don't you get married again if you're so restless?" Alan teased. He sniffled noisily in a manner that would be vulgar anywhere except in cocaine culture. "Have a kid or something."

That was a sore topic. Buddy's ex-wife had taken him to the cleaners in the divorce settlement. He could afford it, but the unfairness still rankled.

"With who? Another bimbo who wants to be on TV?" Buddy stared into space, lost in thought. The game show gave way to a Feed the Children ad. "You know," he finally added. "Between my ex-wife and all the others, I can't remember a single one ever just asking me, 'How are you?' I mean, is that all there is? More money? More drugs? More women?"

"Little Mikael doesn't know where his next meal will come from—" the commercial intoned mournfully.

A sad, brown-skinned boy stared out from the television at Buddy.

6

"They ought to have the kid talk directly to the audience," Buddy said to no one in particular. "Tell them himself what his life is like. Even if they have to subtitle it."

"Please help Mikael and thousands of children like him live—" With a final appeal to call a phone number displayed on the screen, the commercial ended.

"Thirty seconds? You can't tell that story with a thirty-second spot."

Miami Vice started. Its pounding theme song promised action to come.

"I ought to do a documentary," Buddy said. "Something serious."

"A documentary? About what?"

"Maybe the famine in Africa."

Alan looked at him as if he had gone crazy.

"It would be an adventure," Buddy persisted. "You don't think I've got the guts?"

"You don't start with nothing and wind up on top in Hollywood without having guts. Just don't do your thing, okay?"

"What thing?"

"The thing where you get all obsessed and everything."

"You'd come with me?"

Alan gave him a weary look. "You're kidding, right?"

"Maybe not," Buddy said. "Would you come?"

Alan cradled the back of his head with his hands. "Hey," he reminded Buddy, "who had your back when they tried to take the go-cart?"

Youthful memories clicked through Buddy's mind. He could still see them, twelve, and Buddy's younger brother, Steve, then a wide-eyed ten-year-old, on the Bronx's Tremont Avenue with an illegal go-cart they'd built. A couple of older kids, tough types, had tried to take it away from them. Alan had jumped on the biggest kid from behind and jerked him backwards onto the ground like one of the muggers who haunted their neighborhood.

Buddy remembered the day in high school when Alan excitedly pulled out of a shopping bag the 16mm movie camera he had

7

bought in a pawn shop. How they'd opened it on his mother's kitchen table and tried to figure out how it worked. The years after college when they were trying to break into the business, waiting for the phone to ring in a one-bedroom apartment on Sunset that smelled of cats from the last occupant. They'd sat on the bed because every chair was piled high with scripts. It was eight years before a phone call from Paramount Television informed them their first show was a hit.

Buddy compared Alan's hand-stitched, Italian suit to his own jeans, sneakers and the cashmere sweater he wore indoors for the air conditioning. He sure dresses better than when we were back on Tremont Avenue, he thought.

Alan melodramatically thrust his hand out to display a scar.

"Who got this when that crooked union guy tried to shake us down, and we threw him out?" Actually, it had been Alan who'd done most of the throwing with Buddy helping the best he could. "Who's been with you every step of the way?" He sniffed more of the cocaine. "And you want to know if I'm going to Africa with you?" He chuckled and finished the circle. "Are you out of your fucking mind? No way I'm going to Africa."

Alan took a handkerchief from his well-tailored jacket and wiped his nose. "You're doing your thing," he declared accusingly.

"I'm not doing my thing."

"You're doing your thing."

"Yeah," Buddy admitted. "I'm doing my thing."

Chapter Two

"IT'S GETTING HILLY now," Buddy yelled over the noise of the Cessna's engine. "Is this TPLF territory?"

It was 1987, almost a year later. Sitting beside him in the cockpit, the Kenyan pilot he'd chartered in Khartoum nodded. The pilot had once flown for Ethiopian Airlines where he'd endured enough abuse to sour him forever against the Marxist government that owned it. His current gig with Kenyan Aviation wasn't piloting a 737 in a snappy uniform that impressed the ladies. But at least he was flying again. He'd seen Westerners like Buddy before. A bunch of naive do-gooders.

When they had first approached Ethiopia from Sudan, the arid earth streaking by under the plane was only occasionally punctuated by brush or an animal skeleton. But after they'd traveled east for a couple of hours, the pilot had increased their altitude to climb over the Ethiopian plateau. The Nubian Desert's sand and stones had turned to dry grass and scraggly trees. Striking, red hills cropped up. In the valleys, the round, thatched roofs of mud huts dotted yellow plots of sorghum and millet.

There, the Marxist dictatorship the pilot so resented was in a life-and-death struggle with the Tigrayan People's Liberation Front, or TPLF, the student-led rebel movement that was Buddy's host. The group controlled much of Ethiopia's hunger-stricken north.

Behind Buddy in the plane slept Cal, his cameraman, and the sound technician, Meir. Their equipment was strapped down under nets. The two weathered, British expats, East Africa veterans, had been hired through a friend of a friend at a Nairobi news agency. The taciturn pilot didn't have much to say, and Buddy wished they'd wake up so he'd have someone to chat with.

He tapped Cal's arm. "You want to get something out the window?"

Cal wore a decrepit vest with innumerable pockets. He woke and glanced out the window. "We can use stock footage," he mumbled and closed his eyes again.

"Sure is dry," Buddy remarked to the pilot. Morbidly, he imagined his mother back in New York learning the plane had crashed. He pictured Alan telling mourners at his funeral he had warned him to forget the whole crazy project.

His thoughts turned to his ex-wife. It had been a fairly standard Hollywood marriage between a high-powered producer and a gorgeous starlet. The inevitable divorce had cost him seven million dollars and sold a few extra copies of the *Enquirer*. Older and wiser now, he'd learned seven million lessons that good looks were not enough. Even four years later, the hurt look on her face when he'd blurted out he didn't love her still gnawed at him. Momentarily forgetting the bitter legal wrangling that had ensued, he thought guiltily he could have been nicer. He hadn't loved any of his girlfriends, either.

An hour later, the Cessna bumpily landed on a dirt airstrip in Tigray Province in the northern Ethiopian highlands. They'd been advised to arrive near sundown, when the danger of an air attack had subsided, but it was still light. The agreeable, dry weather was typical of Tigray. Parched scrubland and hills extended in every direction. A far-off mountain range formed a scenic backdrop.

From his research, Buddy knew even further to the north was an important TPLF ally, the breakaway province of Eritrea. The Tigrayans sought to capture Ethiopia's capital, Addis Ababa, to the south, and conquer the rest of the country. But the Eritreans fought for a different objective—independence for their 761-mile-long strip of coastline along the upper rim of Africa's Horn and the Red Sea.

Eritrea's hardy, resilient fighters had opened up a valuable, second front in the war. It was an open secret that the coalition of the two guerrilla armies, the Tigrayans' TPLF and the Eritrean People's Liberation Front, was funded by the CIA. The American president, a conservative, supported anti-Communist movements around the globe.

The pilot opened the plane's door and turned to help his passenger disembark.

"I'm fine." Buddy backed down the plane's ladder. The wind carried the odor of death, sweat, excrement and burning wood. Faint wailing floated on the unpleasant breeze.

The airstrip was defended by low, sandbag bunkers from which ugly, black machine gun barrels protruded. Sinewy Ethiopians in brown shirts and shorts, some with wild Afros, crouched under spreading acacia trees with AK-47s in their hands. Guns made Buddy nervous, and he had never seen so many at one time. Everybody looked so young. Where were the adults?

Hanna, only twenty-two and slim in a khaki shirt, trousers and a captured officer's cap, stepped out from under a tree. "Mr. Schwartz?" She mispronounced his name with her soft lisp and offered a firm handshake. "I'm Lieutenant Ashete. Public Affairs Officer for the TPLF."

Her startling beauty reminded him of a bust of Nefertiti he had once seen in a Berlin museum. Doelike eyes, set in a blushing, copper face, shone with humanity. She seemed more confident around Westerners than the other Africans he had met so far on the trip, and he guessed at a childhood spent among sophisticated people. A sleeping gown that would double, if needed, as a burial shroud was wrapped around her neck like an oversized scarf.

"Thanks for helping arrange this," he said, hiding his surprise. "And please call me Buddy."

A camouflaged Nissan pickup truck was parked under a tree. Branches were tied to its roof and a 50-caliber machine gun was mounted in its bed. Its driver watched them with his rifle laid across the dashboard.

"Did you have a good flight?" Hanna asked politely as they walked toward the Nissan.

"We were grounded for a long time in Khartoum before we could make the transfer." He surreptitiously looked her over again. An electric tension gripped him. The same thing had happened when he'd met his former wife. Get it together, he told himself. You've got a job to do.

"Your first name's Hanna, isn't it? Is it all right if I call you Hanna?"

"Yes. Would you like to rest before we begin?"

He shook his head.

The soldiers threw a camouflage net over the Cessna and everyone waited in the shade of the acacia trees until sunset began. The pilot stayed with the plane while Buddy left with Hanna in the Nissan for a tour of the refugee camp. Cal and Meir hunched in the truck's bed beside the machine gun.

A mile beyond the airstrip began a gray sea of hovels made of recycled, burlap grain bags stretched over branch frames. The tent city included many grass huts and housed thirty thousand Tigrayans. Divided into sections by unpaved roads, it was one in an archipelago of feeding centers where people from remote, drought-ruined villages turned up daily in desperate search of food.

Hundreds of pairs of eyes followed the slowly moving pickup then lapsed back into indifference. With sundown near, those who had gotten a chance to settle in, still thin and weak from lingering malnutrition, rested, talked or cooked in a listless manner. Here and there, a mother or father in used Western clothes whose cheerful colors mocked their predicament sat dejectedly in front of a tent. Wordlessly mourning a son, daughter or parent who hadn't made it, their slumped shoulders and downcast faces were testaments to unspeakable grief. Sympathizers squatted near them and stared at the ground, unable to find words of comfort suitable for such monumental loss.

"We are responsible for the people here," Hanna explained. The light was fading, but she still checked the sky for enemy aircraft. "And the rains did not come this season."

"What about the US and Europe?"

"They give us something. But, as you see, it is not enough. More than two hundred people die every day." She took off her cap to wipe her brow, revealing the short haircut favored by the TPLF's female fighters to contend with lice and a lack of water. It gave her a boyish appearance. "Many of the dead are children."

They came to the end of one rutted lane. In an open field, new arrivals sat helplessly on the bare earth. They had covered their heads with old tarps, blankets or robes to create private spaces where they could hide their misery and humiliation.

Hanna pointed. Far behind the new arrivals, tiny figures cast long shadows on the bleak horizon. "More are coming."

A well-thumbed book lay on the truck's console.

"*Principles of Entrepreneurship*?"

"I have an idea for a business after we win the war," Hanna confided. "The tourists will come, and we will take them to different restaurants where they can try the food from all the different regions of Ethiopia. I will name it, 'Tasting Tours of Ethiopia.' What do you think?"

Tourists with people starving everywhere? "Just what they need," Buddy said.

Hanna's confused look suggested she didn't understand sarcasm. "I brought my textbooks when I went into the bush. My father was a professor of English at Addis Ababa University."

"Does he still teach?"

"The Derg executed him during the Red Terror."

"I'm sorry."

From the reading he had done, Buddy knew the Derg was another name for the military dictatorship in Addis Ababa—the TPLF's enemy. Its leader was Colonel Mengistu, a name that would send chills down Ethiopians' spines for generations to come.

Sometimes known as The Butcher, sometimes as The Black Stalin, Mengistu, despite a reputation for insubordination, had risen through the army's ranks to emerge as the power behind the scenes in the 1974 overthrow of the 2,500-year-old Ethiopian monarchy. Led by the elderly Emperor Haile Selassie, the monarchy had been intertwined with Ethiopia's history and culture since time immemorial.

The class distinctions of Ethiopia's antiquated, semi-feudal system reminded Mengistu of the racial discrimination he'd experienced during a six-month military training course in America. After seizing authority, he'd passionately avowed at a meeting with his fellow Derg members at the Addis Ababa Fourth Division headquarters, "In this country, some aristocratic families automatically categorize persons with dark skin, thick lips and kinky hair as slaves. Let it be clear to everybody that I shall soon make these ignoramuses stoop and grind corn!"

Mengistu had summoned Addis Ababa's population to watch him smash bottles of pig's blood to symbolize what he wanted done to the "traitors." Then, with an uncanny sense of what Ethiopians called *aradanat*—street smarts—he'd ruthlessly set about implementing his vision.

First to die were his former commanders who had elevated him from obscurity. They'd awakened to find their homes surrounded by heavily armed Mengistu loyalists and were killed in shootouts or summarily executed. Next to be shot were fifty-nine former imperial ministers and officials. The defiant patriarch of the Ethiopian Orthodox Church, *Abuna* Theophilos, was strangled with electric wire.

The Butcher smothered the ailing Haile Selassie to death with his own hands and hid the emperor's corpse. He'd been broadcasting on television old newsreels of Selassie feeding his pet lions spliced together with film clips from the famine to make the public believe their Emperor was indifferent to his starving people. But hunger under the Derg would be much worse. The massacre of many more former nobles and bureaucrats followed.

Finally, assisted by his Soviet and East German advisers, Mengistu had turned on the general population. His notorious "Red Terror" that claimed Hanna's father saw more than one hundred "exploiters of the people and counter-revolutionaries" executed daily. Each dawn found students, suspected rebel collaborators and other opponents hanged from lampposts. The jails and torture centers overflowed. Hyenas and jackals feasted in the gutters of Addis Ababa's suburbs on the one thousand children Mengistu slaughtered. Families paid the five hundred *birr* "wasted bullet" tax to redeem the bodies of their murdered relatives.

Mengistu's killing methods ranged from simple executions and assassinations—many committed himself to set a good example—to war and genocide by starvation. No one knew the real total, but estimates of the number of the Derg's victims ranged from half a million to over two million.

With all real and imagined opposition dead or on the run and his terroristic stranglehold on the population secured behind a smokescreen of Marxist rhetoric, Mengistu now presided over the second-largest army in sub-Saharan Africa.

This was the foe the students of the TPLF had vowed to destroy.

"Almost all of us here have stories like mine," Hanna continued. "That is why we fight for a new Ethiopia." She carefully recited the slogans. "With unity and human rights and economic development." She pointed at a tent. "There is the clinic for the babies." The driver, familiar with the VIP routine, shifted gear and they lurched toward it.

Some of the refugees they had seen earlier came into view. Three young men and a girl dragged a skeletal man—their father or grandfather, perhaps—on a litter made of branches. Every few steps, they stopped and whisked flies from his face. Maybe this elder had given up his food ration on the long journey so the young ones could survive. Further on, a mother tried to quiet an inconsolable child. One woman held a dead baby so thin it looked like a large, featherless bird.

"They have nothing," Hanna said.

15

In a makeshift cemetery, no headstones dignified the rows of mounds. Grim volunteers sweated from exertion as they dug graves in the pitiless soil. Six corpses were wrapped in colorful blankets. Two were long and the others were short.

"Get that," Buddy ordered Cal. The video camera whined.

An elderly Ethiopian man leaned on a stick to shuffle over to the Nissan. Despair was in his rheumy eyes. Smallpox scars pitted his gray-bearded face. His odor assailed Buddy.

He held out an open palm.

"Many others will ask you," Hanna warned.

"I can't say no to him." Buddy took out his wallet and gave him some money.

Painfully, the old man tried to kneel in gratitude. Buddy opened the Nissan's door and gently stopped him.

"Come on, don't do that," he said, embarrassed.

The man grasped both of Buddy's forearms and said something in an urgent voice.

"What does he want?"

"He is telling you what happened to his family."

"Yes, it is very difficult to see," Hanna said as they left. "But after we have liberated the country, our movement will help every Ethiopian."

They wheeled up to a large, white tent stenciled with Tigrinya's Hebraic-looking script. Its open entrance exposed an Ethiopian nurse weighing an emaciated baby on a battered scale. A line of mothers in stained shawls clutched sick and dying infants.

"When we win the war, all this suffering will end," Hanna promised. "Now I will take you to a feeding tent."

"You're from the capital?" Buddy asked as they bounced over the stony terrain.

"My father was Tigrayan and my mother is Amhara from Addis Ababa. The people here are Tigrayan."

At the foot of a rocky outcropping rested what looked like a black dummy.

"What was that?"

"That is nothing. Here is a feeding tent."

"Go back. I want to see what it was."

"It is not on the program."

"I want to check it out."

Hanna reluctantly gave the driver an order. The pickup turned and proceeded toward the strange object.

It was a half-charred corpse with its hands tied. A tattered shirt, a sandal, a ballpoint pen and scattered cigarettes littered the ground. Three vultures hopped on and off the body with a single flap of their wings and pecked at it.

Hanna unemotionally regarded the blackened remains. "He was a traitor."

"I want to get this," Buddy instructed Cal.

"I am sorry," Hanna said. "Filming it is not permitted."

"We agreed I would have full cooperation."

"This is not about our work to feed the people."

Buddy fought the desire to please this beautiful woman. "If I'm not going to have cooperation, I can't do this project."

"I have to get permission."

"Then get permission."

With the disagreement hanging in the air, they finished the tour in a restrained tone.

The Nissan finally deposited Buddy and his crew at a camp set up for them under camouflaged canopies. Their fatigue made the canvas cots hung with mosquito nets feel like downy mattresses.

Soon, all three men were asleep.

The snarls of two animals, maybe dogs or baboons, fighting viciously outside his tent woke Buddy. Moonlight streamed through the tent's opening. Meir slept nearby. Cal's cot was empty.

The fighting abruptly ceased. There was the faint wailing Buddy had heard before. He put on his pants and shoes and went outside.

The evening sky held more stars than he had ever seen. Cal sat in a camp chair with a beer and contemplated the mountain range's dim silhouette. A servant lay on a blanket near a campfire.

"Where'd you get the beer?"

Hal pointed to the servant. Buddy used hand gestures to imitate drinking. In the firelight, the servant's face brightened with comprehension. He rose, extracted a beer bottle from a plastic cooler, opened it and gave it to him.

"*Yekenyeley*," Buddy thanked him, proud to have learned a few phrases. He felt the glass bottle. "I guess it would've been too much to hope it'd be cold," he said to Cal and took a swig.

The servant poured some hot water from a kettle suspended over the campfire into a basin and set it on a flat rock. He placed a towel beside it and pantomimed for Buddy to wash.

Hal eyed the basin suspiciously. "Be careful you don't get any of that in your mouth."

"It's boiled, right?"

Hal shrugged.

Headlights glimmered in the distance. They recognized Hanna's truck when it got closer. The Nissan screeched to a halt.

"I will bring you to meet our commander, Meles Zenawi," she said to Buddy.

"I need to get the crew together."

"No filming. Only you, to talk."

"I thought I'd interview him."

Hanna shook her head.

"I have to get some stuff cleared up," Buddy told Cal.

"See if you can score us some real booze."

"I'll get dressed," Buddy said to Hanna.

"Meles is not his real name," she explained as they drove along a well-beaten trail, following the Ethiopian habit of calling people by their forenames. "He took the name of a classmate who was killed by the Derg. Before the war, he was a top student here in Tigray who won a

18

lot of scholarships. He went to medical school and was involved with the student movement fighting the dictatorship. The TPLF army—" she searched for the correct word—"'developed?' Developed from it."

The truck's headlights illuminated a line of prisoners herded by guards. Despondent faces, pitifully thin frames and ragged uniforms appeared like phantoms out of the darkness then disappeared. One prisoner gave the American a desperate look.

Holy shit. Buddy wished he could free the man.

After an hour-long, uphill ride, they parked beside a brush-covered jeep and hiked another ten minutes to a large, boulder-strewn cave in the mountainside. Soldiers of both sexes stood guard with automatic weapons. One peeked from behind a rock.

Hanna greeted the guards in Tigrinya with a wisecrack that made them grin. They allowed her and Buddy to enter.

A low-ceilinged passageway opened onto a rock-hewn, smoky kitchen where two female cooks prepared a meal under the supervision of another soldier. A dangling string of light bulbs along the ceiling flickered. Somewhere, a generator hummed.

Hanna led Buddy through the kitchen to a larger chamber. There, scruffy rebel leaders in military garb sat on a coarse carpet covered with papers, maps, a compass and a digital calculator.

A thoughtful-looking man in an unadorned army uniform rose to shake hands.

"It is a great honor to meet you, Mr. Schwartz," Meles Zenawi said. Slightly younger than Buddy, his steady gaze and self-reliant air engendered confidence. A Che Guevara-like beard and thick, arched eyebrows distracted from a balding forehead that encroached on unruly hair.

"Call me Buddy."

"All right, Buddy, then." There was a radar-like quality to the alert way the TPLF commander watched and listened. Everything was data to him. He looked at Hanna. "Is she taking care of you?"

"She's fine."

"Smart as a whip, as you say." Meles' expression hinted at humor.

"But you never know what she's really thinking." He patted his shirt pocket. "Say, uh, you wouldn't happen to have a cigarette?"

"Sorry, I don't smoke."

Meles sighed. He introduced some of his officers. The two cooks entered the room with covered tin pails. Meles motioned for Buddy to sit and they joined the others on the carpet. The cooks handed out tin plates. Large platters held the spongy bread, *injera*, a berbere-spiced bowl of chickpeas and some kind of bush meat stew.

Before they could begin, Meles nodded at the cooks. With tarnished spoons, the two women tasted each dish. At first, Buddy thought it was a chivalrous gesture to feed them first. But from the way everyone relaxed after the cooks had sampled the meal, he realized they had proven it wasn't poisoned.

"Okay," Meles declared. As Hanna and another officer put their hands together to say grace, he and the others pounced hungrily on the meal. With their hands, they tore off pieces of injera, wrapped bits of food in them and devoured them.

Meles winked at Buddy. "You can tell who are the godless Communists at mealtime," he joked.

The stew smelled gamey. Not wanting to insult his host, Buddy dug into the meal and pretended to relish it.

Satisfied his guest was enjoying his dinner, Meles turned serious. "How do you find Ethiopia?"

"There's a lot of people who've got nothing to eat. And a guy somebody used for firewood."

Meles dabbed his lips with a cloth napkin. "That was an enemy spy," he explained. "Rough justice here, I'm afraid. We're still a revolutionary movement, not a government yet."

"I need to know, am I going to have freedom to film what I want? 'Cause if not, I don't think this is going to work out."

"You're here to film hungry people," Meles said. A smile played on his lips. "That was not a hungry person."

Did this sonofabitch just smirk? "I've got to have creative control over my work," Buddy insisted.

Meles' quick brown eyes measured him. "Millions are at risk," he said. "If we confuse the foreigners and they don't help us, all those people will die. So you see, there's a certain logic to our request." He put another piece of bread on his guest's plate. "Here, take some more injera." His hand was soft and well-manicured like the doctor the guerrilla had once planned to be.

"Thank you."

"You've got no idea what I have to do to get a penny out of these rich people who know nothing about Africa." Meles used the bread to scoop more food into his mouth. A smear of grease on his cheek betrayed the decisive manner. "Our problems make more sense when you look at our history," he went on. "Fighting off the colonial powers. Centuries of Amhara feudalism. Now, a terrible dictatorship. But this is also the world's oldest civilization. We gave birth to Egypt. The Queen of Sheba ruled right here in Tigray. In the south is where the first human beings walked—the original Garden of Eden."

They ate for a few moments in silence. "Why did you want to come here?" Meles asked.

"I saw a horrible picture of a starving kid on TV. I don't understand how anybody can sit by while people are hungry like that."

Meles gave him an approving look, took a final bite and sat back on the carpet. With anticipation, he drew from his pocket two small bundles of magenta and green twigs wrapped in a wide leaf with twine.

"Khat," he said. "Do you chew?"

"Never tried it."

"Good and fresh." Meles removed the leafy wrapping to reveal lime-colored, oval leaves. He peeled off two sprigs and offered one to Buddy.

"Here. We share it to say we are friends." He stuffed a wad of leaves in his mouth and chewed them to show how it was done.

The leaves were bitter, and Buddy worried he'd get sick from them. He felt a rush of adrenaline. "This stuff's like speed, isn't it?"

Meles called out in Tigrinya. One of the cooks brought two bottles of orange soda.

"Sorry there's no ice," he apologized in a strained voice that sounded a little like Alan when he was coked-up. "Now, you're well known and people in the West listen to you. If you want to help us, tell them to send us more money so we can feed these hungry people."

The soda was sticky. Buddy wished he had a toothbrush.

"You're asking me to make a commercial. Not a documentary."

Meles rose and held out his hand. "Come with me."

A bit awkwardly, Buddy took it. The Ethiopian's grip was firm and dry. He led Buddy out of the cave.

At a nod from their commander, three bodyguards followed them to the jeep hidden beside Hanna's pickup. Meles got behind the wheel and told Buddy to take the passenger seat. The guards climbed in the rear.

Their khat-fueled conversation felt extraordinarily intense as Meles eased the jeep down the mountainside under the dazzling night sky.

Soon they rejoined the trail. Trucks and a heavily laden mule train went by. The warring parties had an internationally brokered agreement not to attack the other's feeding centers. But to play it safe, most of the TPLF's military movements and food distribution took place late at night when Mengistu's Cuban pilots didn't fly their Soviet-supplied MiG-21s. Buddy wondered what had become of the column of prisoners.

After a while, they parked near a feeding center. The low wailing drifted their way.

"Do you hear that?" Meles asked.

"What is it?"

"It's hungry children." Meles spoke rapidly in a way Buddy suspected was from the khat. "They're sick and they have no medicine. They have no home. They don't know what will become of them."

Buddy looked over the miserable encampment. The urge to cry nearly overwhelmed him.

"They are dying in front of me," Meles said. "And I've got enemies, powerful enemies, trying to stop me from feeding them."

They entered a pediatrics tent. The nurses and parents fell silent at the sight of them. Meles paused by an infant care unit. He picked up a baby boy who resembled a tiny, wizened old man. The baby might have been around two, but it was hard to tell Ethiopian children's ages because so many were stunted from malnutrition. A string around his neck bore a single, blue ceramic bead, evidence someone had once loved him.

Meles chatted with a nurse. She gave him a chipped teacup.

"We feed them honey," he explained. He dipped his finger in the cup and tenderly put it to the child's lips. The boy greedily sucked it.

"That's right," Meles cooed. "Suck. Take the honey." He looked pleased. "We have wonderful honey here. The best in the world. See how he likes it?" He gazed fondly at the baby, handed him back to the nurse, and they continued their stroll.

"It's not just a matter of food," Meles said. "They need clean water. Hygiene. Medical care. And contraception." His voice grew passionate. "But they need more than that. They need human rights. And freedom."

A weeping mother kissed her dying child's face with broken desperation.

At that moment, what had begun as an adventure became for Buddy a mission

"I swear to God—" he muttered.

"We want the same thing," Meles said. "To feed the people. That's all I'm trying to do."

Buddy regarded the hellish scene.

"We've got to think bigger," he said. "We've got to think a lot bigger."

Chapter Three

"HER NAME IS Desta," the television narrator said. "She hasn't eaten in two days."

On a monitor in Buddy's production office, a grungy Ethiopian girl spoke in Tigrinya to the camera. A subtitle read, "Mommy is dead. Who will take care of me?"

It had taken a year of hard work to organize one of the largest worldwide broadcasts in the history of television. He had called in every favor he was owed and twisted friends' arms to make the necessary contacts with the top names in music, persuade them to perform for free and overcome their hard-headed managers' objections to waiving their royalty rights on the subsequent album. There were egos to be stroked, especially when deciding how many songs to allow each artist and the order in which they'd appear. But Buddy had cajoled, negotiated and begged his way through the thicket of creative and legal demands with skill.

And so, by limo, helicopter and private jet, their personal assistants barking into the bulky mobile phones just coming into widespread use, David Bowie, Freddie Mercury, Ashford and Simpson, George Michael, Roy Orbison, John Denver, Jerry Garcia and twenty-five more of the industry's biggest stars had come that day to Culver City for the Help Ethiopia telethon. The line of limos outside the studio was so long, Alan had jokingly asked where the funeral was.

Buddy had decided to use a television studio with a live audience instead of staging a concert. He felt more in control and feared the complications and liabilities of an outdoor event. As a teenager, he'd been at a chaotic outdoor Rolling Stones concert where someone was stabbed and hadn't liked crowds ever since.

The studio he'd leased was on the 40 Acres backlot in Culver City. Once home to Desilu Studios and, before that, Howard Hughes' RKO, its large outdoor sets had accommodated everything from Cecil B. DeMille's biblical Jerusalem to King Kong's jungle. *Bonanza* and *Star Trek* had been shot there before the old scenery, like Rhett and Scarlett's Atlanta, also filmed at 40 Acres, was swept away by the winds of economic change. An industrial park had replaced it in the `60s, followed by television studios in the `70s.

Even within the contained environment of a studio production, it hadn't been easy for Buddy, acting as executive producer, to keep the project on track. There'd been hair-raising technical difficulties, from a camera breakdown to blown fuses, involved with the live shoot. Alan, stronger on the engineering side than Buddy, had rolled up his sleeves and been a lifesaver.

There had been controversies, too. During a pre-broadcast press conference, one reporter had questioned why money was being raised for foreigners when there was hunger at home.

"People aren't dying in the streets here, you idiot!" an overworked Buddy had retorted. The plain-spoken remark had made the news and stirred public debate.

Furnished with state-of-the-art digital editing equipment, the production office that adjoined the stage was otherwise unassuming. But today it was a madhouse. Entertainers and staff tried to make themselves heard over the din as they dashed in and out.

Buddy cradled a phone receiver against his shoulder, held another in his hand and minded the television monitor amid the pandemonium. "Latin America's not getting a signal," he complained into one of the phones. "I need a signal down there now."

On a sofa, a long-haired George Harrison, in a wide-brimmed red hat and black vest, sat with his backup band and watched the fundraising commercial.

"I don't care what it costs," Buddy snapped, uncharacteristically curt under the pressure. "Hold on." He took the other phone and brusquely answered, "Schwartz."

It was Kurt Cobain. The singing sensation's latest hit topped the charts, and Buddy wanted it on his show. He listened impatiently. "You've got a cold? We've got millions of people starving. You going to punk out on them?" He checked the typed schedule taped to the wall beside his desk and silently mouthed, "you're on" to the former Beatle.

"Come on, then," Harrison said to his band members. They gathered their guitars and sauntered out the exit to the stage.

The television monitor switched to images of starved Ethiopians from the documentary Buddy had shot on his trip. Donations were surging each time the commercial and film clips interrupted the musical performances.

The phone number 800-HELP-ETH scrolled across the bottom of the screen. Good optical, he thought. Nice and clear. "Do you want me to send a car?" he said into the phone. "We'll be on another eight hours. Never mind about your fucking cold." He remembered almost weeping with Meles at the feeding center and wished crossly he could better explain what he had witnessed.

The monitor changed to a live shot of Harrison as he prepared to play to enthusiastic applause. Behind him, a banner read, "Help Ethiopia."

"That's it," Buddy said into the phone, his eyes still on the screen. "I knew I could count on you." Live music and applause came from the stage and amplified the cacophony. A dial on a console told him audio levels were holding. He briefly reflected with a touch of pride on his multitasking honed from years of experience.

He hung up, ignored the blinking calls on hold, strode down a utilitarian corridor and waited in the wings until Harrison finished his set. An assistant director cued Buddy. He walked onto the stage to a spot marked with two strips of yellow tape.

A camera swung towards him. A small, red light indicated it was on. Buddy faced the lens.

"He's the greatest!" he exclaimed with a flourish as Harrison left.

When the applause died down, he spoke soberly to the camera. "Let's remember why we're here today. We can save the Destas of this world if we all get together. Remember, the number's 800– HELP– ETH. And now, a song from Tom Fogerty!"

The studio audience cheered and clapped. The singer joined Buddy onstage, slipped his guitar strap over his head and began one of his crowd-pleasers.

Buddy retreated backstage. Waiting reporters surrounded him.

"How many people are tuning in?"

"How did you get so many big stars to work together?"

"How much do you hope to raise?"

"Just tell everybody to keep the money coming," he replied. "There's a lot of lives depending on us."

"The White House has invited you for dinner," a reporter from the *Wall Street Journal* pointed out. "Your face is on every magazine in the country. You're nominated for all those humanitarian awards. What about those who say you're doing this for the publicity?"

The question stung. Buddy knew, in the deepest recesses of his heart, part of him secretly enjoyed the status and adulation that media coverage of the event had brought him.

"I'm not that good looking, and I'm not that smart," he replied disarmingly. "I can produce and write a little. This is probably the only chance I'll ever get to make a real difference. We've got to ask ourselves if we're doing all we can. So please get the word out. The world needs to hear this."

The world did hear it. According to Nielsen, nearly half the planet's television sets tuned in to the telethon—a much bigger audience than anyone had expected. Buddy had brought the world together in a common act of compassion.

Even more important was the project's financial success. The album became one of the highest-grossing ever and generated forty-eight million dollars. Domestic and foreign sales of the television re-broadcast rights brought in another eleven million.

The donations proved the most remarkable source of income. Like some undersea explosion fueled by years of simmering disgust and frustration over world hunger, the Help Ethiopia telethon set off a global tidal wave of giving. Big corporations and convenience store clerks donated. Millionaires' foundations donated. Florida retirees living on social security donated. Yuppies. Hippies. Teachers and secretaries. Factory workers and firemen. *I can't afford much, but here's ten dollars.*

Thousands and thousands of people called the 800–HELP– ETH phone number to give their credit card numbers to eight-dollars-an-hour call center operators reading from scripts. *Hello, are you calling to help a hungry Ethiopian child?*

Envelopes poured in from every corner of the world. Many enclosed cash. Most held a check or postal money order made out to Help Ethiopia, some carefully written, some in a hurried scrawl and others in a shaky hand. South Americans sent money. The British sent money. Irish, Germans, French and Italians sent money. People from Samoa and from South Africa. From Andorra and Afghanistan.

Especially the schoolchildren.

Dear Mr. Schwartz, we are in the fifth grade. Our class collected this money for Ethiopia.

"Jeez, they even got coins in here." College-age interns and volunteers, sustained by late night beer, coffee and office romances, tried to keep up with the deluge of mail. They heaped it on folding tables in the foundation's temporary offices near the studio and dumped more onto the pile every day.

"I guess it's hard to be funny when we're talking about hungry people," Johnny Carson said with uncharacteristic seriousness.

It was Buddy's third talk show appearance in a week, and he was tired. "What's funny," he replied as he took a sip from the coffee mug with the NBC logo, "is we're supposed to be living in modern times and this sort of tragedy is still going on."

The dapper comedian spoke to the camera. "We're going to show the Help Ethiopia phone number for those viewers who want to contribute."

Say something memorable, Buddy told himself. "Imagine if it was your child," he said. "Or your parent that was hungry. It's life or death."

The studio audience grew quiet.

"We're going to take a break," Carson announced. "And when we come back, we're going to have Mr. T."

The audience applauded.

Despite Buddy's anxieties, people must have gotten the message.

For the money continued to pour in.

A few weeks later, Buddy examined an accounting statement in his office with Alan. "Sixty-eight million bucks in four months," he read aloud. He stared at the piece of paper.

"What?" Alan asked.

"Nothing."

"What?"

"I'm...happy."

Chapter Four

WHEN BUDDY WANTED to relax, he went surfing with The Gandel. Alan was Buddy's oldest friend, but The Gandel was Buddy's surfing friend.

The Gandel was actually Richard Kleinman, MD, adjunct clinical professor at the UCLA Neuropsychiatric Institute and Hospital. It was the "grommets," the young surfers, who first called Richard a "Gandel"—someone with the wisdom of the waves. Buddy had picked up on this nickname. The two friends liked to sprinkle their conversation with surfing slang as a private joke.

Buddy had just started out as a production assistant at *60 Minutes* when he met The Gandel in 1973. Richard, then a senior resident in neurology at Cedars-Sinai Hospital, had been on call the day the future television producer was brought in after getting clocked in the head by a swinging boom mic.

Only recently arrived from New York, Buddy wanted to learn to surf. But he lived far from the beach and didn't know how to get started until his follow-up visit to Richard. They'd pulled into the hospital parking lot at the same time, and Buddy, in his beat-up, used Volkswagen, had recognized on the rear bumper of the doctor's vintage woodie station wagon a patchwork of decals from surfing havens around the world.

Before long, Richard had become his surfing teacher and friend. By the time of Buddy's 1987 telethon, the ponytailed medical resident, who had once looked like he belonged in one of the surfing magazines Buddy avidly read, had begun to morph into the wiry, balding, acclaimed doctor and scientist he would later become.

An empathetic personality had prompted this Arizona native to endure the eleven years of grueling, post-graduate study his dual medical specialty demanded. But besides his deep insight into the workings of the human brain, part of The Gandel's mystique came from his professional interest in spirituality.

His choice of residence, up a narrow canyon above Malibu's Surfrider Beach, encouraged this sideline. The famous surf spot where seagulls soared over spectacular coastline and movie stars' beachfront mansions, with its breathtaking views of the Santa Monica Mountains colliding with the Pacific, stimulated The Gandel's desire to understand the cosmos and how humans perceive it. But he approached the subject like a scientist. Many Saturday afternoons were spent in his lab taking brain scans of meditating priests, rabbis and Buddhist monks. The whirring, magnetic resonance of the MRI revealed neural patterns he thought held clues to experiencing God.

"Just because God allows evil doesn't mean there isn't one," he'd once explained to Buddy as they sat on Surfrider's sand discussing the Holocaust. The Gandel had converted many an agnostic and atheist by proposing they abandon their preconceived definitions of God and decide whether nature had a collective intelligence. He could interpret dreams, believed they contained coded, unconscious guidance and helped his friends understand their own. Buddy had come over the years to trust and rely on his advice.

Friendship with The Gandel conferred another advantage. Locals jealously guarded most of the great surfing beaches against outsiders in the belief that more people got in the way and left less good waves for them. Some locals, the "Surf Nazis," even formed gangs to defend what they saw as their turf from vacationers or surfers from neighboring towns. Occasionally, they went so far as to puncture tires or pick fights.

Fortunately for Buddy, Richard had helped spur a UCLA study that led to well-publicized environmental improvements at Surfrider and was popular among the surfers. As a well-known, respected local, The Gandel provided protection against the Surf Nazis. But Buddy was careful never to surf there without him.

Because of the classic wave conditions, by sunrise each day a handful of other boards already bobbed behind the dark silver breakers along the ten mile strip reserved for surfers. Despite their demanding work schedules, Buddy and The Gandel joined the lineup at least once a week.

Later in the day would come the surgically-enhanced housewives, topless or long-haired Europeans in skimpy bathing suits and picnicking families with children. The smell of suntan lotion would mingle with the ocean air. But this early, only a few health nuts jogged along the damp high tide mark on the sand. There was fog, and the two friends wore wetsuits to protect them from the chilly air.

The wind, the waves and the cries of the sea birds helped Buddy forget about Ethiopia and its problems.

But not for long.

While Help Ethiopia transferred the millions it had raised to the British bank account of the TPLF's relief organization, a good harvest and the influx of refugees that had joined the movement led Meles and his CIA advisers to conclude TPLF capabilities now matched the Soviet-equipped Derg's in northern Ethiopia. To break the stalemate, they went on the offensive.

Previously buoyed by the promise of an easy victory in compulsory propaganda meetings, Mengistu's troops quickly became demoralized when they encountered stiff resistance. Many were conscripts, students and professionals press-ganged off city streets. They became reluctant to fight. Defections grew weekly.

Sensing weakness, the TPLF and its Eritrean ally pushed southward into the provinces of Wollo and Gondar with its medieval castles.

In the summer of 1988, the Derg began a major campaign, but Meles' TPLF stole a march on its enemy. The guerrilla army seized three towns that included the region's logistical center, Mugulat.

It turned and bagged Ethiopia's ancient capital, Axum, where the Queen of Sheba had embarked on her journey to meet Solomon in Jerusalem.

The next city to fall was Adwa where the nineteenth-century Emperor Menelik II had astounded the world and shattered the paradigm of European superiority with his triumph over Italian invaders.

Like a cornered animal, the Derg unleashed an even bigger army in a fresh attack. But this, too, was parried. Meles' Eritrean allies killed or captured eighteen thousand government troops, their armor and artillery.

Desperate, Mengistu took off the gloves. On April 6, 1988, he ordered all foreign aid workers to leave the parts of Tigray and Eritrea he still ruled for "security reasons."

He didn't want the outside world to see what was coming.

Buddy didn't hear about the foreigners' expulsion. En route to Meles' base camp near Mugulat to inspect feeding operations, he was cut off from broadcast media.

The Derg's attacks and forced resettlement of villages had left millions of people without food, water or shelter.

Refugees were streaming into TPLF relief camps.

It was a refreshing, Tigrayan morning with wispy clouds in the sky. Hanna waited by the airstrip with her truck and a half-dozen TPLF fighters.

The white, single-propeller Cessna landed, took two long bounds and stopped. The propeller quit, the door opened, and Buddy emerged.

She made the trilling howl used in that part of the world to express strong emotion and waved.

The TPLF controlled the one good road through the area. Soon, Buddy surveyed for the first time a Help Ethiopia-funded feeding center. The temporary warehouse's gates, fences, doors and roof were in good condition. The locks looked secure, the floor was clean and the open ground was tidy. Piles of woven hemp sacks were stacked on pallets and covered with plastic tarpaulins. Each bag meant another week of life for a family.

Hanna pointed to a frayed hole in one leaky bag. "We keep it dry from mold, but we have the rats."

Sagging trucks dropped off heavy cargoes. The Derg still held Eritrea's Red Sea port of Assab, loaned to the Soviets for a naval base. The long, hazardous trip over bad roads from the alternative harbor in Sudan, where chartered ships unloaded the food, exhausted the drivers.

The warehouse manager wrote out and gave a receipt to one truck driver, a Sudanese Dinka with V-shaped facial scars. The driver had a seven-hundred-mile drive back to the port in his now-empty truck to get paid, drunk and laid.

"At first," Hanna explained, "we had to give each family cooked meals. But that was expensive. Now we give them the grain and a can of cooking oil once a week, and they can prepare it themselves."

"I'd like to see how it looks when it's cooked."

She led him behind the warehouse. They cut through an open field that stank of human waste, dodged barefoot children playing soccer with a donated ball and entered an open-air communal kitchen.

Refugees ate in small groups around a kerosene stove. Hanna led Buddy over to a careworn woman in a threadbare dress that years ago had been white. The woman carefully fed three frail children with a tin spoon from a blackened cooking pot that had accompanied them on their long trek. Their distended bellies, reddish hair and skin ulcers were signs of malnutrition.

"Shouldn't those kids be getting emergency treatment?"

"They will be all right." Hanna pointed at one child's leg. "See? The sores are healing." She politely asked the woman to show them her food. The woman tipped the pot so they could peer at its contents. "We've increased our feeding from one hundred thousand people a day to one hundred and twenty-four—"

The woman and her children showed no pleasure in the bland preparation. They glanced at the tall *faranj*, as they called foreigners. Buddy remembered his own childhood dinners busy with jokes, arguments and his mother scolding him to finish his food.

"...thanks to you," Hanna concluded.

The meal didn't look like much. "That's enough nutrition?"

"It has vitamins added. We are trying to get them vegetables." She looked at her watch. They had to be back at Meles' camp at nine for a press conference.

"My pilot told me the government tried to send food in here. And the TPLF attacked their convoy?"

"They were using it as a cover to move military supplies," Hanna replied stiffly. "It was necessary."

The mother scooped a speck of cereal from one child's chin and put it back in his mouth.

"More money's coming," Buddy said.

There was admiration in her gaze, and he wanted to take her in his arms. But this was not the place for it.

The dry wind sweeping across the Red Sea from the Arabian Peninsula assaulted eyes, nose and ears with a fine dust that would have been farmland if the rains had come this year. Meles and the reporters were late for Buddy's press conference at the rebel commander's tent.

After an hour, a caravan of six camouflaged trucks appeared. Their round, canvas canopies resembled covered wagons from the old American West. Four reporters climbed down from the lead truck. They wore sunglasses to protect against the dust. One was Ethiopian, one was French and two were British. They stretched sore muscles.

Hanna greeted them and introduced Buddy. "We will begin when Meles arrives," she said.

Inside Meles' tent, she handed out mimeographed press releases. The tent's edges flapped loudly in the wind while everyone made small talk about the war and speculated about the foreigners' deportation.

Meles' jeep drove up. He'd put on a well-pressed uniform for the occasion but looked tired. His face lit up when he saw Buddy.

"Thank you so much," he exclaimed with a hug.

"Let us do the photo now," Hanna suggested.

Meles and Buddy posed together. Cameras clicked.

"How have you spent the money from the telethon?" one of the British journalists asked. He had a pale, jowly face, sported a safari jacket and seemed old for such a hardship assignment.

"I'll let our public affairs officer answer that," Meles said.

"Thanks to Help Ethiopia, we cut adult mortality by nineteen percent," Hanna told the reporter. "Infant mortality in the liberated sector is down by almost one-third. We distributed fifty thousand vaccine injections for typhoid, diphtheria and measles."

The man from Agence France Presse, a dashing adventurer type, raised his hand. "Can you confirm your plans to have your own trucks and teams on the ground?" he asked Buddy in French-accented English.

That was the new strategy. Help Ethiopia had bought a fleet of trucks and would manage its own aid distribution. This would give Buddy and his board of directors—Alan, who had stepped in to help administer the US side of things, and some other friends—more oversight and flexibility in responding to the crisis.

"We're good at logistics," Buddy said. "It's like shooting on a remote location. Get your equipment in. Your power. Your water. Your people."

"Are you satisfied the money has been spent properly?" the older British reporter persisted.

"Of course."

The Ethiopian journalist, a friendly guy with an impish smile named Abey, raised his hand. He was from the diaspora that had fled the Red Terror for new homes in America and Europe where they'd been exposed to ideas like democracy and human rights.

"What about the mass killings of civilians in the mountains by your forces?" he asked Meles.

"We're here to talk about hungry people," the TPLF leader replied in an irritated tone. "Not foolish rumors."

Buddy answered more questions. Hanna handed out the press release. "We have lunch for you," she told the reporters and steered them out of the tent.

The moment they were alone, Buddy turned to Meles.

"What the hell was that?" he asked, upset by the Ethiopian reporter's question.

"Propaganda," Meles said. "Don't worry about it."

Wearily, the guerrilla leader sat down on a carpet spread across the earthen floor. He gestured for Buddy to join him, took a bundle of khat from his shirt pocket and offered it to the American.

"Good and fresh," he said.

Buddy stripped off a sprig. The two men sat and chewed quietly. Outside the tent's opening, soldiers unloaded grease-covered guns from wooden crates.

"About those government food convoys—"

"They use them to sneak in men and supplies."

"You're guaranteeing us safe passage in the MOU," Buddy reminded him, referring to the memorandum of understanding Help Ethiopia had signed with the TPLF. "Your men are going to accidentally shoot up one of our trucks, and somebody will get hurt."

"We'll work something out."

A rebel officer, his chest criss-crossed by a bandolier loaded with ammunition that reminded Buddy of a Pancho Villa movie, entered. He knelt beside Meles and whispered in his ear. Meles listened gravely then rose to his feet.

"The government is launching another attack," he said. "We're going to give up some of the towns and move back into the mountains."

"What?"

"Come with me, please." Meles ushered him out of the tent.

"I want to see the other feeding centers."

"Not now," Meles said tersely. He gave his lieutenants orders.

The camp stirred into action. Soldiers broke down the tents and collected provisions.

Hanna wiped her mouth with her sleeve as she emerged from the kitchen tent with the journalists.

To lift everyone's spirits, one of Meles' officers made the trilling howl. First one soldier, then another and another joined in until the entire camp rang with the earsplitting sound.

Two jeeps rolled up. Hanna directed the journalists into one. She opened the door of the other for Buddy, and they got in. Three bushy-haired fighters with rifles squeezed in with them, smiling apologetically at the cramped situation.

Once assembled, the column of jeeps and trucks threw up a shower of dirt as it sped out of the camp. Buddy looked back. Hundreds of TPLF fighters were forming rows. An officer yelled orders.

"Where are we going?"

"A town to the west called Shire. It will be out of range."

A disturbing and unfamiliar sound—*thump, thump, thump*—began.

"What's that?"

"They are mortaring the airfield."

The convoy raced across the rugged landscape. Buddy wondered if his plane had escaped. This was going to be a long ride.

"What about the feeding centers?"

"The government will probably burn them."

"Christ."

The TPLF soldier beside him had a bandage on one forearm and held his rifle pointed skyward for safety. The weapon radiated the menace of something dangerous to touch like a resting serpent. The soldier's eyes were bloodshot, and Buddy suspected he'd been smoking grass. That's nice, he thought sarcastically. There was no point in asking.

They drove for hours. The wind subsided, and the blue sky returned. Buddy's tongue was gritty. His sides were sore from the jolting ride. They stopped to eat and refuel. Then the column, its engines grinding and spitting black exhaust, climbed higher into the mountains.

Despite the danger, the vast, wild panoramas and utter absence of urbanity created an exhilarating sensation of freedom. Biblical-looking shepherds wore toga-like, white cotton shammas to signify their Christianity. Flocks of goats nibbled grass between red sandstone boulders. Herds of gazelles scattered. A leopard flashed between the boulders.

There was no road for long stretches, and the trip took most of the day. It was afternoon when they came out from behind a craggy mountain into a broad valley with a few thousand low-slung, gray, white and blue houses. Several stone churches, minarets and yellow-green trees formed a meager skyline. A falcon slowly circled above the town.

"Where are we?"

"In the middle of Tigray."

The line of vehicles pulled onto the main street. The scent of incense used in the coffee preparation ceremony mixed with the smell of burnt charcoal. A flock of brown and sky-blue birds swooped back and forth over their heads.

"Come," Hanna said. "We will find you a comfortable place."

She barked an order, her soft voice authoritative, as TPLF soldiers took up positions around the town. One of the fighters grabbed Buddy's suitcase and showed them down a side street. Four armed pickups blew past them headed for the overlooking hills.

The box-like stone house had two sparsely-furnished rooms. In one, an adolescent girl sat on the bed nursing a baby. Next to her, an inflatable Santa Claus sagged incongruously.

The soldier plunked the suitcase down. Hanna said something to the young mother, and she rose to leave.

"I don't want to push her out of her own house," Buddy protested.

"She doesn't live here."

The girl, holding the baby to her breast, gathered the inflatable Santa with her free arm and left with the soldier.

"You will sleep here," Hanna said. "I will be in the other room."

The rough-hewn bed had leather straps instead of a mattress. A rudimentary table held a lantern.

"I am sorry my country has so little hospitality to give you," Hanna said.

"I'm not here for a vacation." The floor was carefully swept. "Where are the people who live here?"

"They will sleep someplace else."

He wondered who had been displaced so he could have their house.

"You are hungry?" Hanna asked.

"Yeah."

Dusk fell as they strolled down the street. They stepped around different kinds of manure. A miniature parade of naked children with runny noses tagged after them. The now-familiar sound of other kids bawling from hunger drifted through the town.

"How do you stand hearing them like that?"

"We are, how do you say it—'used?' We are used to it," Hanna admitted. "But it hurts us when we think about it."

Shire was otherwise peaceful, its usual population of 10,000 depleted when many inhabitants and farmers from the surrounding districts had run away to escape the fighting or the famine. High wooden or corrugated tin walls protected ramshackle buildings. Gates displayed advertising signs in Tigrinya with hand-painted pictures copied from Western magazines. A hairdresser styled a woman's hair. An electric lamp. European style shoes. A 1930s CocaCola sign.

A *gari*, a horse-drawn cart with two rubber tires used as a taxi, went by. Jingling bells on the horse's collar reminded Buddy of the young mother and her inflatable Santa Claus. Where would she go? The gari driver sized them up to see if they wanted a ride. Hanna shook her head, and he urged his horse on with a flap of the reins.

Freshly bullet-pockmarked walls testified control of Shire had recently passed back and forth between the TPLF and the Derg.

The town had seen war before. Elders remembered Haile Selassie's Imperial Army, a half century earlier, readying spears and thick, hippo skin shields as Mussolini's *Regia Aeronautica* approached with poison gas, eighty tons of explosives, fire bombs and low altitude strafing. The stench of thousands of rotten corpses in the hills had made what was left of the town unlivable for weeks.

Many homes doubled as shops. Their inhabitants sat outside in the mountain air and waited for business. Some fussed over cooking fires. Others drank coffee or chewed khat and gossiped. Two men argued as they banged a car part with a hammer.

Residents of the town lowered their gaze as they walked by. Some carried bundles on their backs. A boy led a camel burdened with firewood by a rope. A goat wandered across the road to graze in someone's yard.

Down the road stood a makeshift inn. With its rickety, wooden frame and dilapidated roof, it was indistinguishable from the other houses except for a white flag, the local sign liquor was served.

A dwarfish innkeeper shook hands with his important guests with Ethiopian formality. While he and Hanna chatted, Buddy admired a Bob Marley poster, the precious gift of some friend or relative abroad, which took pride of place on one wall.

"Do you eat chicken?" Hanna asked. "With some spinach and yams? That is what he has."

"Just not spicy, please."

Hanna ordered the food, and the innkeeper stepped into a yard to prepare it.

"I've got commitments back in LA," Buddy complained. "How long do you think we'll have to stay here?"

A squawk outside told them a chicken had been dispatched.

"We will counterattack soon," Hanna assured him. "Then we will push them back. We did it before."

An open doorway framed a swarm of flies on a pile of peeled yams.

"Is there a phone here?"

"It is probably down. I will go to look."

"After dinner's fine."

"They have some barley beer. Or would you like *tej*? The beer is probably warm."

"What's the tej like?"

"It is a wine we make from honey."

"I'll try it."

"Tej!" Hanna called.

"You seem pretty calm," Buddy observed.

"I fought on the front line for three years before they assigned me to the propaganda section."

The innkeeper brought the tej in glass goblets. Buddy wiped the edge of his glass with a napkin and sipped it.

"It's sweet."

"Do you like it?"

"It's kind of weird. But not bad." The drink had a real kick. He began to enjoy the inn's strange, yet homey, atmosphere. The Bob Marley poster grew radiant. The dreadlocked, Rastafari singer's carefree grin hinted at some pleasurable, secret knowledge.

Buddy was acquainted with a Rasta carpenter at his television studio and had learned a little about the religion. It took its name from Haile Selassie's birth name of *Tafari* in Amharic, Ethiopia's *lingua franca*. Ras meant "Prince." It had begun in Jamaica in 1931, Selassie's coronation year. Four street preachers, each unknown to the other, had turned up in Kingston. All proclaimed the young king's inheritance of Solomon's title, "Conquering Lion of Judah," and his accession to the House of David's Rainbow Throne fulfilled Biblical prophecy of a Messiah.

The faith had spread among Jamaica's poor, thirsty for a symbol of black dignity and independence. Now it numbered a million believers. Yet considering the crucial role Ethiopia had played in black history, surprisingly few Rastas, or African-Americans for that matter, generally knew, or even cared, about Ethiopian current events.

A deep rumbling sound made his glass of tej vibrate.

"That is enemy artillery," Hanna said.

Buddy looked out a window. Soldiers dug trenches by flashlight.

"Look," she said. "The others are here."

Abey entered, followed by the old British reporter and his younger colleague, an intellectual type with wire-rimmed spectacles.

"Hey, Buddy," Abey said cheerfully.

"Front row seats to the show," the older reporter said. "What are you having?"

"We might have gotten the last chicken," Buddy said. The French reporter was missing. "Where's Jacques?"

"Dysentery. Thank God it didn't start till we got here." The elderly Brit turned to Hanna. "Think you can use your influence to get us something?"

Hanna conferred with the innkeeper, gave him some money and he scurried away.

"He has another chicken. And spinach."

"Chicken and spinach. Right."

"Any chance of some mash?" the younger journalist asked.

"He has yams."

"Yams, then."

"Where are you guys staying?" Buddy asked them.

The old British journalist pointed. "They've got us in a cottage down there. Not the Hilton exactly. But I've been in worse. At least they've got the breeze up here. Keeps away the mosquitoes. I spent a night in Lagos once during the Biafran war. No screens or netting. Over a hundred bites by morning. Lucky I didn't get dengue."

Buddy imagined the man's life as a monotonous series of flea-bitten hotel rooms, lonely drinking and mediocre food. His attention returned to the soldiers digging trenches.

44

"What's with the digging?"

"Just in case," Hanna said.

It took a second for her meaning to sink in.

"Right." He tried not to sound worried.

The stewed chicken with spinach was a comforting sight. Hanna closed her eyes and prayed silently. Piety was not something Buddy saw much in LA. Contemplating her composed, gentle face, he attempted to imagine her thoughts.

She opened her eyes and smiled at him. "Eat," she urged.

The food was so spicy he could hardly stand it. The ever-present crying waxed and waned. Everyone pretended to ignore it.

"What do the people here eat for dinner? The regular people?"

Hanna indicated her plate. "The rich ones eat this."

"And the ones who aren't rich?"

"If they have animals, they can trade milk for honey to make tej and for *teff* to make injera. The poor people eat a weed that grows everyplace. Especially the farmers if the rains do not come. I do not know the word in English."

"They live on weeds? No wonder they're crying." The half-eaten chicken suddenly looked repulsive. But hunger won out. I can't help everybody, he reminded himself. And I've got to keep myself alive. Maybe alcohol would smother the guilt. "I'll take another tej."

"That's the idea," the old Brit said. "These kinds of nights go easier if one's plastered."

"You'll have one, too?" Buddy asked Hanna.

"I am not permitted."

Before dinner was over, everyone except Hanna was drunk. The two British journalists sang tipsily.

God bless our gracious Queen, long live our noble Queen.

"Just because you Ethiopians murdered your own monarch," the older one told Abey, "doesn't mean you can't toast our queen, goddammit!"

The Ethiopian reporter laughed and joined in.

God save the Queen.

"What do you usually do at night in these sorts of situations?" Buddy asked Hanna over the singing.

"I study my textbooks if I have light." She rose from the table. "I will find you a phone." She excused herself to ask the innkeeper.

After she'd left, the old British journalist smirked. "Meles is brave when it comes to sending others out to fight," he declared drunkenly. "But you never see him with an AK in his own hands."

"His father was a fascist collaborator, you know," the younger one chimed in.

Hanna returned. "The police have a phone that might work."

"You're off?" the old Brit asked.

"Got to find a phone."

The journalists resumed singing.

Outside, soldiers worked on the entrenchments. Flashes of fire illuminated the horizon. The rumbling sound reverberated a few seconds after each flash.

A cordon of soldiers guarded one of the houses. Three jeeps were parked beside it.

"Meles is here," Hanna said. "He must have a phone."

"I hope so."

She led Buddy to the house. The soldiers let them pass.

Inside, Meles huddled with aides over a map. His look of annoyance at the intrusion gave way to friendly acknowledgment when he saw who it was.

"Apologies for the detour," he said with an ironic smile. "Did you get here okay?"

"No problem."

"Buddy needs to use a phone," Hanna said.

"No electronic communications," Meles apologized. "They might target us for shelling."

The room fell into polite silence. Buddy was holding up some busy people. "Well, I'd better let you get on with your work." He turned to Hanna. "Do you have to do anything for those reporters?"

"They are drunk."

Buddy and Hanna headed back to the stone house.

"These lands belonged to the monarchy," she explained as they carefully crossed a wobbly plank over an open sewage ditch. "Then the colonels overthrew Haile Selassie, and everyone thought our lives would be better."

Tiny fires lit the evening like fireflies. The crying sounds picked up.

"But the colonels—'expropriated'?" She pronounced the word with difficulty. "They expropriated the people's property and forced everybody into the army. They killed and tortured many students and teachers. That was when I ran away to join the movement."

"How long have you been fighting?"

"They have been fighting for ten years. But I have been with them for the last five. I love the TPLF."

The deep rumbling grew emphatic.

"They are moving up," she said.

"Can they get us here?" Buddy asked apprehensively.

"We are out of range. And we are going to counterattack in the morning before they come closer."

The roosters crowed before dawn and woke Buddy. For a moment, he forgot where he was, his disorientation compounded by the din he mistook for thunder.

He got out of bed and went over to the window. There were bursts of light on the distant plain, and he remembered with a sinking feeling what made the noise. He went back to bed and lay there, frightened, as he listened to dogs bark and cows bellow.

How did I get here? he asked himself.

The room was filled with sunlight. He'd fallen back to sleep. The battle sounded further away. Somewhere outside, a muezzin chanted a prayer.

He dressed and went outdoors. Hanna sat on a rock in her uniform and read her book. Her beauty tugged at him like the undertow at Surfrider after a storm.

"How are you?" she asked with a smile.

A desire to propose marriage to this woman he barely knew stirred in him.

"I guess I'm okay."

"You slept all day." She pointed to a plastic bottle. "Clean water," she explained. "Would you like some breakfast?"

"Definitely."

A half hour later, the innkeeper placed coffee, eggs and injera on the table. Hanna bowed her head again and prayed. Buddy wondered what his Hollywood friends would think if she prayed like that at one of their dinner parties.

She ended her prayer, and they ate. The eggs were the freshest he'd ever tasted.

"Do you need sugar for your coffee?"

"Thank you."

She asked the innkeeper, and he brought some in a paper bag.

The sugar had probably arrived by a trading route used since the days of Sheba. Buddy poured it into his coffee, stirred it and took a sip.

He remembered his schedule, now irretrievably screwed up. "There's a lot of stuff waiting for me in LA. Lawyers. Accountants. Publicity. Isn't there a car I can hire?"

"We are cut off from the airfield. To get out, you have to go through Sudan to the coast. It is about six hundred kilometers. The roads are bad. And there are *shiftas*. Bandits. We would have to give you an escort. I will ask Meles."

Hanna finished her coffee. Even this simple act was charming. She put her cup down. "Ready?"

They left the inn and walked toward Meles' command post.

"We pushed them back nine kilometers—" she began when a whistle shrilled. More whistles joined in.

"What's that?"

"Air raid," she grimly replied.

"What?"

"We have to take cover." Hanna glanced at the cloudless sky and calculated the likely angle of attack. She nudged Buddy toward one of the trenches.

He tried to control his anxiety as they walked quickly toward the ditch. "What's going to happen?"

She yanked his arm. "Hurry, please."

They got in the trench and nervously looked up.

Meles and his staff came out of his headquarters. They stood in the road and studied the sky with binoculars. He gave his aides orders. They ran to their jeeps and took off in different directions. Other soldiers dashed for cover. A hand-cranked siren yowled hysterically.

Meles trotted over to the trench. With athletic grace, he jumped in beside Buddy and Hanna. The rebel commander took a bent cigarette from his shirt pocket and carefully straightened it. He lit it, took a grateful drag and exchanged a tense look with Buddy.

"Welcome to my world," he said.

A squad of TPLF fighters ran up and dropped into the trench with them. The four men and two women steadied their AK-47s against the berm and scanned the heavens.

The seconds ticked by.

There was a low-pitched buzzing sound.

Hanna pointed. "There it is."

A dot in the sky grew larger.

Its triangular shape became clear.

"MiG," Meles said. "Keep your mouth open, and take small breaths."

Before Buddy could ask what he meant, the buzz became a deafening roar as the metal monster came straight at them.

An orange light flickered under its belly.

Hanna pushed Buddy down. Chunks of plaster from nearby houses, dirt and rock rained on them.

The MiG roared by overhead. The rebel fighters leaned back and fired at it.

"Jesus!"

The jet climbed and lazily circled in the sky. It dove at the town once more. The rebels shot at it again without result.

A gray cylinder tumbled from under its wing.

Buddy cringed. "Watch out!"

Everyone ducked.

A tremendous explosion rocked the earth.

More explosions boomed.

Shrapnel tore up the ground.

Hanna's lips moved. Buddy couldn't hear anything. Then his hearing returned.

"Cluster bomb," she said.

Screams sounded throughout Shire. A half-naked boy with a red hole in his stomach limped up the road. Babbling tearfully, he tried to slide into the trench. One of the soldiers dragged him in.

Hanna tried to comfort the child and pressed her shirttail against the wound. The hole welled up every time she let go. Her blouse became drenched in blood. It smelled metallic. The boy's shrieks were maddening.

"What is he saying?"

"He is asking who will bury him."

Buddy stared in horror at the child.

Meles, who had medical training, took over. Soon his own shirt was blood-soaked. His face told the others it was hopeless.

The buzzing sound started again. He looked up.

"Get down. Get down!"

Another series of explosions resounded. More screams rang out.

Just as Buddy thought it couldn't get any worse, the explosions and screaming got louder and louder until they seemed to combine into one long howl.

Sometime later—Buddy didn't know whether it was minutes or an hour—it was quiet except for the incessant jingling of bells on a wounded gari horse thrashing in agony down the street. Shadows

50

had settled onto the ditch. All that was left in the sky was the lingering white jet plume dissipating into the pink and golden hues of sunset.

"I think it is gone," Hanna said.

The boy was dead in a puddle of blood.

Buddy peeked over the berm. Shire was in ruins. Bodies lay everywhere, cut down in mid-activity like animals culled from the herd. His knee hurt where he'd knelt on the trench's stony bottom.

Survivors emerged from the destroyed houses. They checked the sky and examined their gashes and scratches. Some searched through the rubble for family members or friends and called their names with heartrending urgency. Now and then, a keening voice signaled another had been found dead.

"They won't come at night," Meles said. His pants were wet. He had peed himself.

So had Hanna. Buddy looked down.

So had he.

The night became an unending, hallucinatory tunnel as they helped the wounded. Buddy's arms and back throbbed from digging through rubble by the time he and Hanna returned to their cottage after midnight.

One wall and part of its roof had caved in. They entered cautiously and tried with the lantern to inspect the house for signs of possible further collapse. Hanna's room was demolished. Buddy's was damaged but stable.

They found her scant belongings and the bottle of water amid the debris and organized the remaining room to make it habitable.

Hanna offered the water bottle to Buddy.

"You first," he insisted.

"I am used to no water."

"No. You take some."

Half the bottle was soon gone.

"We're going to need more."

"There was a pump near the police station."

The police station's wooden framing stuck out of its wreckage like broken bones. Rebels and townspeople, shocked and angry yet orderly, waited in the dark for their turn at the pump. The moans of the injured haunted the scene.

The Ethiopians gestured for Buddy to go first. His legs felt unreliable, but he declined and took his place at the end of the line.

Hanna spoke to a woman with a kettle. "She can get us some more bottles."

Buddy had forgotten about his home and life in California. Now their safety beckoned. "What about that car?"

"We will try to convoy you and the reporters out tomorrow."

They returned with the water bottles to the house. The baying of jackals and hyenas blended with the whimpering of the wounded. They found clean clothes. Hanna modestly stepped outside, and they washed up the best they could with their scarce water.

The single bed presented an awkward dilemma.

"You take it," Buddy proposed. "I'll sleep on the floor."

"There are scorpions. You take it. I will sit up."

"Look. We'll share the bed. Back to back."

"You are our guest. We want you to be comfortable."

"I wouldn't be able to sleep knowing you're without a bed."

"I am used to it."

"Please."

Hours later, they rested, still dressed, on the bed. The anguished noises outside had died down. Despite their fatigue, they couldn't fall asleep.

"Hanna?"

"Yes?"

"I'm sorry. I can't sleep on this side. I've got to turn over. Is that all right?"

"Yes."

Buddy shifted and faced Hanna's back. Calmer now, he could smell her—pungent, earthy and strangely attractive. He felt the magnetism of her small waist and hips inches away.

You're in a war zone, he thought. Don't do anything stupid. "So this is your life?" Moonlight revealed where she had neatly mended her khaki shirt collar. "Fighting, running, hiding?"

"I love my country."

"Don't you miss your home?"

"I miss my brother."

"No husband? No boyfriend?" What are you doing? he asked himself fiercely. Don't go there.

"I was engaged once. But he is missing for three years now."

"I'm sorry." They lapsed into an uncomfortable silence. "I don't like to leave you," he finally added, unsure what to say.

"You must go. Tell our story. Help us feed our people. I do not sleep at night, thinking about how they suffer."

"Neither do I."

They lay quietly together on the bed. "I can't understand this country," he admitted.

"In Ethiopia, what seems real is not always real. There are layers and layers before you get to the final truth."

"Like you, I think."

"Like everyone."

With her exquisite profile in shadow, she looked like a princess from the Arabian Nights tales. Her soft breathing whispered an invitation.

"That question the reporter asked," she said. "About the killings in the mountains. There were some people who didn't want to join with us."

She grew very still.

"I think Meles killed them."

The convoy was organized early in the morning to avoid the heat that would come when they descended from the mountains and

53

entered Sudan. The reporters got into a jeep with rusted wheel wells.

A second jeep was loaded with food, water, medical supplies and extra ammunition. A pickup truck, painted mottled brown for camouflage, led the column. A two-man crew manned the machine gun in its bed. Another similarly-armed truck took up the rear.

Buddy tried to memorize every detail as Hanna completed the preparations. The painstaking way she inspected their provisions and sternly gave orders to the muscular bodyguards who would accompany him. The way her expression softened when she was satisfied.

This one is special, he thought. This one is really special.

"Well, it's been a lovely visit!" the old British journalist joked.

Buddy went over to Hanna to say goodbye.

"It is a long ride," she warned him in a motherly tone. "Be careful with your food and water. You have to make them last."

Go for it, a voice in Buddy's head told him. "How'd you like to come back to Los Angeles with me?"

She smiled in kind refusal. "I cannot leave my country."

"Take a little time off. See America."

She seemed surprised by his interest then gave him an appraising look.

"Come with me," he repeated.

She stroked his arm in the Ethiopian custom and took from around her neck a carved, wooden cross that hung by a leather string beneath her bloodstained shirt.

"Do you believe in God?" she asked.

"Yes. But it's not a very nice God that lets people suffer like I've seen here."

"You must not say that," she admonished him. She pointed out the cross's elaborate lattice design traditional to Ethiopian Orthodoxy. "The edges are especially very beautiful. To remind us of God's endless mercy."

She moved to put it around his neck. "Take this."

Buddy stopped her. "I'm Jewish," he explained more brusquely than he intended. "We don't wear those."

She held the cross uncertainly. It was probably her most precious possession.

"I'll keep it with me for good luck," he promised, afraid he had hurt her feelings.

She pressed the cross into his palm and closed his fingers around it. His hand felt warm where she had touched it. His chest ached.

"Is there anything I can do for you when I get back?" he asked.

"Remember us."

"Come on, Buddy!" the old British journalist shouted. "Let's get the show on the road!"

Hanna walked Buddy to the jeep. He got in and lowered the window. It was already hot.

"Write to me," he said.

"I will."

The convoy started its engines and took off.

It disappeared down the trail in a cloud of dust.

Chapter Five

"TV Producer in African Relief Plea," the *Los Angeles Times* article's title read. "Don't Forget ' Em, Sez Buddy," said the *New York Post*. "Famine Hero Meets President," proclaimed *USA Today*. Piled next to a stack of neglected production reports and a long letter from Hanna, the other newspapers on the glass table in Buddy's bedroom had versions of the same story. But although he'd kept a close eye on his press coverage since his return from Ethiopia a year ago, they lay unread that morning.

The television commanded his attention.

Grainy news video showed Meles' soldiers sprinting through brush like mountain goats with pointy-nosed Chinese rocket launchers over their shoulders. Some hid behind trees and boulders to fire automatic weapons.

"And in Africa," a reporter announced, "rebel forces successfully ousted the dictator of Ethiopia today, ending a seventeen-year civil war—"

The news piece cut to a clip of two of Meles' captured Soviet T-54 tanks, still camouflaged with branches from their operations in the countryside. They smashed through the royal palace's gates— Mengistu's headquarters.

"Holy shit."

Another good harvest had permitted Meles to recapture the cities he'd abandoned the previous year. Soon he had seized others, some only one hundred miles north of the ultimate prize, Addis Ababa. By late May of 1991, after a months-long campaign in which TPLF forces moved inexorably further and further south, his army perched on the capital's outskirts. It was ready to move in when the dictatorship, demoralized by the string of military defeats and defections, its Soviet aid withdrawn, simply crumbled.

At a London peace conference on the eve of Meles' triumph, the State Department had sought the rebel leader's commitment to include Ethiopia's biggest tribes, the Amhara and Oromo, in a democratic system. Their two-thirds of the population was needed to stabilize the country. Meles had made promises. But his foreign backers couldn't stop him from taking his hard-won victory on his own terms. A resigned US Assistant Secretary of State for African Affairs had given Meles a green light he no longer needed. TPLF armor, flanked by foot soldiers, had rolled into the capital. They'd overwhelmed the last pockets of resistance from Mengistu's elite troops at the palace and defense ministry.

The Butcher had escaped to Zimbabwe a week earlier with a multimillion-dollar payoff from Israel to let Ethiopia's Jewish community emigrate.

Once the news report ended, Buddy's gaze fell on Hanna's letter. His thoughts turned to her as they so often had since he'd come home. They had written each other for the past year, each envelope taking a circuitous, ten thousand-mile trip by jeep, truck, air, sea, truck again and, lastly, by hand, to reach its recipient.

Her first message had arrived six weeks after Buddy's ride down the mountains and across the desert fringe to Port Sudan. Its businesslike discussion of Help Ethiopia's work seemed to confirm his fears that his sentiments were not reciprocated. But their handwritten correspondence had soon taken a personal turn. With trepidation, he had confessed his fondness for her. To his delight, this had elicited a similar response. Now each envelope contained two letters, one official and the other private.

The ignored production reports on the table were a testament to his preoccupation with Hanna. Over and over, he'd imagined her admiring him in Help Ethiopia meetings as he saved her people. Usually a workhorse, he now relished his bedtime when he could close his eyes, think about her about all he wanted and hope she would appear in his dreams.

Occasionally she did, but the circumstances were always peculiar. In one dream, they'd stood in his backyard while he explained he had to take his car to the mechanic. That was not the script he would have written.

But this morning, he only wished he could speak to her to celebrate the joyous news. He felt almost as if he, too, had fought and won the war.

With sullen suspicion, the residents of Addis Ababa watched the victorious TPLF parade through the streets. As much as they hated the dictatorship from which Meles had liberated them, tribal divisions die hard in Africa. The Amhara and Oromo, who made up most of the capital's population, distrusted these Tigrayans from the north. The news that Meles had ceded Ethiopia's historic coastline to his Eritrean allies—that their northernmost province would now be an independent country that left them landlocked—hardly endeared him to them, either.

Later that day, TPLF and Eritrean units captured police headquarters. They took over the television studio. The newspaper office. Control of the airport soon followed.

The city was speedily pacified. Special squads arrested those Derg officials too dumb or too slow to flee.

The former regime was finished for good.

Meles was the most powerful man in Ethiopia.

A fortnight after Meles occupied the capital, Buddy had a beer in the first-class British Airways lounge at Los Angeles International Airport while he waited to board his flight to Addis Ababa. Absentmindedly, he felt in his pocket and ran his thumb over the cross Hanna had given him. He'd removed its string and carried it every day as a keepsake.

59

He took a small packet of her letters from his jacket pocket and selected one to re-read. Touching the cheap writing paper she had touched, seeing her feminine handwriting that hinted at an artistic side, reminded him he would soon see the object of his desire.

This was his favorite letter because it was the first time she had written she loved him, too. He had read books and screenplays in which people fell in love through letter writing but had never dreamed such a thing could happen to him. Yet, miraculously, it had. He scrutinized her words. Had he misread their meaning? He'd know soon enough, he decided.

For the thousandth time, he imagined what she looked like naked. What she was like in the throes of passion. Had she and her fiancé been intimate? They had both been young and it was a conservative society. C'mon, grow up, he told himself.

"Going to Ethiopia?"

A clipped British voice interrupted his reverie. It was the captain. To Buddy's chagrin, the flight crew and some of the other first-class passengers—American journalists, development program experts and charity executives—had recognized him.

"They're swearing in the transitional president."

The lounge had no Ethiopians. Now that it was safe to return, they flew coach to family reunions or to cash in on connections to the new regime.

"It's a great thing you're doing over there, Mr. Schwartz," a flight attendant gushed.

More passengers spotted the celebrity in their midst and eyed Buddy.

He forced a polite smile and wished they'd leave him alone.

It was one in the morning when a flight-weary Buddy stepped out of Customs. The terminal was eerily quiet—the public was barred by a ring of TPLF soldiers and tanks. The disembarked passengers' footsteps echoed in the cavernous hall.

Hanna's government credentials allowed her inside the arrivals lounge. She wore an inexpensive, green dress and a cardigan. In civilian clothes, she looked unfamiliar.

Raised in a culture where public displays of affection were frowned upon, she made sure no one was watching before she let Buddy embrace her. Their first kiss began clumsily, but it quickly told him everything he needed to know about her feelings. Finally, she remembered propriety and reluctantly pushed him away.

"I missed you so much," he said. Her beauty seemed to bloom before his eyes. He opened his jacket to show its inner pocket stuffed with air mail envelopes. "I've been carrying your letters with me."

"All of them?"

"I read them when I'm lonely."

"I have been lonely all the time without you. I thought I would be crazy."

They kissed again. He pressed against her.

"Let's go to the hotel," he said.

A worried look crossed her face.

"What's the matter?"

"Maybe you want to eat?" she asked.

"I'm not hungry."

"You are probably tired." She straightened his jacket collar with her hand. "Maybe you should go and rest first."

"I'm tired. But come with me."

She caressed his shoulder but didn't answer.

"What is it?" he asked.

"Only I am not so beautiful," she said.

He kissed her forehead. "You're the most beautiful woman I have ever seen."

They didn't say much while he waited for his bag but glanced at one another as if to make sure they were really together.

The suitcase slid down the chute onto the slowly-turning carousel. An elderly porter in patched trousers wrested it from Buddy with calloused hands.

"I'll take it for you," the old man insisted in good English that hinted at a professional career disguised during the Red Terror by his menial trade. Buddy relented, and they followed the porter as he toted the bag outside with surprising strength.

The air outside smelled of diesel fumes. A few official vehicles idled in the terminal access lane.

Hanna waved over a black Mercedes appropriated from the vanquished government. The driver, a gangling youth rewarded with the job for his English skills and valor during the assault on the defense ministry two weeks earlier, got out.

"Hello, sir." He opened the sedan's rear door for them.

Buddy tipped the porter. They got in the car. The driver put the bag in the trunk, got behind the wheel and they took off.

Inside the Mercedes, Hanna checked if the driver could see them in his mirror. Then she met Buddy's slow, deep kiss with uninhibited warmth. Their pent-up longing weighed on them.

The car stopped at a security checkpoint by the airport exit. The driver spoke to the lieutenant in charge of the post and pointed at a pass taped to the dashboard. The lieutenant guided the car between two piles of sandbags and sent them on their way with a friendly wave.

It was two a.m. when they cruised through the wealthy Bole neighborhood near the airport. The Mercedes' strong springs turned the uneven road into easy jounces. Its interior turned silvery then plunged into shadow each time they passed under a street lamp.

Even in this well-to-do enclave, the less fortunate slept on sidewalks, in alleys or under tarps. Here and there, a petty trader dozed with an arm guardedly draped over a few cans of food, fly-covered meat, bundles of khat or cigarettes.

"All I could think about," Buddy said as he held her, "was when your next letter was coming. I knew I'd never be happy unless I had you with me."

The country was not yet fully secured, but the capital was unexpectedly tranquil except for the soldiers and armored vehicles posted on street corners.

The car entered the hilly Piazza district in the middle of the city. At last, it pulled into the unpaved lot in front of the old-fashioned Taitu Hotel.

Despite the late hour, the Mercedes was swiftly surrounded by a gang of aggressively friendly, barefoot orphans in tattered clothing. They offered chewing gum, boiled potatoes, khat, ganja or merely an outstretched palm. Hanna shooed them away. They retreated a few paces and stared at the rich faranj like a pack of hungry animals. The recent visitors from the United States and Western Europe tipped better than the Eastern Europeans during the Derg.

If he gave them all something there would be a hundred kids waiting when he left the hotel. "Here." He pointed to the suitcase his driver had removed from the car's trunk. "Take this in for me."

The bigger kids rushed forward. Three of them triumphantly bore the bag into the lobby.

The Taitu had been built in 1907 by Empress Taitu, wife of the great Menelik II who had defeated the Italians' first invasion at Adwa in 1896. The Empress, deeply proud of her traditions, had directed an artillery battery herself. The white stucco building was encircled by a quaint, wooden balcony and looked like a hunting lodge.

Buddy gave each of the kids five dollars, enough for a week's worth of food for a poor person in Addis Ababa.

The receptionist snored on a sofa in the antique-filled lobby. Buddy prodded him, and he awoke with a start. Yawning, he registered the American in a timeworn ledger.

The couple followed the uniformed bellboy as he lugged the suitcase up a broad staircase of burnished African redwood.

Each step brought Buddy closer to being alone with the woman he'd longed for all year.

Seconds felt like hours.

They reached the door to his room. The bellboy opened it with a key and let them in.

Ethereal in the moonlight, the hotel room had a mini-fridge, writing desk and set of chairs. A mosquito net hung over an ornately carved bed. An open screen door, wreathed by long drapes that billowed in the breeze, led outdoors to a balcony beyond which Addis Ababa sprawled. There were remarkably few electric lights on for a city of 2.5 million people. The dark hills resembled the back of a slumbering behemoth.

Illuminated areas on one hill were ringed by parkland. One was probably the former royal palace. There, Meles had now replaced Mengistu, and it was where the inauguration ceremony would take place later that day. Boxy, modernist buildings were probably government ministries from the Selassie era. Broad boulevards enclosed a large, triangular plaza.

"Here is the light," the bellboy said. He turned on a lamp by the bed. Brightness dispelled the mysterious atmosphere. "Here is the mosquito net. The bathroom."

Masking his impatience, Buddy gave the bellboy a tip.

"Thank you, Mister." The bellboy backed out the door and closed it.

Buddy and Hanna faced each other. He took her in his arms and kissed her.

She drew back. "Maybe you want a beer," she suggested.

"No, thanks."

She went to the mini-fridge and removed a bottle. "This is a good one." She examined the label. "St. George."

Buddy pushed the mosquito net aside, sat on the bed and watched her.

Hanna picked up a bottle opener. "We have a famous church in Lalibela called St. George." Her hand trembled as she opened the bottle. "It is carved from the rock."

She presented the beer. Buddy put it aside and gently caught her wrist.

Hanna sat on his lap, put her arms around his neck and met his questioning gaze.

"There is something I want to tell you," she said. "I am not so beautiful. I am different from Western women."

64

"What?"

"My body. It is different."

"What do you mean?"

"They cut me. When I was young."

"What?"

"They cut me."

Seeing his look of incomprehension, she took his hand and placed it between her legs. "Can you feel?"

The color drained from his face.

"Are you all right?" she asked in alarm.

"They circumcised you?"

"It is the way my people do with the young girls here. "

Be there for her, he thought desperately. "It must have hurt," he managed to say.

"I screamed when I saw the razor. They had to hold me down."

"Then why'd you do it?"

"I was only a child. They said it would honor my family. We say women who are not cut are dirty."

"Can you feel anything there?"

"A little. You look so angry."

"Doesn't it bother you?"

She didn't reply.

"You don't care?"

"It is our way. But maybe you will not like it." She searched his face. "If you do not want me, I will go."

She rose to leave, but he grabbed her arm.

"Don't talk like that," he said. "I wouldn't care if you were missing your legs, your feet or anything. I love you. Do you understand?"

He turned off the lamp. Enveloped by the mosquito net, they fell back on the bed.

"Are you sure it is all right?" she asked tremulously in the dark.

"Of course, it's all right," he lied. "I'm just so pissed off anybody would hurt you like that."

"Hold me, Buddy," she pleaded.

He took her in his arms.

"I love you," she said.

A shaft of light from the bathroom revealed his stricken face. Outside their window, a dove cooed. He listened to its sweet, plaintive sound.

A mosquito buzzed his ear, disturbingly loud and close. Furiously wondering how it had gotten through the net, he tried to swat it.

A minute later, it returned.

When he awoke, Hanna slept nude with her arm thrown across his chest. Buddy marveled at her physical elegance. As a kid, he'd sat, bored, in Temple beside his parents on Jewish holidays, but some of the more entrancing turns of phrase had stuck with him, and he remembered a passage from the Song of Solomon, *the joints of thy thighs are like jewels.* He tried not to wake her as he disengaged himself. She murmured something in Amharic and pulled the sheet around her shoulder.

He got up and stepped onto the balcony. Addis Ababa stirred in the early morning light. Like trails of ants, thousands of small, faceless figures, some holding lunch pails, trudged to work seemingly indifferent to the momentous political change taking place.

He went into the bathroom, its dinginess exposed by daylight, and rummaged through his kit bag for his shaving gear.

A stifled cry came from the bedroom.

He found her awake. "What happened?"

"I had a bad dream."

He sat on the edge of the bed. "Tell me."

"It is nothing." She turned away as if to go back to sleep.

Buddy had interviewed enough people to know when to keep quiet.

"It was very dangerous living in Addis with the Derg government," she finally said. "The Derg soldiers raped some of my friends. One girl I knew, they tore a hole in her when they raped her and then she could not control her bowels. No one will marry her. Even her family avoids her because of her smell."

Hanna stared at the wall. "The soldiers ran the government. Even Mengistu was a colonel. The government forced many people to be a spy with threats to their family. You could only talk about food and how much you loved the Derg because maybe somebody would report you. Then you would be executed. Everybody paid a soldier to protect them and gave him barley beer to drink and money. And if a soldier wanted your daughter or your wife, you had to give her."

She sighed at the memory. "Many soldiers liked my father because he was a good man," she continued. "But Mengistu brought new soldiers into the city to represent their military camps to the Derg committee. These were the worst people who were sent to the Derg when nobody believed it was important. But it made the coup and these terrible people became the rulers. They did not know my father. One of these representatives, a captain—his name was Wondwosen—came to our house. He was drunk and said he had observed me for a long time."

Hanna rolled over to face Buddy. "I was studying at the university. And planning to marry my fiancé. But Wondwosen told my father he wanted me. That day, I was in the neighbor's house. So Wondwosen said he will come again the next day and I must be ready to go with him."

She sat up and hugged her knees. "In the night, my father gave me money to run away with my fiancé. We decided to go north to Tigray and join the TPLF. I did not know about my father for two years. Then a man came to the women's camp to look for me. He was a prisoner in Alem Beqagh with my father."

"Alem Beqagh?"

"It is a special prison for the most serious cases. Alem Beqagh means 'goodbye to the world.' This man knew one guard from when they were children. And the guard helped him escape. This man also joined the TPLF in Tigray. Before he came, he visited my mother, and she asked him to bring to me a letter."

Her voice drifted off. "The letter said," she resumed after a few moments, "when Wondwosen came for me the next day, my father told him I ran away. Wondwosen said there is no problem, Ethiopia is a free country, and he talked very nice. But a week later, soldiers went to the university and said my father was TPLF. They put him in Alem Beqagh."

Buddy rubbed her arm soothingly, but Hanna appeared not to notice. "Her letter said she went to the prison to bring him food. But the guards told her he didn't need the food and to go home. Then my mother knew he was dead."

Hanna's smiled bitterly. "I should have gone with Wondwosen. I could have saved my father." She studied Buddy's face to see if he understood. "My fiancé was good to me. Many times, he brought me food and gave me barley beer to drink. And said kind words to make me feel not so sad."

She smoothed the sheet with her hand. "I want to find my father," she whispered. "And my fiancé. And bury them correctly."

Buddy kissed her forehead. "I'm going to take you away from all this," he promised. "Someplace beautiful." A recurring anxiety resurfaced. "You don't think I'm too old for you?"

"You are not too old," she said to his relief. "But I cannot go. I must help my country."

He nodded understandingly to hide his disappointment.

"The sacrifice of so many of our fighters—"

Hanna quietly translated Meles' speech for Buddy as the new president, dressed like a statesman in a navy blue suit, the wild hair cut short, addressed a crowd of foreign dignitaries, supporters and freshly-minted government officials.

The inauguration was held in a glorious reception hall of the Jubilee Palace whose lights Buddy had seen the night before. The long, cream-colored building had been Haile Selassie's residence. It boasted fountains and a zoo. Giant tortoises crawled through its lovely grounds. Ten low-ranking military officers from the Derg had confronted the Emperor in its library and read him the statement that deposed him. When he scolded them, they'd imprisoned him in an older royal compound built by Menelik II.

To broaden its national appeal, the TPLF had cobbled together a few token political groups from Oromo and Amhara prisoners of war to join it in a coalition they named the Ethiopian People's Revolutionary Democratic Front, or, EPRDF. But tribal rivalry still prevailed. The gilt-embossed invitations to the palace function read "EPRDF," but the Tigrayans' TPLF ran the show.

Buddy, also in a suit and tie, and Hanna, looking adorable in a dress and shoes he had bought her that morning, sat in the VIP section. The large room smelled of cooked onions, beer, perspiration and women's perfume. Down the hill beyond the palace's big iron fence, the bodies of the Derg's last defenders had been cleared away only days before. Curious passersby inspected Mengistu's smashed, gray-green, Soviet-donated tanks abandoned on the road. With their drooping, silenced cannons, they looked like disappointed beasts.

Meles' speech ended to a standing ovation. "Now we begin a new war. A war on poverty. Because this is the gold standard by which any Ethiopian government must be measured. I say to you, humbly, aware of the challenges ahead, I cannot do this without your help. I call on every Ethiopian and every foreign friend of Ethiopia to join me in this campaign. I promise I will not rest until it is won."

Buddy and Hanna rose and joined in the applause. "There are many people I wish were alive to see this," she said. With a twinge of jealousy, he realized she had an emotional attachment to Meles and the TPLF cause he could probably never match. Was she secretly in love with the new head of state? In the TPLF, fraternization between the sexes had been punished and relationships kept hidden. Even Meles' own violation of the rules had gone undisclosed until the birth of his first child with Azeb Mesfin, a typist from Propaganda Section Four, three years earlier in 1988.

The ceremony gave way to a party featuring music that had played a part in the war. The guests greeted their favorite performers, some just off the plane from exile, with enthusiasm. They trilled and joined in whenever a particularly meaningful song began.

Respected bards, called *azmaris*, played traditional warrior ballads on the old instruments. The bamboo flute's notes fluttered between the one-stringed lute and the ten-stringed lyre's age-old, meandering melodies. The eccentric harmonic spirals of Ethio-jazz played by Western instruments sounded almost Arabic while bongos threw off hints of Latin rhythm and funk.

Especially cherished were "wax and gold" songs whose lyrics' sly double meanings insulted the Derg. Sung during the struggle by the regime's opponents without Mengistu's spies and censors catching on, they still delighted the crowd.

Most of the music's significance was lost on Buddy, but he felt the triumphant spirit in the room as he and Hanna sipped bottles of beer. The war was really over. The sadness of last night and that morning seemed long past.

"It's quite a day," he remarked.

"It is the happiest day of my life."

Buddy reflected on the price in blood and years Hanna and her comrades-in-arms had paid for this victory. He squeezed her hand with an empathy that needed no words.

Many guests performed *eskista*, Ethiopia's popular dance. The basic move involved shaking one's shoulders without moving the hips. Every Ethiopian at the party could tell from which part of the country the other dancers came by their eskista style. Some loosely swung their heads or danced with their hands on their hips. Others put their hands together as if praying.

"Do you know how to do eskista?" Hanna asked. With uncharacteristic impetuosity, she grabbed his hand. "Look."

She swayed in an achingly sensual manner that made Buddy think of ancient Egypt. The thought of her sexual disfigurement stung like a wasp bite.

"Like this," she purred, oblivious to his distress. "And this. See?"

Not wanting to spoil her fun, he put down his beer and tried to imitate some of her moves.

"Very good," she coaxed.

"For a faranj, you mean."

They danced together, awkwardly at first, but with growing familiarity.

"There is Meles." Hanna pointed across the room. The new president was surrounded by a thick circle of supporters.

"Excuse me," someone shouted over the din into Buddy's ear. It was Abey, the Ethiopian reporter. "Remember me? I interviewed you during the war. Up in Tigray."

"Sure. Nice to see you. Are you living here now?"

"Yes. I'm starting my own newspaper," the reporter explained. "I'm working on a story about the Help Ethiopia telethon money being used to buy guns. Any comment?"

"What are you talking about?" Buddy asked sharply.

"My sources say the TPLF used that money to buy Russian light weapons from a Bulgarian arms dealer."

"I don't believe it. And you can quote me."

"You're sure?"

"Of course, I'm sure." Annoyed, Buddy held up his nearly empty beer bottle. "I need to get a drink." With ill-concealed disrespect, he headed for the bar.

Hanna joined him. "You should not have said that."

He stared at her, stunned. "What are you saying?"

"They bought a lot of weapons after the telethon."

"They did?"

"We had to fight."

"You knew about it?" he asked incredulously.

"They do not discuss with me about subjects like that. But I know they bought many weapons."

His face flushed. "Where's Meles?"

Ethiopia's leader was across the congested room. Buddy attempted to reach him through a forest of precariously held cocktail glasses and plates heaped with *tihlo* barley dumplings and spicy stew.

Hanna, confused, followed him. "What is wrong?"

"I'm a nice guy. But I don't like being screwed around." He tried again to cut through the party, but it was too dense.

"I'm going," he declared in disgust.

He pushed his way out of the room and strode down the lengthy corridor decorated with European furniture and African treasures.

"Why are you angry?" Hanna asked as she trailed him. "We should be happy today."

He stormed out the building's rear entrance where the guests' cars were parked. Under the guards' vigilant gaze, he looked for his Mercedes.

"Where the hell's my driver?"

The young man was smoking a cigarette under a tree with some other chauffeurs. He rose and flicked the butt away. A parting joke made the other drivers laugh.

Hanna caught up to Buddy. "If they spent the money on weapons, it was necessary."

The car pulled up. Buddy opened the door, and they got in.

"The hotel," he told the driver sourly.

"I do not understand why you are angry," Hanna said.

"You don't understand what it means in my world to break your word."

"Los Angeles is a different world from an African war," she reminded him as the Mercedes took off.

"I wish you would not go this way," Hanna said miserably in their hotel room a short while later.

Buddy ignored her remark as he packed his bag. "It'll take a few months to get you a visa." He had just tried to call the front desk to tell them to have his bill ready. No one had answered. He darkly wished everyone in this God-forsaken country would act more responsibly. "Then I'll send you a ticket."

"I cannot go to America."

"We'll come back as often as you want. And I'll help you with your Tasting Tours."

Hanna didn't respond.

"What is it?" he snapped, his patience exhausted. "I'm giving you a chance most Ethiopians would kill to get." He was ashamed of his words as soon as he said them.

"I have to help Meles. I will be here when you come."

A knock sounded at the door.

"Now what?" he asked irritably as he opened it.

An Ethiopian lieutenant in dress uniform stood there.

"Mr. Schwartz?"

"Yes?"

"I am here to take you to see the president."

"Tell the president I went home."

"The president insisted you please accompany me."

"I have a flight to catch."

"The flight is delayed."

Buddy's folded his arms and leaned against the door jamb. "The president wants to see me?" he asked scornfully. "Fine. I'll be glad to see the president."

The celebration was still going on noisily in the reception hall when the lieutenant led Buddy and Hanna back into the palace.

They returned down the stately corridor and entered an antechamber. A secretary sat at a desk.

"Just a minute, please." The officer disappeared into the next room.

Hanna knew the secretary and, while Buddy sulked, they gossiped in Tigrinya until the lieutenant reappeared to usher them into a grand office.

Meles waited behind a big desk covered with files and documents. He smiled and came around the desk.

"Why did you leave before I could see you?" he asked, clasping Buddy's shoulder.

Buddy stiffened at his touch. "I went on national TV and told the world their money would feed hungry Ethiopians. And you used it to buy guns?"

"Why do you say that?" Meles asked innocently.

"That reporter, Abey, is investigating the story. When it comes out, Help Ethiopia will be finished. People from coast to coast will sue me. And I'll have on my conscience the rest of my life all the people who died of hunger because of this."

"The money was spent on humanitarian aid," Meles assured him. "But it freed up other money we had for arms." His eyes glistened with appreciation. "Thanks to that money and thanks to you, we saved the entire country." He took Buddy by the arm. "Come. I want to show you something."

Escorted by his security detail, Meles led Buddy and Hanna down the red-carpeted hall.

"We're going to build schools," he said excitedly. "And roads."

He opened the door to another office. Its walls were covered with maps and engineering plans. Meles produced from his pocket some khat, tore off a sprig and gave it to his guest. He stuffed one in his own mouth and pointed to an architectural rendering of a colossal dam.

"The Renaissance Dam," he announced, chewing. "It's going to provide power to half the country. And enough left over for export. With all this electricity, we can build hospitals. Factories. People will have jobs to feed their families." He patted his pocket. "You don't have a cigarette, do you?"

"I don't smoke," Buddy reminded him curtly.

"I've got to quit," Meles sighed. "I've started playing tennis with the American Ambassador." He turned to a map of Ethiopia with areas outlined in red. "Here, we're bringing in modernized farming," he explained eagerly. "We're going to lift tens of millions of people out of poverty. Move them where they'll have clean water. Health clinics." His passion reminded Buddy of their visit to the feeding center during the war. "We're going to make history. You and me. Together."

Ethiopia's president thought for a moment. "There's a billion-dollar aid package we need from your government. The world listens to you. You must make sure they help us."

"How can I help you when that reporter's going to destroy my reputation?"

Meles said a few words to his bodyguards. They saluted and left the room.

"Don't worry about the reporter," Meles promised once they were alone. "He's not going to publish it." He returned to the map. "How we struggled in the early days," he mused as he studied it. "The brave classmates we lost—"

A man in an ill-fitting suit stopped in the doorway and spoke in Tigrinya to Meles.

"I have to meet some people," Meles said, his mood broken. "They're on my back about holding elections."

He held out his hand. "Can Ethiopia depend on you?"

Buddy hesitated.

"Don't do it for me," Meles said. "Do it for the poor and the hungry."

Buddy reluctantly took his hand.

"Our work has just begun," Meles said.

Buddy held the Ethiopian leader's hand.

Finally, he managed a small smile.

Two days later, a heavy, steel door opened in Zone Five of Kaliti prison in an Addis Ababa suburb. Prison guards shoved a man with a torn shirt and a bloody face into a dank cell. The door slammed shut behind him with a clang.

It was Abey, the reporter.

Chapter Six

In 1993, BUDDY, along with millions of other shocked Americans, watched on television as jubilant Somalis abused the mutilated bodies of US Special Forces in the streets of their capital, Mogadishu.

Somalia, Ethiopia's neighbor to the east that jutted into the Indian Ocean like an arrowhead, had descended into a violent contest between its tribal warlords. Among the spoils at stake were the routes used by international relief convoys and the opportunity they offered to loot food donations intended for the country's famine victims. When local warlord Farrah Aidid pillaged the convoys, the Pentagon had sent its best young men into the maelstrom to ensure the aid reached the poor.

The infamous "Black Hawk Down" debacle, in which eighteen US Special Forces troops were killed while they hunted Aidid's lieutenants, had led to the awful display on television. Public revulsion forced a precipitous US withdrawal from Somalia and left American officials unwilling to solve Africa's problems with American troops.

The fiasco marked the real start of the West's dependence on Meles as a military partner able to fight on its behalf in the Horn. With Mengistu's Soviet and Cuban advisers recalled, Meles' new Ethiopian army became an essential source of manpower, intelligence and logistics for a number of urgent African missions. Western governments came to rely on the former guerrilla fighter and his circle of battle-hardened military officers.

The battalion Meles contributed to the UN's mission to Rwanda after the 1994 genocide reinforced his status as the West's go-to guy in a treacherous corner of the globe. Of course, he had been an

American intelligence asset even before his conquest of Ethiopia. But with the resources of a state now behind him, the stream of intelligence that flowed from NISS, Ethiopia's National Intelligence and Security Service, to the US Embassy's CIA station became a river. Real and suspected terrorists' names, addresses, financial assets, license plate numbers, connections, phone numbers and intentions were identified in ever-increasing numbers to the impatient Americans, British, Israelis, Germans and French. Long-shuttered, covert US surveillance outposts, designed to listen in on phone calls across the region, reopened around the country.

The TPLF's humanitarian relief apparatus made Meles doubly useful. His on-the-ground infrastructure provided far-reaching security and operational support to non-profit groups like Help Ethiopia that supplied millions of needy Ethiopians with food, water, contraceptives and medical treatment. The network was invaluable to foreign governments pushed by the media to respond to the AIDS epidemic with HIV prevention and treatment in Africa.

While Buddy devoted himself to building Help Ethiopia into an effective and influential organization, Meles became the poster boy of the international community's hopes for Africa. After the horrors inflicted on the continent by Mengistu and other dictators, Ethiopia's young president was hailed as a new, progressive African leader who promised democracy and development.

Western officials, goaded by Buddy and other celebrities, loosened their purse strings and gave Ethiopia levels of financial, humanitarian and military aid not seen since the Imperial era.

One evening, after a series of meetings, Buddy relaxed in the Taitu's jazz club with Hanna and some officials from USAID, the American international development agency. He was enjoying the beer, the music and the conversation in the converted ballroom when he was struck by a burning pain in his gut that felt like he'd been knifed.

A terrible urge to move his bowels quickly followed.

Unsure he'd make it in time, he abruptly excused himself, dashed to the men's room and sat down. A cramp doubled him over as a torrent of liquid rushed from his body.

Again and again came the pain and diarrhea until he could barely imagine a world outside the bathroom stall.

The runs and cramps gradually subsided. He finally dressed, washed his hands and, feeling unsteady and apprehensive, returned to the bar.

The USAID officials were arguing about rainfall projections. Hanna gave him a concerned look.

"Something's wrong with my stomach," he said, embarrassed.

"Diarrhea?" Hanna asked matter-of-factly.

"I'd better go lie down."

"I'll come with you."

"I'll be all right."

But he wasn't all right. The moment he ate or drank anything, it went right through him.

Later that night, a bedridden Buddy was reassured when he recognized the sturdy, distinguished-looking man with a broad, good-natured face who had answered Hanna's summons. He'd seen his photos in opposition newspapers hawked on the streets of Addis Ababa. It was Ethiopia's most famous doctor, Asrat Woldeyes.

Haile Selassie's former physician and the dean of Ethiopia's first medical school, Dr. Asrat was so universally esteemed that even Mengistu had left him alone when he'd challenged the Derg's claim that the assassinated emperor had died of natural causes.

"I'm sorry I couldn't come earlier." Asrat placed his medical bag on the bed and shook Buddy's hand warmly. "I was giving a speech."

The illustrious surgeon's disapproval of the government's plans was big news. He'd criticized Meles' constitutional convention which cut the majority Amhara and Oromo tribes out of the power-sharing arrangements. He had publicly objected when Eritrea was allowed to secede without a referendum. He'd protested the lack of human rights.

Now, Asrat and his followers opposed Meles' partitioning Ethiopia, Africa's historic symbol of unity, into ethnic regions. They charged it was a form of apartheid calculated to divide the population and leave the minority Tigrayans in control.

"I apologize for bringing you out at this late hour," Buddy said. The sixty-five-year old's vitality at one in the morning, after what must have been a long day, was remarkable.

Also relieved by the doctor's arrival, Hanna took a seat across the room, too respectful to interrupt.

"I am happy to do it," Asrat said. He expertly palpitated his patient's abdomen. Removing a thermometer from his medical bag, he placed it under Buddy's tongue.

"A little high," he said as he read it. He felt the glands in Buddy's neck and took from his pocket a small glassine envelope containing some pills. "Take one after the next bowel movement. Then one every day until the symptoms are gone."

"Amoebic dysentery?"

"Probably. If you're not better in a couple of days, we'll run some tests." Dr. Asrat closed his bag and stood up. He had the straightforward way of a man who fixes things "Rest for a while. Drink plenty of fluids. Do you like juice?"

"Any special kind?"

"Mango. Papaya. Guava. Pineapple." He smiled at Hanna. "She knows."

"Thank you, Doctor," Buddy said. "What do I owe you?"

"Nothing. Her father was a friend of mine."

Hanna's face fell at the reminder. The macabre opening three years earlier of the dozens of mass graves around the prisons had uncovered such an enormous jumble of decayed bones and rags it had been impossible to identify the victims. Television cameras had broadcast the crowd of horrified family members watching a bulldozer refill the holes while priests prayed.

"And you're a good friend to Ethiopia," Asrat added.

"How is the convention coming along?"

"Not very well. Our complaints and proposals were dismissed. The government is killing Amhara in Arba Gugu."

Buddy had heard about Amhara farmers and villagers being thrown off high cliffs to their deaths. "They said the Oromo did it."

"The TPLF stirs them up." The doctor grimaced. "Some women had their breasts cut off and were forced to eat them." Seeing the American's appalled expression, he changed the subject. "If there is anything else you need, please let me know."

And with that, the good doctor left.

After a week, Buddy still didn't feel better. Despite Hanna's ministrations, he couldn't remain more than a few steps from the bathroom. To his annoyance, he was forced to cancel his flight home. Meetings back in the States had to be postponed. He asked Hanna to arrange the follow-up tests with Dr. Asrat, glumly realizing their purpose was to determine what type of parasite had occupied his colon.

"I made the appointment," she informed him when she returned to the room with a stool specimen jar from the pharmacy and a large can of mango juice. She gave him the jar. "You know what to do?"

Buddy nodded.

"It will take forty-eight hours before they have the result. Then they will give you a new antibiotic."

"How about a new intestine?" he grimly joked. He contemplated the jar in his hand. "Did Dr. Asrat say if he wanted to see me again when they confirm the diagnosis?"

"A different doctor will come."

"Too bad. I liked him."

"He is in jail."

Buddy looked at her in surprise. "In jail?"

"I found out when I called his office. The prosecutor said he was starting a war against the government. They arrested him this morning."

"Starting a war against the government?"

Hanna gave a puzzled shrug. "They say he made a speech calling for a violent revolution." She opened the can of juice and poured him a glass. "I found another doctor for you."

"I wonder what they'll do with his patients." Ethiopia was notoriously short of physicians, most of them having fled to America or Europe long ago.

"I don't know," she said ruefully.

His gut cramped up. "I gotta go." He swung off the bed.

"Start a war," he muttered, shaking his head. "Christ."

Buddy admired Asrat's world-renowned expertise in public health and was thankful for his visit. But although he was dismayed to learn the doctor with the sympathetic bedside manner was a warmongerer, the strange episode was soon nearly forgotten under a blizzard of more immediate problems.

For there were still millions of sick and hungry Ethiopians in dire need of help.

Chapter Seven

Now that Ethiopia's contacts with the West had resumed, a number of prominent actors, musicians, entrepreneurs and other personalities wanted to help its poor. Some did it for the publicity. Some did it out of personal conviction. Others were moved by a combination of both. But his world-famous telethon and the relationship he'd formed with Meles during the war had made Buddy the best known.

Making the difference between life and death for hundreds of thousands of people was a grave and heady responsibility. Once he recovered from his illness, guided the enlargement of Help Ethiopia's logistics and supply chain and returned to Los Angeles, the burgeoning charitable organization and the demands of his production company were hard to keep up with. He only made it back to Ethiopia for field inspections or media events a few times each year while local managers ran things inside the country.

Hanna played her own part in the nation's renaissance. As head of the public affairs office in the Ministry of Health, she handled the unceasing requests for information and tours from the foreign politicians, journalists, aid officials and celebrities interested in Ethiopia's notorious poverty.

She and Buddy spoke daily by phone. Their affectionate, often humorous, chats were the high point of their day. Every so often, he still asked her to come live with him in the States, and she continued to refuse. When they did see each other in person during his visits, their rendezvous took place under the pressure of grueling schedules because they shared a sincere desire to improve life for Ethiopians.

Buddy's prior romances had been heavy on the lovemaking but lacked an intellectual connection. His and Hanna's common interest kept their bond strong despite a sex life constrained by work, separation and her physical limitations.

Still, he had read more than his share of romantic screenplays. Might the distance, planning and anticipation each reunion demanded, he occasionally wondered, also have something to do with it?

Chapter Eight

MELES' VICTORY MEANT it was now possible for Help Ethiopia to expand beyond Tigray. Buddy was keen to do it. Hunger and disease were rampant in the country's other regions, too.

By 1995, after a widely boycotted election, the transitional government had become permanent. Meles, now calling himself Prime Minister, had at first been reluctant to divert much assistance from his Tigrayan homeland and political base. But he needed to polish the image of the capital, Africa's diplomatic center, where the international media was always present.

So with the government's support, Help Ethiopia opened three feeding centers in Addis Ababa. And it was Buddy's inspection of one on a spring-like day in late February 1996 that gave him and Hanna an opportunity to do what both enjoyed most—observe operations helping real people.

When Hanna and her important faranj arrived, a long line of Ethiopians already stood outside the new, two-story building in the capital's *Woreda*, or District, Seven. Most were mothers with babies in their arms or slung on their backs. They waited to enter the triage section where they'd be evaluated and, depending on the patient's age and condition, referred to the various programs provided by the center.

Inside, Buddy was pleased to find the site manager, a stocky Tigrayan with an enterprising air, personally supervising the intake process. He'd been recommended by the Ministry of Health and spoke English well.

Flustered by the presence of the executive director, the manager offered his eminent visitors coffee. Once that was politely tasted, he dutifully awaited their orders.

Buddy tried to put the man at ease. "I just want to look around."

The manager called over a woman with a kind face and elaborate braids who held a clipboard. "This is Beselot, the health assistant. She places the people who come here into nutrition groups and teaches them how they should feed their children at home."

"Do you speak English?" Buddy asked.

Beselot shook her head no.

"Ask her how often the patients come here."

The manager and Beselot chatted in Amharic, the language commonly spoken in the capital. Their speech was crowded with guttural sounds and hard consonants.

"She says they come once a week for feeding and instruction. The parents do not understand about nutrition or are too poor to provide it. We make the food together, so they learn how to do it. Then we give them vegetables and fruits to prepare at home."

The next woman in line was in her early twenties. She wore a dingy shamma and held a lethargic infant boy of perhaps three with a distended stomach. His skin hung loosely over his forehead and cheekbones.

"What's wrong with him?"

The manager talked to the woman. "Malnutrition," he reported. "The parents do not have much work."

"They'll see our doctor, right?"

"The first aid may be enough."

"No. Send him right away."

The manager recorded this order in a notebook. Shyly, the mother said something.

"She is very worried," the manager translated.

"Tell her we'll do everything we can." Buddy hoped his comforting look would overcome the language gap. She responded with a frightened stare.

The manager led them on a tour of the first-floor school and orphanage. Children drank with giddy excitement from a new clean water station. They fell quiet at the sight of Buddy. Their newly-washed faces pleaded for affection. Those experienced at begging grinned and winked.

In the second-floor vocational school, occupational skills were being taught to adults and teens.

An open window revealed the line of people outside had grown. Some, too weak to stand, lay on the ground.

For a second, Buddy fantasized giving all his money away until nothing was left.

"How long do they have to stand out there before they're seen?"

"Usually, it is only thirty minutes," the manager replied. "But it is longer today because the Oromo Relief Center closed. Many of them are coming over here."

The Oromo inhabited most of Ethiopia's southern half. With a distinct culture shaped by their traditional *Gaada* system of governance, an oral history covering four thousand years and a resentment by some of nineteenth-century conquest by the northern "highlanders," their loyalties were divided. Many wanted to stay within a united Ethiopia. Others wanted to declare independence like the Eritreans had done.

Buddy frowned. "Why'd they close the Oromo Center?"

"I am sorry. I don't know."

"I think it was political," Hanna said.

In the street below, a man, whose bright, white T-shirt, sunglasses and clipboard set him apart from the others, slowly passed down the line. Each person showed him a small, green card.

The man questioned a mother cradling a baby. He wrote the woman's answers on a form attached to the clipboard. She let him hold the child while she signed it.

"Who is that?" Buddy inquired.

"He is from the government," the manager explained. "He makes sure they belong to the EPRDF, to the government's party. If they don't belong yet, he registers them."

"What if they don't want to join?"

"They don't say no."

The manager escorted them to the freshly-painted dining

room. It served breakfast to a thousand street kids every morning and lunch to another thousand men, women and children.

Nearly everyone who ate at the long tables was homeless. Many were street orphans. Always saddened by their plight, Buddy examined their tin plates. On each rested a good-sized piece of injera made with vitamin-enriched teff and a portion of bean stew.

"Do they get meat?"

"No."

"It doesn't seem like much."

"There are so many people."

A teenage boy walked by on his hands. The youth's legs, shriveled from polio, were so thin and rope-like they were tied in a knot behind his head. Buddy imagined what it would be like to walk on his hands over the rocks and broken glass of Addis Ababa's streets his entire life. Yet the boy waddled up to the counter where they handed out the plates and injera, stuck a plate under his chin, thanked the server with a sweet smile and made it back to the table. With strong arms, he hoisted himself onto a bench, slid the plate on the table and waited expectantly for the staff to ladle the bean stew onto it.

The man in the white T-shirt and sunglasses entered the dining hall. He began to check the diners' membership cards.

One family caught Buddy's attention. A little girl with a cherubic face fed her blind mother. The father's hands rested in his lap while his boy fed him devotedly.

"What's the matter with them?"

"I don't know."

Followed by Hanna and the manager, Buddy strolled over to the family. The father looked up in surprise.

"Tell him he has a beautiful family."

The Ethiopian blinked uncertainly.

The tall American didn't want to tower patronizingly over the man, so he crouched beside him.

"Does he work?"

Some discussion ensued. "He does not work now."

"And before?"

More discussion. "He was a farmer."

"What happened?"

Once this question was translated, the father entered into a long discourse in Oromo. His wife and children watched intently as he showed Buddy his deformed fingers.

"He had an accident," the manager said. "With some equipment and hurt his hands. He could not work any more."

Hanna's expression darkened.

"Equipment? What kind of equipment?"

"Farm equipment."

Most Ethiopian farmers used a crude wooden plow pulled by an ox.

"But couldn't someone help him? Why did he lose his farm?"

The government official who had been registering people drew near. He and the manager exchanged a look.

"He could not handle the work," the manager finally answered.

"Let him see one of our doctors," Buddy instructed. "Maybe we can help him."

The manager spoke to the father again. The father covered the ears of his older child with his mangled hands. Indicating his wife, he explained something at considerable length.

The manager's eyes darted between Hanna and the official in the white T-shirt.

"He thanks you," he said uncomfortably when the father finished.

"Thank you?" Buddy repeated, puzzled at such a short translation.

The manager nodded.

"God bless you," Buddy said to the father. He thought the man would at least understand his friendly tone. But the Ethiopian seemed to expect something more.

Hanna appeared preoccupied as they completed their visit.

"Are you okay?" Buddy asked quietly. She didn't reply.

Putting aside his curiosity, he made a few suggestions for improvements. The manager wrote these down in his notebook and promised to report to the organization's district administrator when they were implemented.

With some words of encouragement to the manager, Buddy and Hanna said goodbye and left.

As soon as they were out of earshot, she turned to him. "He did not translate what the man said to you," she confided in a low voice. "The man in the dining room with the injured fingers."

"What about him?"

"The man was a farmer from Nedjo district in Oromia. But he did not say he hurt his hand in an accident. He said he was arrested by soldiers. They accused him of being a member of the OLF."

The OLF, or Oromo Liberation Front, had been another ally of Meles during the war. But the powerful role in government the Oromos were promised because they represented more than a third of Ethiopia had been denied them. Instead, they were ruled by a despised TPLF-appointed administrator. The lion's share of national resources went to Meles' Tigray, which made up only six percent of the population. To enforce their rights, the Oromo had taken up guerrilla warfare against their former partner.

"He said they took him to the police station," Hanna continued, "and—how do you say? 'Hanged?' They call it the 'Number Eight.' They hanged him on a stick and forced him to eat human waste. They broke all of his fingers. They raped his wife and many other women in his village. The wife became blind after she was raped. He does not understand why. That was what the man said."

"Why didn't the manager tell me?" Buddy demanded.

"Did you see that other man who was standing behind us? With the white shirt? He was government security. If the manager said the wrong thing, he could have a problem."

Buddy stared at the feeding center. He took a step toward it then hesitated.

"I think," Hanna said, "they closed the Oromo Relief Center because it was helping the OLF."

A meeting with the mayor kept them too busy to discuss the incident further. They finished their appointments around six and, mercifully, had the rest of the evening free. Buddy was tired, and by unspoken agreement they talked of other matters during dinner at a good Italian restaurant. They returned early to his hotel and went to bed.

"Turn over. I will rub your back," Hanna said later that night. Buddy complied, she knelt beside him on the bed and pressed her fingers into his shoulders. His muscles were tense. She thought how hard he drove himself on behalf of a people who were not his own.

"Strange about that man today," he said sleepily.

"Which man?"

"The man with the broken fingers. Did you believe his story?"

"I don't know." She pushed the heel of her palm against his spine and worked her way down his back. "Did you hear about Dr. Asrat's trial?"

He shook his head.

"The witnesses confessed in the court what they said against Asrat was not true. They said the police forced them to say it."

Buddy had heard the doctor's health had deteriorated in the harsh prison.

"That's good. They'll let him out now."

That night, he dreamed he was in the feeding center's dining room. He was supposed to put injera on each plate, but now it was his own fingers that were broken.

Panicked, he looked for Hanna. Searching desperately for her, he stumbled into the kitchen, and there she was.

Her eyes were closed.

In terror, he realized she, too, was blind.

BOOK 2

Chapter Nine

THE NEXT TWO years slipped by in a blur of meetings, press conferences, airports, plane rides, reports, financial statements, correspondence and phone calls. The man with the broken fingers receded in Buddy's memory.

In 1998, the Ethiopian-Eritrean alliance snapped over economic and trade disagreements. Now an independent nation, Eritrea invaded Badme, a town on a disputed border it shared with Ethiopia, in an attempt to humiliate and undermine Meles.

The trench warfare and human wave attacks, reminiscent of the First World War, that resulted over the useless, rocky sliver of land killed one hundred thousand people. The mutual expulsions of citizens suspected of ethnic descent from the enemy destroyed tens of thousands more lives.

By then a decade into his mission, Buddy had become so enmeshed in Ethiopia's affairs he felt as if his own identity were bound up with the country's fate. He despaired as the two impoverished allies brushed aside the pleas of their foreign sponsors and wasted hundreds of millions of dollars urgently needed by the poor on war. His inability to influence Ethiopian policy was frustrating.

But foreign and military affairs weren't his thing. The clash touched deep chords of Ethiopian pride beyond the understanding of foreigners. He simply had to hope Meles knew what he was doing.

Once the fighting ended with a shaky, UN-brokered peace, there was little left for Help Ethiopia and the rest of Ethiopia's charitable community—the donor nations, the non-governmental organizations and the activists—to do but pick up the pieces.

They helped the new refugees, the war orphans and the maimed. They replaced the wasted money.

They pressed on with their work.

Help Ethiopia, now a globally-recognized brand, continued to bring in millions with new fundraising campaigns. Its work expanded every year. But while Buddy and Meles still greeted each other with a hug whenever they met, they spoke less often as their other responsibilities multiplied.

The last time he'd seen Meles, during a joint press conference to announce a large loan from the World Bank, Buddy had been struck by the Ethiopian leader's transformation. Now in his seventh year of power, the prime minister looked confident and distinguished in an expensive suit. His face was rounder, and the wild hair had given way to a bald pate. His mustache and goatee reminded one of Lenin and gave him a slightly devilish air. Behind the spectacles, the high, arched eyebrows created a perpetually surprised look. At forty-two, he had aged more quickly than Buddy who retained that preternatural, Southern California youthfulness characteristic of Hollywood's elite.

Meles' worn appearance was understandable. He'd moved to the more secure Menelik Palace, a wooded compound of modern and antique buildings on a hill overlooking the city, where he was up late at night with his military planners and ever-present CIA adviser. Somalia had degenerated into further turmoil as its warlords fought for control. Cross-border clashes between Ethiopian forces and Somali clan leaders had inflamed sentiment among the xenophobic Muslim Somalis against the Christian Ethiopian "highlanders." Now, in addition to tensions with Eritrea and a simmering Oromo rebellion in the south, Meles had on his hands a resurgent guerrilla insurrection by Ethiopia's own Somalis on his side of the border in the Ogaden desert.

Ethiopia's Muslims had historically gotten along well with the much older Christian community. Their mild, tolerant version of

Sufi Islam had enabled the two great religions to co-exist more or less peacefully in towns and villages throughout the land for twelve hundred years.

This changed with the advent of fundamentalist Salafi Islam in Saudi Arabia in the nineteenth and twentieth centuries. Saudi funds for mosque-building had helped this ultraconservative creed take root throughout the Horn, especially in Somalia. This opened the door to radical thought.

And through this door, like a deadly serpent, violent Muslim extremism slithered during the late 1990s from Saudi Arabia and Yemen, across the Red Sea, into Africa.

It wasn't long before the serpent bit. In August 1998, a light brown Toyota truck rolled up to a security gate at the American Embassy in Nairobi, Kenya. Its driver threatened to shoot the security guard if he didn't open it. When the guard refused, the terrorist fired at him, threw a stun grenade at other embassy guards, fled and left the truck behind.

The explosion of the twenty wooden crates inside the truck packed with five hundred soda-can-sized cylinders of TNT, ammonium nitrate, aluminum powder and detonating cord devastated the embassy building and an adjacent secretarial college. Its heat surged between the buildings and incinerated a bus filled with commuters on nearby Haile Selassie Avenue. The blast shattered windows up to a kilometer away. Two hundred and thirteen people were killed. Four thousand were wounded, most of them Africans. Some CIA and US military personnel were also injured. Many suffered eye lacerations when they went to their office windows to see what had happened when the grenade went off before the truck detonated.

Ten minutes later, a smaller attack at the US Embassy in Tanzania killed another eleven and wounded eighty-three.

For the first time, the American public heard on the evening news strange-sounding names like Osama bin Laden, Ayman al-Zawahiri and al-Qaeda.

Western defense analysts began to worry radical Islamists could take over the Horn's Red Sea shipping lanes, on which the international economy depended, and even Ethiopia's Blue Nile River headwaters on which Egypt's survival relied. Like the river's cascading falls which hurled precious water downstream to anxious Egyptian wheat farmers, such defeats would set in motion their own, awful chain of catastrophes. Egypt's pro-Western government would collapse and open the door to another extremist takeover. That would spell the end of the Israeli-Egyptian peace treaty and spread mayhem throughout the Middle East.

Thanks to Ethiopia's strategic location, Meles became more important to the West than ever. The United States and Europe would pave his way with more money, training, signal intelligence and arms.

The deal had a bonus. Ethiopia's leader could use this pumped up military muscle for any domestic problems of his own. That was a godsend to a young leader struggling to govern sixty-two million far-flung subjects, most of whom did not know, like, or trust him.

Chapter Ten

ETHIOPIA WAS CAUGHT in a vortex of greed, violence and, of special concern to her Western partners, spreading Islamic radicalism. The fighting in the Ogaden desert that adjoined Somalia produced a new wave of war-weary refugees. They plodded slowly westward across the arid Ogaden plateau on sore, sandaled feet with crying, diseased children in tow or on their backs. A scrawny, tethered goat ambled behind if they were lucky. They were hungry and thirsty. Their illnesses and pains demanded medical attention. They needed food, medicine, water and shelter.

And so one January morning in 2001, fifteen years after he had first gone to Ethiopia, Buddy stood on a hastily-constructed wooden stage under a Help Ethiopia sign at the inauguration of his charity's new Teferi Ber refugee camp in eastern Ethiopia near the Somali border. Moldy-looking hills, littered with rusted military vehicles from past conflicts, surrounded the camp. A temporary parking lot held a small fleet of pickups and SUVs. Their drivers napped, smoked, or chewed khat behind the stage.

Help Ethiopia had opened the site to take up the overflow from an overcrowded UN camp sixty miles away. Buddy and Hanna were there to join the Ethiopian deputy minister of health, the town's officials and the charity's local representative in welcoming the first convoy of a thousand Somalis from the UN site. Another five thousand would join them over the next two weeks.

The Help Ethiopia representative, an idealistic Methodist from Minnesota, had chosen this spot because it had water. A road, rough but drivable, was busy with trucks smuggling khat from Ethiopia's north to customers in Somaliland, a breakaway part of Somalia that had miraculously escaped the rest of the country's chaos.

The Minnesotan planned to work with the UN to build a school and clinic. Buddy admired the willingness of such employees to suffer the hardships of a remote post.

Teferi Ber meant "Gate of Fear." Haile Selassie had conducted secret reconnaissance of Italian positions near the ancient city in the early days of the 1935 fascist assault.

Because of Buddy's fondness for reggae music, which often celebrated the Rasta god, he was intrigued by Ethiopia's legendary emperor whose clandestine operation was a footnote to events that had shaken the world.

Mussolini, greedy for more territory to satisfy his grandiose ambitions, had set his sights on Ethiopia. The Italian lines Selassie observed near Teferi Ber would soon advance. Poisoning rivers, lakes and crops, they began the extermination of Ethiopia's defenseless people while the bombastic tyrant proclaimed the kingdom part of the new "Italian Empire."

Haile Selassie had personally commanded his troops in the final battle and even operated a machine gun himself. But the invader's technologically superior forces overwhelmed his antiquated Imperial Army.

That was the backdrop to Selassie's dramatic 1936 appeal to the League of Nations in Geneva that aggression against one state be regarded as an attack on all. The United Nations would later be founded on this principle.

"Today, it is us," the diminutive, yet regal, Emperor had warned the indifferent European delegates who were already cynically colluding with the Italians. "Tomorrow, it will be you."

The conquest of Africa's only independent state was widely expected to extinguish the last flicker of African freedom. Africans, the West believed, would soon go the way of the American Indian.

But from exile in England, Haile Selassie kept the dream of African liberty alive with speeches and diplomacy. A few years later, when all of Europe recoiled under the fascist onslaught, many came to see the words of Solomon's heir as prophecy. His cause turned the

Ethiopian emperor into a global symbol of collective security. The British, finally awakened to the wisdom of his prediction, placed men, money and matériel at his disposal.

In 1941, Haile Selassie re-entered Ethiopia at the head of a tribal uprising. The Lion of Judah flag was raised again. Together with allied units, Ethiopian patriots pushed deep inside the country and defeated Mussolini's army.

Selassie's triumphant return to Addis Ababa and the Rainbow Throne had given a frightened, besieged world its first victory over fascism. It gave the African continent hope that one day it, too, would be free.

Loud trills cut short Buddy's musing. The first convoy of trucks had arrived to howls from the surprisingly kind local residents who had come for the occasion. Their welcome was heartfelt because they shared a culture similar to their tribal compatriots' along the border. The camp would be good for the local economy, too.

Slim, male Somali refugees in white skullcaps, light-colored tunics and sarongs jumped down from the trucks. Their easy manner hid their distress at being dispossessed. The women, garbed in brightly dyed robes, were more obviously depressed. Each household would receive food, tarpaulins, blankets, sleeping mats, kitchen sets, jerry cans, kerosene stoves and soap.

It was Buddy's turn to speak to the assembled foreign press, executives from foreign aid organizations and Ethiopian officials. His hair had begun to gray. He had gained weight and his trousers chafed. He counted the number of years he'd been doing this and vowed to get more exercise.

He'd also changed in other ways. He appreciated having water every time he turned on a shower. He rarely ate without remembering there were hungry people at that same moment around the world.

A billion of them.

Everyone who had come from the capital was tired. They'd had to get up at five a.m. for the ninety-minute flight from Addis Ababa's Bole International Airport to the airstrip at Dire Dawa, followed by a bone-rattling, three-and-a-half-hour, hundred-mile drive to the feeding center.

To a smattering of applause and clicking cameras, he took out his notes and adjusted the microphone. The day was warm. Beads of perspiration dotted the deputy minister's forehead. Behind the audience, a feeding tent efficiently served refugees. We've come a long way, Buddy thought.

Off to one side, Hanna oversaw the proceedings she had arranged. No longer the fresh-faced young woman who had first captivated him, she was still very beautiful in her late thirties. She gave him a quick smile.

"The US Congress has approved substantial aid bills for Ethiopia since the end of the civil war," he began. "The opening of the Help Ethiopia Teferi Ber Center is an opportunity to remind the world that Congress must approve this year's increased aid bill as well—" Applause interrupted him. "And take a leadership role in the campaign to forgive another billion and a half dollars owed by Ethiopia to multinational institutions."

He finished his remarks and shook the deputy minister's moist hand.

"It's a beautiful day," the deputy minister commenced in English. "And I want to thank my friend and partner in our fight, Buddy Schwartz—"

Workers unloaded trucks by the feeding tents. Balancing the fifty-pound sacks of grain on their heads, they walked rapidly on skinny legs to relieve their burdens as quickly as possible.

The trucks were further away from the tents than necessary, creating extra work for the men. His producer's habits aroused, Buddy stepped off the platform and strode over to the unloading operation.

The supervisor came up to him. "Mister?"

Buddy gestured at the trucks. "Move the trucks closer. They won't have to carry the bags so far. See? Closer. Closer."

"*Ish*," the supervisor agreed. He signaled the drivers.

"Ethiopia is moving toward a new future—" the deputy minister read.

The trucks started up. Playing traffic cop, Buddy directed them himself.

"But we cannot make this journey alone—"

Hanna joined him. "You have never met my family. And next week is *Timkat* festival. Will you come and eat with us?"

"I would love to." He guided the trucks some more until they rested in the right spot. "That's it."

He forgot his chafed thigh. With a feeling of gratification, he watched the refugees wait uncomplainingly for their supplies as the ceremony continued in the background.

Buddy's Cessna soared back over the Ogaden plateau toward Addis Ababa, where a drink, a good meal and a comfortable bed at the new, opulent Sheraton hotel awaited. It had been a grueling day. After the long road trip back to Dire Dawa, he and Hanna were exhausted.

Only minutes into the flight, lulled by the engines' monotonous droning, Hanna slumped, asleep, against her shoulder harness. Buddy fought the urge to doze, too.

They flew without talking much. The pilot chewed gum and hummed Kenyan Migori Super Stars *benga* tunes. Garbled messages stuttered once in a while over the radio's open emergency channel. The radar transponder beeped at intervals.

The sky was bright and clear. But half an hour later, a brown streak that hugged the curve of the earth appeared on the horizon like sediment at the bottom of a glass.

"Sandstorm," the pilot said. He scrutinized the band of Somali dust, swept in on Indian Ocean wind currents, that blocked their way. "We'll have to change our route." He picked up his microphone and pressed the transmit button. "Alpha Delta Tower, Alpha Delta Tower," he said, using the ground station code for Bole. "Acknowledge."

An Ethiopian-accented voice broke up amid static. "This is Alpha Delta Tower."

"This is Tango Alpha Two Four Six Four Alpha, presently route Victor one two. Heading west Victor twelve. Position six one three. Heading three six zero. Speed two five zero knots. We're encountering sandstorm and wind conditions. Request route change to Juliet five thirty-three. Over."

"Verify."

"We're at four thousand five hundred. Over."

"Maintain heading three six zero," came the order. "Climb and maintain six thousand. Over."

The pilot frowned at the refusal. "Unable," he said into the microphone. "Wind direction five five zero. Request route change to Juliet five thirty-three. Over."

"Maintain heading three six zero," the crackling voice said. "Climb and maintain nine thousand."

"Something wrong?" Buddy asked.

"Unable," the pilot repeated, ignoring him. "Request route change to Juliet five thirty-three. Over."

The brown wall got bigger and bigger.

"Negative," came the reply from the tower. "Juliet five thirty-three is closed. Climb and maintain thirteen thousand. Over."

"He doesn't want us to change our heading," the pilot grumbled.

"Can we go over it?"

"The wind is too much." The pilot pushed the button. "Unable. Minimum fuel. Request pilot options. Over."

"Negative."

"What is wrong with this guy?" the pilot exclaimed. "How do you hear me?" he asked the controller.

"I hear you."

"Say again."

"I hear you. Juliet five thirty-three is closed."

"He's saying the other route is off limits," the pilot explained. "Probably something military."

Now the sandstorm's monstrous, looming clouds resembled a 1950s atomic bomb newsreel.

"What do we do?" Buddy asked.

The pilot glanced at a photo of his girlfriend taped to the instrument panel. "We'll have to cross some restricted airspace, but I'm going to divert south. It's the only safe course." The pilot pulled at the controls and turned the plane left and southward. "I'm not letting that moron fly us into that or make us run out of fuel." He turned off the transponder and squinted at the radar display. "They can still pick us up on the secondary. We may get a fine when we get back to Bole."

"How much?"

"Maybe twenty-five hundred dollars."

Buddy shrugged.

"Say heading. Over," came the controller's voice after a few minutes.

The pilot winked at Buddy. "I can't read you."

"Say heading. Say heading. Over." A long pause followed. The microphone crackled again. "Radar contact. Squawk 7421."

The pilot shook his head. The plane continued south.

The flight became uneventful again. The sparse, Ogaden scrubland gave way to the arable Oromo south. They sailed over rectangular fields of yams, cassava and corn in forest clearings, their yellows, tans and greens vivid in the late afternoon. The occasional village's scattered roofs went by, the inhabitants too small to see.

A column of black smoke rose in the distance.

"What's that at two o'clock?" Buddy asked.

"Probably clearing a field," the pilot replied, referring to the slash-and-burn method used to convert forest to farmland throughout much of the developing world.

Buddy sighed. The traditional technique destroyed roots and temporary water storage in tree canopies that prevent nutrients from being washed away.

He craned his neck to view the flaming field far below. Instead of a burning plot, thirty or forty separate, small fires formed a flickering orange ring. "Look at that." The pilot tried but couldn't see it from where he sat. "It's like a bunch of fires."

Buddy watched the strange constellation of flames until it was behind them.

They flew in silence another minute or so.

"Can you go back?" he asked the pilot.

"Hm?"

"I think that was a village on fire. Can you go back? I want to take another look."

The pilot was tired, but the American was a good customer. He turned the control wheel to the right.

The spiraling smoke came back into view. The plane headed for it.

"I'll go over it low." The pilot worked the rudder pedals and opened the throttle for descent.

"Where are we?" Hanna murmured.

"We had to take a detour," Buddy told her. "We're in Oromia."

The plane banked and circled the site. Smoke billowed from huts. In a dirt clearing, a few tiny figures looked up at the plane.

"Yeah, it's a village."

Hanna peered out the window.

"Okay?" the pilot asked Buddy.

"Can you land it down there?"

The pilot shot him a surprised look.

"They might need help."

"We're in restricted airspace. It's not a place to be hanging about."

"There may be injuries. We have a medical kit."

He was too distracted to notice the pilot roll his eyes. The plane banked again. They descended to a hundred feet.

The jungle canopy rushed by under them.

"There's a spot." The pilot pointed to a patch of farmland outside the village. "You sure you want to do this?"

"Maybe it is not a good idea," Hanna said warily.

"Is it smooth enough to land?" Buddy persisted.

The pilot circled the field to inspect it. Five hundred meters long with neat furrows, its ground-hugging, yellow leaves promised a crop of yams ready for harvest.

He'd landed on worse. "That will work."

He put the plane into a final turn and aligned it with the end of the field.

They came in nice and slow. As they crossed the edge of the yam patch, the pilot pulled the power back to idle.

The Cessna glided for a few seconds, touched down hard, jostled along the ground and braked just before the jungle resumed. The pilot cut the engine. The propeller slowly stopped turning.

They unbuckled their harnesses. With the power off, the cabin began to swelter. The pilot scrambled past them to the plane's rear, grabbed the first aid kit and opened the door. They climbed down.

Up to their knees in yam plants, they surveyed the area. Oromia was a different Ethiopia—hot, green, fertile, real jungle. The Africa of adventure stories. The setting sun made the field glow. A monkey's screech came from the nearby forest.

Not a soul was in sight.

The plane had cut a long trail through the plantings. "Some farmer's going to be pissed," the pilot said.

Hanna carefully looked around.

"You'd think somebody would already be here to see what's going on," Buddy said.

Beside the field, a red clay road, fiery in the dying light, led in the direction of the village.

"Do you want to wait here?" Buddy asked Hanna.

"I will come with you."

"Wait a minute," the pilot said. He climbed back into the cabin and re-emerged a moment later with a pistol. The Kenyan tucked the gun into the back of his pants and pulled his shirttail out to hide it.

"Let's go," he said.

The road passed tall, shaded forest, the tree trunks long and white. Monkeys whooped and birds hooted.

Buddy watched the sides of the road for snakes. The aggressive black mamba could be ten feet long and sprang up to bite people on the head. Its venom would kill a human in four ghastly hours. The spitting cobra's poison, even if the bite missed, could blind a man if it got in his eyes. No medical help, let alone anti-venom medication, would be found here. He glanced down at Hanna's bare legs protruding from under her dress as she trudged beside him.

They walked about half a mile to the edge of the now-abandoned village. The charred remains of a few dozen huts smoldered. By the first burned hut, the body of a teenage boy hung upside down by his ankles from a tree branch. Blood dripped from his head. His face was purplish black. His eyes bulged hideously. His tongue dangled past his chin. His white trousers were soiled.

For a moment, Buddy felt as if he'd left his body.

"Let's get out of here," the pilot said.

They retraced their steps as fast as they could looking over their shoulders and flinching at every noise.

When they reached the yam patch, an Oromo man in a shamma and knee socks waited by the plane. His lanky build, high forehead and deep-set eyes made him resemble Abraham Lincoln. He appeared unarmed as he watched them approach.

The pilot spoke some Oromo and greeted him.

"I speak English," the man said. "I am the school teacher."

Buddy pointed. "There's a dead boy there."

"They killed many boys," the Oromo replied. "Many boys are dead."

"What happened?" the pilot asked.

"The soldier came and they made a fire to all the house. All houses have fire."

"Soldiers burned the houses?"

The Oromo nodded vigorously. "They burned the house. They killed many men. I—" He crouched to demonstrate what he was trying to say.

"You hid."

"Yes. I hid. I hid. The soldiers rape all women. And the men—" He raised a fist beside his neck to simulate a noose.

"They hanged the men?"

"Yes, yes. They hanged some men. And they shoot some men." He fearfully scanned the road. "They say we give food to the OLF."

The OLF was engaged in a low-intensity war for autonomy in Ethiopia's south. But Buddy had never heard of such atrocities.

A motor growled down the road.

"Let's move," the pilot said.

"Please. I go with you," the Oromo pleaded.

The pilot looked at his client.

"Okay," Buddy said.

They clambered into the plane.

"You take me to United Kingdom?" the Oromo asked Buddy.

"We're taking you to Addis."

The Oromo gulped. "Addis Ababa?"

Buddy looked out the aircraft's window. An army jeep with two soldiers sat in the road.

"Go," he said sharply to the pilot.

The pilot closed the door, jumped in his seat and started the engine. The Cessna slowly swung around to get ready for takeoff.

One of the soldiers in the jeep fired a shot in the air.

The pilot applied the brakes, and the plane shuddered to a halt, its propeller still spinning.

"Go!"

"They'll shoot the plane." The pilot shut down the power.

Events seemed to happen in slow motion. Another jeep with two more soldiers joined the first one. Their drivers briefly conversed then both jeeps rumbled across the yam patch to the Cessna. The soldiers got out. One banged with his rifle butt on the cabin door, the thumps loud and terrifying.

"Open the door," the pilot told Hanna, who was nearest it. She jerked the handle down, and the little door swung outward. The soldier motioned with his AK-47 for them to get out.

"Can't you talk to them?" Buddy asked Hanna who, after all, was a high-ranking government bureaucrat. She attempted a few words of Amharic with the two soldiers but got no response. This far to the south, Tigrinya was useless.

"I'm an American," Buddy told them.

Disregarding him, the soldiers directed him and Hanna to get in the back of one jeep. The pilot and the school teacher were put in the other.

"Speak English?" Buddy asked the two soldiers in the jeep's front seat with forced friendliness.

No reply came. A mobile radio sat on the jeep's dashboard. The soldier in the passenger seat picked up its handset and spoke irately into it.

"Tell him I'm a friend of the prime minister," Buddy urged Hanna. She tried again. The soldier shouted angrily at her in an unfamiliar-sounding language.

"They don't speak Amhara."

"Meles Zenawi," Buddy said deliberately, hoping the soldiers would understand him. "I'm a friend of Meles Zenawi."

"Wait," Hanna advised him under her breath.

Both jeeps tore through the field, turned onto the road and headed toward the village.

Soon the road took them into the ravaged hamlet. The soldiers hardly glanced at the hanged boy. In the central clearing, where the town's citizens met to trade and share the day's gossip, two men and another boy lay dead. Their clothing was disheveled, and their limbs splayed in unnatural positions. A chicken pecked at the ground beside the dead boy.

At one end of the clearing stood a mighty sycamore tree known as the *Oda*. Its shade was a sacred place where laws and important decisions were announced. Four more men hung like Christmas ornaments from its branches.

Buddy fought hysteria. "Somebody's got to tell Meles about this," he said to Hanna.

"Tell him? I think he ordered it."

They continued through the village. A few hundred meters up

the road, the jeeps stopped at a one-story cinder block building. A blackboard was set up under a tree with the English alphabet neatly written on it. Two soldiers guarded its entrance.

At least they hadn't been taken into the forest, Buddy thought.

"Is this your school?" he asked the teacher as they got out of the jeeps.

Weeping, the Oromo nodded.

With their guns, the soldiers prodded their prisoners inside the schoolhouse.

Moths flitted a round a light bulb. Night had brought the musty smell of decayed vegetation into the empty classroom in which they'd been held for hours. Tired and sweaty, nobody was in the mood to talk. Buddy's chafed thigh stung.

The soldier in the doorway appeared to be no more than twenty. He wore camouflage gear and smugly cradled an AK-47 in his arms. His body odor was rank.

Except for one older man in civilian clothes who had come in, made them write their names on a sheet of paper and left, no one had spoken to Buddy and his companions.

The teacher's hands had trembled so badly he'd scarcely been able to write his name. He'd begun to belch out of fear. Each burp sounded like a warning from some dark place of what was to come. Buddy wondered what the tearful Oromo knew that they didn't.

Through an open window came the sound of soldiers talking and laughing. Their youthful exuberance reminded Buddy of Meles and his young TPLF fighters during the war. But these recruits from the southwest were darker skinned, their features broader and less Semitic. They were more volatile. Their argumentative style of speech suggested an utter lack of social restraint.

Over the chatter of the soldiers, an unearthly wail pierced one of the classroom's walls. Like a siren, it rose in volume, fell, then intensified again.

"What the hell is that?" Buddy asked the teacher.

The teacher belched. "They rape a lady."

As the wailing continued, the soldiers outside began to quarrel.

"What are they saying?"

"One want to shoot us. The other soldier say they need—" He struggled to find the right word. "Permission," he finally said.

"Shoot us?"

"We see too much. He said they will do—" the teacher struggled again for the English phrase. "Like to steal."

"To steal...you mean, a robbery?"

"Yes. Yes. A robbery."

"They will rob us?"

The teacher tried again. "They will make all people believe a robbery."

"They will make it look like a robbery?"

"Yes. Yes."

"These are government soldiers?"

"These are soldiers."

Enraged, Buddy indicated the guard. "Tell him," he loudly instructed the Oromo. "We are very good friends of the prime minister." The guard eyed Buddy and tightened his grip on his weapon. "And if they hurt us, they will be punished."

The teacher translated, but the guard didn't seem impressed.

"Do you understand?" Buddy furiously asked the guard. "I am a friend of Meles Zenawi."

The wailing coming from the next room stopped. A younger female's moans began.

"Christ! What are they doing?"

The teacher leaped from his chair. "I know that lady." He ran to the wall, pressed his cheek against it and hollered the same word, perhaps her name, again and again.

"They rape all lady," the teacher said. He pointed to his groin. "They put pepper in the lady." Crying, the Oromo sank to his knees and prayed.

At a loss for words, Buddy looked to Hanna. Her calm seemed oddly misplaced.

The pilot nervously tapped his foot. Things could quickly get much worse if the still-undiscovered pistol was found.

The noises in the next room tapered off. Time dragged by. Buddy examined the peeling blue paint on the wall. His thoughts fluctuated between apprehension and shame at having gotten Hanna and the pilot into this mess. The praying teacher reminded him of something he'd read about Haile Selassie's last days as Mengistu's prisoner in the palace. The emperor's valets had later testified how he had become despondent when he learned members of his family and top officials had been executed. Realizing his own death was imminent, he had also knelt, at a window overlooking one of the palace chapels, prayed and wept. Buddy pictured the proud monarch, who had done so much for Africa and the world, vulnerable as a wounded gazelle before a crocodile ready to lunge.

Would these soldiers actually harm him? Usually, a white man in Ethiopia was presumed to have powerful connections. Surely that offered some kind of protection. Why, then, were the soldiers arguing over their fate? Why had they been arrested?

Suddenly, it all fell into place. The restricted airspace. The massacre of the village—and God knows how many other villages.

Like the Oromo had reported the soldiers saying, they had seen too much. They were inconvenient witnesses.

The bilious taste of panic rose in Buddy's throat.

Around midnight, they heard a vehicle arrive. A car door slammed. The guard straightened up. A few moments later, an Ethiopian officer and another soldier entered.

"Mr. Schwartz?" To hear someone in authority speak English flooded Buddy with relief. "I am Major Zewdie. I am sorry for your inconvenience. We are taking you and your party back to your plane."

Everyone got up to leave.

The major considered the teacher. "Not him."

"He's with us," Buddy said.

113

"We still have some questions for him."

The teacher tried to stand with Buddy. The guard shoved him back and aimed his rifle at him.

"I can't leave without him," Buddy protested.

"He cannot go," the major said. He grunted a command, and the guard stepped aside to let the others pass.

"He works for me," Buddy lied.

"My orders are to send only you, the woman and the pilot back to the capital."

"I want to call the prime minister."

"Someone spoke to the prime minister. You are free because of him."

The teacher belched.

"He's got to come with us."

"He is a terror suspect, and we must interrogate him."

"That's ridiculous!"

"You must come with me," the major said politely but firmly.

"This is really fucked up!" Buddy yelled.

Hanna's alarmed look told him to get himself under control.

"I'll pay you ten thousand dollars to let this man go," he said to the major in a low tone.

"This is a political case," the major said. "Nobody can touch it."

"Twenty thousand."

The major shook his head.

"Tell me your name," Buddy said to the teacher.

"That is enough," the major warned.

The teacher burped. "Gebru Hailu."

"Gebru Hailu," Buddy repeated.

"You must come with me now, sir." The major gave Buddy a sardonic look. "Unless you want to stay here with him."

"Go," the teacher cried with a crazed stare Buddy would never forget. "Tell Mister President of America everything here."

Buddy jabbed his finger at the major. "I'm going to talk to Meles about this. And I'll want to know if anything happens to this man!" The officer regarded his finger impassively.

"I'm telling the prime minister about you," Buddy promised the teacher.

"Come," the major said.

"We'd better go," the pilot muttered.

"I'm sorry," Buddy said to the ashen-faced Oromo.

"Go and tell Mister President." The teacher belched once more. "Tell Mister President."

With a final look back at him, Buddy reluctantly allowed himself to be herded out of the schoolhouse with Hanna and the pilot. A partly open door gave a glimpse of a soldier standing over a naked man lying on a table. But they passed too quickly to know whether the man was dead or alive.

Outside, they gratefully breathed the equatorial night air. The soldier put them in the back of a late model American Humvee and slid behind the wheel. The major got in the passenger seat.

A loud pop went off.

"What was that?" Buddy demanded.

The major lit a cigarette. "Nothing," he said.

Buddy glanced at Hanna.

Uneasily, she averted her eyes and turned away.

Sipping her macchiato in the Sheraton's garden, Hanna watched Buddy fidget with his spoon. He'd had trouble sleeping and appeared restless since their return to the hotel a few days ago. She'd seen the same signs in TPLF fighters after their first battle.

Meles was tied up hosting the African Union Summit, and they had to wait until he could see them. In the meantime, they stayed close to the hotel. They swam in the sparkling pool, ate long meals in its smart restaurants and rested on its Egyptian cotton sheets, the luxury a reassuring reminder of a safe, orderly universe. Each day helped the recent traumatic events fade from memory.

Finally, the date rolled around and, with Hanna beside him, Buddy had his opportunity to sit across the imposing desk, look

Meles in the eye and ask what had happened to the school teacher.

"I'm sure he is fine," the prime minister replied, unconcerned.

"Can we make sure?"

Meles tiredly pressed a button. An aide entered and saluted. The prime minister gave him an order. The aide saluted again and left.

"Okay, we will let you know."

"And government troops are burning down villages and hanging people from trees?"

"The report I saw says it was the terrorists who attacked the village. Not us. We don't burn villages."

Hanna had read the same thing in *Addis Zemen*, the government-owned newspaper, but didn't believe it.

"That teacher seemed pretty reliable to me," Buddy insisted.

But with Meles' insinuation, doubt seeped in. Maybe the Oromo teacher, however pathetic he sounded, was not an innocent witness but a terrorist sympathizer twisting the truth to protect himself and his OLF terrorist friends. Maybe it wasn't Meles' soldiers who had committed the hangings, as the teacher had claimed, but the OLF terrorists themselves. Maybe those screams had not been innocent rape victims' but Islamo-fascists being interrogated—harshly perhaps, but necessarily so.

Buddy wanted to believe Meles' implication that the Oromo had duped the naive foreigner. Uncorroborated, single-witness interpretation of events, he told himself. You wouldn't have used it on *60 Minutes*. Or maybe, he thought grimly, the soldiers had hanged those men, but they were well-justified executions of dangerous maniacs. Sure, there's a war going on down there, even a dirty war. But it's for a just cause—fighting terrorism.

Counterterror was no Sunday school picnic. The dead bodies, dazed survivors and mounds of rubble left by the embassy bombings had been big news. So were the fifty-six dead and injured American sailors and the gaping hole left by terrorists in the side of an American Navy destroyer while it refueled in a Yemeni port.

In that murky no-man's land, lines got blurred. People got swept off foreign streets into prisons without names where God-knows-what was done to make them talk. When you deal with zealots who put bombs in planes, buses and buildings, there's not always time to read them their rights. You put a bullet in them first and ask questions later.

The competing realities danced round and round in Buddy's head like a dog chasing its tail. Who could tell what was the truth with these people?

He studied Meles. The round, shark-like eyes behind designer glasses. The rich fabric of his suit. The silk tie. The costly, gold watch. The soft, manicured hands restively tapping a Montblanc pen on the desk.

An Ethiopian flag hung limply from a pole beside the prime minister. Even Mengistu had not dared change the red, green and yellow stripes ordered by Menelik II and had merely removed the crowned Lion of Judah, symbol of the Solomonic Dynasty, from the flag's center. No fan of the monarchy either, Meles hadn't restored the Lion but had added instead a yellow star on a blue disc meant to stand for unity. To ensure its popularity, the rubber-stamp Parliament had passed a law that punished anyone who displayed the old flag with a year and a half in jail.

"Maybe you should talk to him yourself," Buddy challenged the prime minister.

Meles nodded thoughtfully. "There will be an investigation," he promised. "And if any human rights were violated, we will deal with it." The former guerrilla leader massaged his temples with his fingertips. "They are very unruly down there," he said in a frustrated tone. He gave Buddy a beleaguered look. "Can you understand my responsibilities?" he asked. "Can you understand what it takes to save sixty, seventy million people? You, with your full belly and guilty conscience. Who sleeps in a clean bed every night."

Was that a confession? "I'm here to feed people," Buddy said. "Not kill them."

"So am I," Meles snapped. He spoke to Hanna in Tigrinya. She answered in a timid tone, and he gave her a displeased look. "Well," he said to Buddy, "if you want to feed them, I need you to do some publicity for the aid package."

Buddy had long noticed his celebrity status attracted Western media coverage Meles couldn't get by himself. And that media coverage was what American and European politicians, who held the foreign aid purse strings, responded to.

A drop of sweat tickled as it crawled down his back.

"Are you all right?" Meles asked. "You look pale."

"Where's the bathroom?"

In the mirrored men's room vestibule, Buddy glimpsed multiple reflections of an aging, slightly overweight, painfully earnest man in a suit receding, like his doubts and questions, into infinity.

Bizarrely, he thought he looked like a pig ready for slaughter.

Moments later, as Buddy splashed water on his face, a disturbing thought crossed his mind. What if he and Meles quarreled? How would he operate here? The government's support for Help Ethiopia was crucial. He needed it to renew the charity's license every year. For security. Logistical support. Advice. To cut the never-ending red tape. The organization couldn't function a day without the regime's help. Whatever the truth of what he'd seen in that village, right or wrong, he had invested years of hard work and his reputation in the massive humanitarian operation he'd built. Countless lives and jobs depended on it.

He thought of the dispossessed Somali refugees he'd seen the week before. The lovable orphans drinking at the water station. The intrepid polio victim walking on his hands through Addis Ababa's streets. The desperate mothers and fathers bringing him their dying children. They relied on him. And he relied on Meles.

The restroom door swung open. Meles entered. "Are you sure you're okay?" he asked as he took a urinal.

"Just felt funny for a minute."

"Make sure you're getting enough sleep," the Ethiopian offered solicitously. An awkward pause followed. "I welcome your criticism," he admitted as he faced the tile wall. "Don't give up on us. My people need you. And I need you. Help us learn to do things better."

What was Meles trying to say? Was he in his own hall of mirrors? Yet to confront him, to push him harder for the truth and risk a falling out was unthinkable. "His" Ethiopians, as Buddy thought of them, still had a chance to live—as long as he and Meles got along. He'd simply have to ignore the confusing, conflicting evidence and take the man's word for what had happened.

Seeing the prime minister at the urinal like any regular guy, Buddy felt a twinge of empathy for this all-too-human man who had risked his life to take on one of the world's toughest problems, Ethiopia's extreme poverty.

The painting of the crucifixion of Jesus by the Renaissance artist Marco Palmezzano came inexplicably to mind. Buddy had seen it once at the Uffizi in Florence when he'd honeymooned in Europe with his first wife. He'd been struck by its spectral, melancholy colors reflecting the unspeakable grief of the witnesses and the naked figure agonizing on the cross. I guess that's why they always paint that little cloth over his loins he mused, glancing over at Meles. Gods don't have genitals—they're a sign of humanity.

This man is my friend, he decided. And friends trust each other.

Relieved, he dried his face and hands with a towel embroidered with Meles' yellow star.

For the rest of the scheduled hour, they discussed Help Ethiopia's operational requirements. There were security issues at the camps. Meles promised to help and dictated a memo to the army chief of staff.

Before he knew it, the details of Buddy's participation in the upcoming press conference had been settled, the meeting had ended with hugs and fond goodbyes, and he and Hanna waited at the top of the long palace driveway for his car to come around.

"I can't believe I agreed to do it," Buddy sighed.

Hanna spotted the car and waved the driver over.

"You were awfully quiet in there," he observed

"You were so cooperative." Her tone hinted this was not intended as a compliment.

"Well, maybe he's right." The comment sounded more like a question.

"The teacher is dead," she said impatiently. "Like Dr. Asrat."

He knew what she meant. The year before, Dr. Asrat had died. Buddy didn't understand why the dedicated doctor had remained in jail after the witnesses against him recanted. But with the constant court delays, he had never been freed. A heart condition had worsened from medical neglect and the damp, cold and lonely prison environment.

The donor nations Meles counted on hadn't wanted to jeopardize the security relationship and had only registered perfunctory diplomatic protests over Asrat's persecution. No one, least of all Meles, took them seriously.

The prime minister had grudgingly released the famous physician on the brink of death to avoid the embarrassment of a national hero dying in jail. The doctor's family had whisked him to the United States in a futile bid to save his life. His loss had crushed the hopes of those who saw his vision of a free and united Ethiopia as the afflicted country's salvation.

"And many reporters are missing," Hanna added. "Now I hear more stories about corruption. Political prisoners in jail. And torture." She bit her lower lip, something she did when she was thinking. "I did not fight in the bush to make another dictator," she said. "You must tell the world what is happening here."

Buddy threw his hands up in a helpless gesture. "I start blasting Meles. He loses the aid package. I can still eat. But what about everyone here who needs the food?"

She didn't answer.

"What was he saying to you?"

"He said I should handle you better."

Buddy's eyes flashed with anger. "Oh yeah? What did you say?"

"I said I would try," Hanna confessed. "You are going back to America," she explained when she saw his annoyance. "But I am here. They could say I am a terrorist. Or accuse me of some crime."

A cool breeze was blowing. From the hill, they looked over Addis Ababa, gray and smoky, so filled with despair and heartache. Buddy realized he and Meles might have been standing on the spot where Haile Selassie's small skeleton had been found under some palace toilet seventeen years after being strangled by his successor.

He took in the leafy royal compound. The modern conference hall built by Mengistu. The royal chapels. The residences for princes and princesses. It had been the Solomonic Dynasty's official center until Mengistu made it his own after the 1974 coup and imprisoned the royal family in its wine cellars. Menelik II's rare, black-maned pet lions had roamed here and occasionally attacked the unfortunate visitor.

How many other bodies were secretly buried on these immaculate palace grounds?

"Anything could happen to somebody in Ethiopia," Hanna said.

Chapter Eleven

BUDDY WAS MORE HURT by Hanna's reproach than he had let on. But by the next day, both had put their misgivings aside in the atmosphere of the Timkat festivities. A time when Ethiopia's Christians tried to forget their misfortune, Timkat, the biggest holiday of the year, lasted three days in January when the weather was mild and dry.

That evening was clear and beautiful. Hanna wanted to show Buddy the Timkat eve public ceremony at Addis Ababa's old imperial racetrack, *Jan Meda*, now the capital's largest park. They left the driver with the car near the university and walked there. Hanna's mother had given her a blanket, a plastic jug of tej and, wrapped in newspaper, a special bread she had baked.

It seemed the entire city had turned out for the celebration. Throngs of men, women and children in white traditional dress headed toward the park. Among them rode medieval-looking, robed men on horseback, their steeds decorated with embroidered saddlecloths, silver bridles and shivering red tassels.

Gaily-dressed spectators camped out along the mile-long meadow that flickered with campfires and torches. It smelled of charcoal smoke, roasted coffee, spicy food grilling on open braziers and incense.

The couple found a low concrete wall to sit on. Hanna opened the jug of tej. They each took a swig.

They'd come in time for the arrival of the ceremony's participants. Bells tinkled and trumpets sounded as riders, on their fancy mounts, galloped onto the field. A sea of purple, red, navy blue and green parasols with swaying fringes followed. Red, green and gold Ethiopian flags bobbed among them.

Beneath the parasols, priests in jewel-colored vestments of satin and velvet carried on their heads puzzling objects hidden under layers of sumptuous cloth. These were the treasured *tabots*, wooden or stone replicas of the tablets bearing the Ten Commandments. Ethiopians believed the original tablets had been stolen from Jerusalem by the first King Menelik, Solomon's son by the Queen of Sheba, and secreted in Axum.

Priests sang, leapt from side to side and rhythmically knocked prayer staffs together. Others shook antique, Egyptian-style rattles or swung bronze censers from which curls of incense smoke floated heavenward.

Solemn old men and women marched in unison. After them, dressed in white, came the congregations of Addis Ababa's churches.

While the vast procession paraded across the field, the spectators partied in what Buddy would always remember as a kaleidoscope of African images. Young couples in casual Western clothes danced on the barren ground in a loose-limbed way while someone played the harmonica. Boys flirted and acted fresh with the unmarried girls to contempt and appreciation. A man strutted around in a pink T-shirt and tie. Friends strolled everywhere with their arms around each other's shoulders, told jokes and belted out songs. One struck a cocky pose in a sparkly, gold party hat. A bearded elder who looked like an Old Testament prophet held a large, cross-topped staff. Men loudly pounded green-painted, goat-skin drums. A white woman, probably an aid worker, kicked a soccer ball around with some kids. Children, fascinated and frightened by the crowd, hugged their mothers tightly.

People chanted hymns all along the park. Each congregation stopped in a different part of the field, erected a tent, devoutly placed its tabot inside and hoisted a flag adorned with a picture of its church's saint.

The park featured a blue, cross-shaped water cistern the size of a swimming pool where the next day's celebration would take place. Blessing its water, priests raised their pastoral staffs or swung the incense burners to send more divine fumes aloft.

124

A shabbily-dressed boy of eight or nine stood near Buddy and stared at him with curiosity. Hanna broke off a piece of the bread and offered it. The boy mutely ate it without taking his eyes off the big foreigner.

Hanna spread the blanket on the grass, and they made themselves as comfortable as the hard ground would permit. She had always appeared unsentimental, sometimes maddeningly so. But as she watched the nocturnal panorama in the dancing glow of a thousand campfires, her eyes glistened.

Buddy covered her hand with his own. "What are you thinking?"

She shrugged.

He lay back on the blanket. How was she affected by the killing she'd done during the war? He'd asked her years ago, and she'd shrugged then too.

Buddy closed his eyes. The hanged Oromo boy emerged from the darkness.

He thought about him all the time.

The priests prayed until two in the morning then performed Mass. Another Mass would be conducted at sunrise, but Hanna quietly told Buddy it was time to go. Celebrants usually waited until morning for the long-bearded Patriarch of the Ethiopian Orthodox Church, in his black, red and gold embroidered robes and dome-shaped crown inlaid with icons of saints, to dip his golden cross in the pool, put out a holy candle and sprinkle water on the congregation. Some of the worshippers, overcome with religious fervor, would jump in the water.

But like the multitude of other early departures, Hanna's was a display of disregard for the current Patriarch, Paulos, a controversial figure appointed by the government. Most Ethiopians revered the former Patriarch, Abuna Merkorios, exiled in New Jersey. He'd been forced out of office by Meles, accused of having been too close to the Derg. Many felt, despite the Abuna's relationship with the despised former regime, he nonetheless represented the authentic line of patriarchal succession. Hanna would go to her family's church for the morning Mass.

They walked back to the car and were driven to the Sheraton. Buddy gave the driver a generous Timkat gift, the amount suggested by Hanna in a whisper during the ride to the hotel, and told him to go home. He wouldn't need him again until the next evening when they'd go to her house for dinner.

Chapter Twelve

"THIS IS MY MOTHER," Hanna said as she introduced Buddy the next day. Her mother was delicate, and he could see where Hanna had gotten her good looks. She limped slightly—from arthritis, Hanna told him later—when she came into the living room to greet them.

After seeing his girlfriend as an object of erotic mystery for so many years, it felt strange to be in her prosaic childhood home. Hanna's mother lived in the Arat Kilo neighborhood near the university where her husband had taught and not far from the racecourse Buddy and Hanna had visited the night before. The modest ʼ50s ranch-style, stucco-and-stone house had an extended, corrugated roof that shaded a long patio. Surrounded by a patch of grass and a cinder block wall topped with barbed wire, it was the sort of modern home an up-and-coming professor would have proudly purchased for his young family in happier times.

"And my brother, Fasika." Hanna presented a gentle teenage boy to Buddy.

Buddy shook hands with them. "Tell your mom she has a nice house."

"I understand," her mother interjected. "My husband was professor of English."

"Yes, I know."

Hanna pointed to a framed, black-and-white photograph on the wall of a reserved-looking man in a suit and tie. "That is him."

"He was handsome," Buddy remarked diplomatically.

"We had a good life." She touched the photo tenderly. "My father was very respected. I had nice clothes and shoes. I went to a good school."

"Do you like Ethiopian food?" Hanna's mother changed the subject to something more pleasant.

"Yes, but not the raw meat."

"*Kitfo*," Hanna interpreted. Everyone laughed. She steered him toward the dining room. "Come, please sit."

A servant girl around Fasika's age served the dinner. She looked down when Buddy smiled at her. The family helped her with the dishes and spoke to her in a familiar way. He wished he could give her some money. A tip he might leave in America would be a godsend to her, but he was afraid it might embarrass his hosts.

Hanna's mother made sure the dining arrangements proceeded in proper fashion. Putting more food on one plate, she ordered that more tej be poured. Buddy imagined the hardship and heartbreak she had suffered during Ethiopia's political upheavals and wished he could do something for her, too. Then he recalled this kindly old woman had pinned her daughter's thrashing arms and legs down while someone hacked at the child's body with a razor blade. An impulse to leap across the table and shake her by the shoulders seized him. He smiled at her with feigned pleasure.

It wasn't long before his stomach was full. Hanna had asked her mother to go easy on the spices, but his lips still burned from the berbere-spiced vegetables that had accompanied the lasagna, a legacy of the Italian occupation, and the roast holiday lamb slaughtered that morning in the backyard by Fasika.

The room was stuffy. Buddy opened another button on his shirt and waited for the inevitable coffee. A family portrait on one wall showed Hanna's parents sitting in the living room. Her father held an infant Fasika on his knee. A cute, fifteen-year old Hanna stood behind them. Next to her was an older sister now married to a computer technician in Germany.

Besides the photo were two paintings. Presumably done by a local artist, one was a rural scene of village life. It reminded Buddy of his macabre misadventure in Oromia.

The second painting depicted, in Communist heroic realism style, Ethiopian farmers cheerfully harvesting corn. Had it been hung there during the Red Terror in an unsuccessful attempt to appease the doctrinaire Captain Wondwosen?

Through the doorway to the kitchen, amid the clatter of cups and dishes, Buddy heard Hanna and her mother argue.

"Everything okay?" he asked Hanna when they returned.

"My mother is Amhara," she reminded him as they moved into the living room and sat on beat-up, upholstered chairs. "She thinks Meles wants to kill the Amhara."

"Meles wants to develop Ethiopia," Buddy reassured the older woman. "They say he's a new type of African leader."

Hanna's mother sat primly without reply.

"Dr. Asrat was her friend," Hanna explained.

"You do not have to worry," Buddy promised. "Your daughter is Meles' friend." She still looked unconvinced.

Fasika wanted to go with some other boys to the racetrack for more of the Timkat revelry. Hanna's mother directed the servant to give him some of the tej and holiday bread. He shook hands courteously with Buddy as he said goodbye. Hanna spoke in Amharic to him in a stern manner, and he answered in an obedient tone. He kissed everyone, including Buddy, three times on their cheeks and left.

"What were you saying to your brother?"

"I told him to be respectful of the women there. Many of the young men are not polite."

The servant called out from the kitchen.

"Excuse me," Hanna said. "I will bring the coffee."

Once she was out of earshot, her mother rose with a wince from her chair and sat beside Buddy. She held his hand and looked into his eyes.

"Can Hanna go to America with you?" she asked in a serious tone.

"I've asked her many times."

"She is a good daughter."

"Yes. I know."

"If you marry Hanna, she could get a visa." Obviously, she had given this a lot of thought. "You want to marry her?"

Hanna entered with a ceramic coffee pot. Overhearing this last bit of conversation, she blushed and spoke sharply to her mother in Amharic. "I am sorry. Please do not listen to her." She put the coffee pot on a side table and returned to the kitchen.

Buddy excused himself and joined Hanna. She pretended to be busy helping the servant put dishes in the sink then gave up and told the girl to attend her mother in the living room.

"I am sorry," she said.

"It's a good idea." He put his arms around Hanna and nuzzled her neck. "C'mon, marry me. And come to America."

To every proposal he'd made over the years, she had pleaded her obligations to her job and country. Now, her slumped shoulders told a different story.

"In America, you live in a big house," she said in a resigned voice. "There is always power. And fresh water. And there are many markets which have all different types of food." She seemed to be trying to convince herself of the advantages of Western living.

"Yes. There's all that."

For a long moment, she judged and balanced two worlds.

"I will go," she said.

"You mean it?" He took her face in his hands and kissed it. "That's great, honey! That's great!"

"How long to get the visa?"

"If we're married, maybe six months."

She led him by the hand into the living room. Her mother and the servant were chatting. Surprised to see Hanna and Buddy wanted to say something, they fell silent.

Hanna made a brief announcement in Amharic.

Exuberant trilling erupted.

Chapter Thirteen

"IT'S A GOOD thing I'm drunk," Alan declared. It was the morning of the wedding, and he, The Gandel and Buddy's brother, Steve, were hanging out with Buddy in a suite at the Sheraton. It had been difficult for these busy men to coordinate a week off. But Buddy had begged them to come and had even offered to hold the wedding whenever they could all make it. Hanna wanted a traditional Ethiopian Orthodox wedding. This took family members and male friends to represent the groom in a series of rituals.

The Gandel knew a Rasta who surfed and had long been interested in Ethiopia. So, if he was ever going to do it, this was his chance to see the place. Alan, who preferred the comforts and vices of Southern California, had needed some real arm twisting. But in the end, he couldn't say no to his friend and partner.

Buddy's mother was too old to make the trip, but at least Steve was there. Two years younger and a shorter, pudgier version of his brother, he was a partner in a large Manhattan accounting firm. Steve had a wife and kids in Scarsdale and the careful manner of a man whose career depended on getting the numbers right. Buddy hardly saw his brother since he'd moved to the West Coast, which made their reunion especially poignant.

Everyone's secretaries had emailed back and forth until they'd found a week they all could block out on their calendars for a trip to Addis Ababa. Buddy could scarcely believe they'd come. From firsthand experience, he knew it was no fun getting the hepatitis A and B, typhoid, malaria, meningitis, rabies and yellow fever vaccinations a trip to Ethiopia required.

But, finally, here they were, relishing the opportunity to loaf around and crack jokes like frat boys half their ages. It gave Buddy warm, decades-old memories of himself, Steve and Alan as kids playing behind P.S. 12 in the Bronx.

They had imbibed so liberally because their host had just informed them that today's Ethiopian wedding tradition demanded they break into a house. Such an undertaking definitely called for getting liquored up.

Buddy, who generally was conservative about alcohol, had decided he was entitled to a drink or two as well. It was the happiest day of his life. For the first time in many years, he had no meetings or interviews scheduled for a couple of weeks. He had his brother and closest friends with him. There was a lovely party coming up. For once, he was going to take a holiday from being a public figure.

His three groomsmen had already completed some of the wedding customs. With Hanna hidden away by her family until the big event, they'd visited her house early on their first morning in town to ask her mother and elderly grandfather to give her permission to marry. This preliminary step was normally taken before any wedding plans were made. But Hanna's priest and family had agreed to consolidate the formalities to fit the groomsmen's travel schedule.

Hanna's mother and Fasika had translated while the three men, despite their jet lag, gallantly performed their roles and secured the requisite assent.

Then came the *Shimagelay*. After brunch, some beers and a swim at the hotel, the groomsmen had returned to Hanna's house. Now that permission for her to marry had been granted, they'd asked for her hand to be given in marriage specifically to Buddy.

In keeping with Ethiopian marriage etiquette, the bride's family had played it cool while the groomsmen, trying not to laugh, listed Buddy's wonderful qualities and assured them he would be a good husband. Hanna's family had given their consent over a spicy lunch her mother had prepared.

The next night had been *Tilosh*, a rite observed on the eve of the nuptials. Buddy's delegation had returned again to Hanna's house. This time, they'd borne a suitcase full of gifts for the bride. Alan had brought his video camera because Buddy had insisted he had to see this scene for himself.

Her family and bridesmaids had greeted them. As a sign of respect, the three Americans had kissed the knees of Hanna's mother and grandfather. Protocol decreed their hosts demand to see what was in the suitcase. Buddy's brother, as the best man, was duty-bound to describe the expensive gifts—a Cartier watch, a Hermes scarf, a Louis Vuitton bag and wallet and other luxuries—in overstated terms to make them seem even more valuable.

Good form obligated the bride's relatives and bridesmaids to belittle the worth of each gift. As Alan's video camera rolled, the watch, the scarf and the accessories had been handled with exaggerated scorn. The Ethiopians had pouted with palpable dissatisfaction. They'd rolled their eyes in derision as a mirthful Fasika and a bridesmaid, a heavyset woman who also spoke some English, imperfectly translated the complaints.

One gift was supposed to be a pair of something, so Buddy had thrown in a beautiful set of Tiffany silver earrings. A bridesmaid had ritually "stolen" one of the earrings so Hanna's family could ridicule Buddy's representatives for the poor half-offering. The Gandel's assignment had been to conspicuously position the earrings to facilitate the "theft," defend Buddy's integrity and blame the jealous bridesmaid for the missing item. This had been done while the translators argued over the right word with laughter all around.

The ceremony had concluded with the gifts being entrusted to the bridesmaids for delivery to Hanna. The family had given its final approval to the match. Everyone had enjoyed another big meal.

All of this had taken place over the last two days. But the wedding day was time for the break-in.

Buddy's groomsmen were incredulous when he'd first explained the process. They would be blocked from entering Hanna's home by her friends, relatives and bridesmaids. Hanna would wait in the house, trembling, at least theoretically, in virginal anxiety. Their mission was to push their way through the resisting revelers, so Buddy could make his way inside and claim his bride. The act represented how Ethiopians in olden days made sure the groom had paid his dowry before he got his hands on his betrothed.

"Wow," was all Alan could say when Buddy described this task. Steve and The Gandel looked doubtful, too.

"I mean," Steve asked, "are they going to put up a real fight?"

"I have no idea whatsoever," Buddy said.

"Gnarly, dude" The Gandel said, using an old surfing term. "I guess we'd better have another drink."

There seemed little reason not to repeat this good idea a few more times. By then it was time to get dressed and go.

When a couple married in the Ethiopian Orthodox Church, they usually donned traditional clothes that included a specially-decorated coat and crown-like hat. But Western attire was increasingly acceptable, and Buddy had received the priest's "economy," or dispensation, to wear a suit.

The scotch complicated knotting the ties and brushing off the suit jackets. Eventually, the four men, ready for whatever this manly Ethiopian duty involved, tipsily crossed the hotel lobby.

After he'd forced his way into the house, Buddy was obliged to give a flower to the bride and gifts to the bridesmaids. He carried a shopping bag with these articles as carefully as his inebriated condition permitted.

The Mercedes waited in the late morning sun. He gave the bag to the driver. They got in the car and departed.

"I forgot," he told the others as they started down the Sheraton's shrub-lined driveway. "You've gotta bless me before we get there."

"How's this?" The Gandel asked. He raised one hand in the Star Trek salute. "I hereby bless you, dude."

"Me, too," Alan chimed in. He took Buddy's head between his hands and kissed the top of it, almost falling over as the car went over a speed bump.

"And me," Steve added. He placed his hand on his brother's forehead as if checking his temperature.

"I guess that will do," Buddy replied. "Oh," he remembered, "we're supposed to sing."

"What, now?" Steve asked.

"No. When we get there. When we're trying to get in. They're going to be singing, and we're supposed to sing, too."

"What do we have to sing?" Alan asked.

"Fucked if I know."

"Like an Ethiopian song?"

"I don't know any."

"Let's sing 'God Bless America,'" Steve said.

"Too chauvinistic."

"How about something by the Beach Boys, dude?" The Gandel proposed.

"Like what?"

"How about 'Help Me, Rhonda?'"

"*Help me Rhonda, help, help me Rhonda*," Buddy tentatively crooned. "Nah."

"I've got it," Steve said. "'She Loves You.' You know, by the Beatles."

"*She loves you, yeah, yeah, yeah.*" Buddy nodded judiciously. "That's good."

"Hold on," Steve said. "What's the rest of it?"

"*You think you lost your love*," Alan warbled, "*when I saw her standing there.*"

"*It's you she's thinking of—*" Steve prompted.

"That's not it," Buddy complained. "That's not it."

Hanna's street was lined with guests' cars. Brassy Ethiopian music came from the house.

"Come on, dammit. We've got to think of something."

"Ninety-Nine Bottles of Beer?" Alan suggested desperately as they parked.

"Ninety-Nine Bottles of Beer?"

"Well, it's a song. And we all know the words."

One faranj melody was probably as good as another for this audience. "Gimme the flower," Buddy told the driver. "We'll give 'em the other stuff later." The driver removed a superb, red rose from the shopping bag and handed to him.

Buddy got out of the car and approached the house. Clutching the rose, he bellowed, "*Ninety-nine bottles of beer on the wall, ninety-nine bottles of beer.*" His groomsmen accompanied him in unmatched keys.

They reached the front door. Party noises boomed inside. Buddy knocked on it. Nobody answered. He pounded harder. Still no answer.

"Maybe it's open, dude," The Gandel said.

Buddy tested the door. It was unlocked. They sang 'Ninety Nine Bottles of Beer,' and he opened it.

The cranked-up music hit them like a blast wave. The foyer was packed with boisterous Ethiopians—Hanna's friends and relatives. Recognizing the groom, they laughed, trilled and cheered. Those nearest the doorway stepped forward and blocked his way. They sang and danced in a taunting manner.

"Well, here goes," Buddy announced. Protecting the rose so it wouldn't get crushed, he tried to push his way through the crowd. The Ethiopians stiffened their resistance. He couldn't even get past the first row of celebrants.

"I need a little help here, guys," he said to his groomsmen.

They gleefully crouched and assumed the two-footed stance of offensive linemen.

"Ready? Set. Go!"

They lunged against the mob. Their momentum carried them just a few inches before strong hands, backs and chests expelled them violently from the house.

The mass of singing dancers mockingly defied them. The heavyset bridesmaid, shaking her big hips and singing at the top of her lungs, joined the defensive line.

Panting, Alan looked her over. "So they want to play hardball, eh?"

"I was afraid of this," Steve remarked darkly.

Alan turned to The Gandel. "You're a man of science. What would you recommend?"

The Gandel looked Buddy over. "Let's use his head for a battering ram."

"Good thing somebody's thinking," Steve, weaving slightly, said.

For a moment, Buddy feared they were serious then they all broke into laughter. The three groomsmen lustily reprised their tune and reorganized themselves into a scrum.

He clenched the rose between his teeth. They faced the door again.

"This is, like, totally rad, dude," The Gandel said. "Ready?"

Buddy extended his thumb and pinky to give the surfer's "hang loose" sign.

"*Ninety-nine bottles of beer on the wall—*"

"One," The Gandel began.

"*Ninety-Nine bottles of beer—*"

"Two…"

"*If one of those bottles should happen to fall—*"

"Three!"

They charged at the crowded doorway.

There was the rush of movement. A scrimmage of tangled arms and legs.

Buddy found himself on the floor inside the house. His groomsmen lay beside him convulsed with laughter.

A chuckling Ethiopian man helped him to his feet and led him into the living room. A slight woman sat there in a white robe with the hood over her face.

Buddy gently lifted the hood and, with a flourish, presented the rose to Hanna. The other guests cheered and trilled.

She examined the flower which had miraculously survived the gauntlet.

"You are my hero," she said.

They married that afternoon in an Ethiopian Orthodox service at Hanna's church. A brightly multicolored, wooden hexagon, its walls were covered with murals of the saints and apostles in iconic Byzantine style.

The family and guests entered first. Hanna's mother, most of the elderly women and the children wore traditional *Habesha* outfits. Everyone else wore Western suits and dresses.

Buddy, now sober and suffering from a headache, came in next with the bridal party. They waited for the bride.

His headache vanished when she appeared in the doorway on the arm of her grandfather.

Hanna wore a wedding dress of Ethiopian fabric. Its top was embellished with crystal beads. With a serene expression, she walked toward him in all her exotic beauty.

The congregation rose to welcome her.

Her mother wiped away tears. They were sad not to have her father there, he realized. Thank God Meles had rid Ethiopia of the Derg that had tormented them.

Hanna met him at the altar and took his arm. They turned to face the priest. His sneakers peeking out from under his vestment, the cleric prayed in Ge'ez, the liturgical language once used in the ancient kingdom of Axum. It reminded Buddy of the Hebrew rites with which he had grown up.

More prayers and interminable blessings he couldn't understand followed. Finally, the bride and groom exchanged their vows in Amharic, the pronunciation spelled out on a card for Buddy to recite verbatim.

The guests sang a wedding song. One took out a saxophone and serenaded the new husband and wife as they left the church.

Buddy had declined to rent for the occasion one of the few limousines available in Addis. His Mercedes sedan, embarrassingly ostentatious amid the city's poverty, was already a magnet for the city's army of beggars.

As usual, on the drive back to the Sheraton for the reception, each time the wedding caravan slowed for vehicles, pedestrians or livestock in the road, needy people converged on the car. He always kept a roll of birr in his pocket, so he could give each one something. By now he knew not to cause a riot by lingering at the scene. He had mastered the art of handing them the money, saying a kind Ethiopian word and moving on.

They passed block after block of derelict shacks, many hidden behind walls. Homeless residents of all ages rested on blankets or newspapers spread on the sidewalk. The odor of sewage drifted through the car's partly open window. Buddy pushed a button and it closed with a soft hum.

"Put on the air conditioner, please," he told the driver.

The car slowed to a crawl once more. An old woman in a man's sweater approached it. Her face was shockingly disfigured by leprous lesions. She was probably the grandmother of the pre-teen girl who grasped her sleeve. Many grandparents took over when the parents had died of AIDS. The child's small size, unsteady gait and vacant expression indicated an iodine deficiency.

The old woman held her swollen hand out to the tinted car window and implored its occupants for help.

Buddy lowered the window again and gave her a thousand birr, enough to feed them for a few days. The girl came up to the car and gaped at its inhabitants.

"Tell them to come to the clinic," he told Hanna.

As she translated, the child coughed and sprayed the sleeve of Buddy's suit with blood.

Hanna waited in the Sheraton's lobby with her bridesmaids while Buddy changed his clothes. The girl probably had tuberculosis, they'd decided, and they were inoculated. But as a precaution, the suit would be put in a plastic bag and incinerated.

A feast was ready in the hotel's garden. The reception would be held under a tent festooned with white paper lanterns. Every detail was exquisite down to the gold napkin rings. Each satin-draped table featured gorgeous arrangements of Ethiopian-grown roses and white lilies. Champagne bottles chilled in ice buckets. The food ranged from Ethiopian to European cuisine. The multi-tiered cake rivaled Paris' finest.

Alone in his suite, Buddy savored the momentary peace and quiet. He thought of his father as he dressed. The owner of a Bronx clothing store, Morrie Schwartz had worked hard throughout the 1950s and 1960s to provide for his wife and two sons in their modest apartment on the Bronx's Grand Concourse.

Family life had been tense and argumentative yet loving in its own way. But as drugs and crime overran the community, his father had become frustrated with their impact on his business. There were burglaries, fights with shoplifters and two armed robberies. What galled him most was the perpetrators seemed mainly to be teenagers devoid of all respect for their elders or society.

"Those damned kids," a young Buddy often heard him mutter. "Those damned kids."

His father had wanted to move his family somewhere safer. But with the neighborhood deteriorating, he couldn't find a buyer for the store. They stayed as the area turned into a frightening world beset by addicts and gangs.

Morrie Schwartz had his first stroke at only forty-six. He mostly recovered, but he relied afterward on his two boys to help with anything that took exertion. Frustration made him impatient and ill-tempered. Buddy tried to avoid him. Their relationship grew strained. The youth did his chores with repressed resentment and tried to shield Steve from the emotional abuse the best he could. Speaking up might earn him a sharp crack across the mouth.

In 1965, a big snowstorm hit New York City. Fifteen-year-old Buddy, with school closed for the weather emergency, shoveled the sidewalk in front of the store with Steve. They took a break so he could show his brother with a series of snowballs how the Yankees' Whitey Ford's sweeping curveball paralyzed righties trying to time the pitch. Their argument over whether Ford was overrated dragged on. They finished their chore late.

Something was wrong when he entered the store to put away the shovels. His father should be scolding them for taking so long.

He found his dad face down on the floor of the stockroom.

The ambulance was late because of the snow. Morrie Schwartz died after four gruesome days on life support.

A brain hemorrhage, the death certificate said.

Even as an adult, the thought that his father might still be alive if he'd not been fooling around and returned to the store just ten minutes earlier haunted Buddy. He pictured him sprawled on the floor while he played just steps away. He suspected Steve felt the same way but, afraid he might plant the suggestion in his brother's mind, had never asked. The entire episode still hung, undiscussed, between them. He sorely regretted he hadn't been more of an emotional support to his father whose stress and sense of isolation he could better understand as he got older.

The family's precarious financial condition had deteriorated after Morrie's death. Worst of all had been the effect of the loss on Buddy's mother. She fell into depression in an era when psychological help still carried a stigma and antidepressants were not commonly used. More and more of each day was spent in bed watching television. The apartment fell into disorder.

It wasn't until both boys were successful men and able to afford psychotherapy that Buddy began to understand the damage these events had caused to his self-esteem. They had turned him from a hardy, self-reliant child into someone in need of others' approval. Meles' gibe about his guilty conscience had struck uncomfortably close to home. With a sense of irony, Buddy speculated hundreds of thousands of Ethiopians might not be alive had he not thrown those snowballs long ago.

He wondered what his dad would have thought of his marrying an Ethiopian. Like many in his generation, Morrie Schwartz had a seemingly unlimited supply of off-color and racial jokes he trotted out after a few drinks. But he'd always been quick to give a shirt or a pair of jeans to a black or Puerto Rican mother who couldn't afford one for her kid.

Buddy's mother hadn't broached the subject of race when he'd given her the news in a phone call to her Westchester nursing home. He imagined she wasn't thrilled about it.

It's my life, he thought defiantly, still worried, at fifty-one, about her opinion.

An hour after the wedding couple made its entrance to much applause and trilling and the first course was about to be served, six bodyguards, their charcoal gray suits matching their automatic weapons, quietly entered the tent. This signaled Meles' arrival.

Buddy and Hanna had debated whether to invite him. They'd finally decided failing to do so would sever an already-tense, yet vital, relationship. The palace had replied Meles would drop by for the reception. A special table had been placed away from the tent's opening, where additional guards were posted, so no one outside could guess his location within.

News that Meles was coming had spread among the guests. Everyone had seen the bodyguards, some uniformed and others in plain clothes, positioned throughout the hotel grounds. A security team from the palace had observed the hotel's gardens and kitchen for the past week, their suspicious attitude, sunglasses and weapons at odds with the festive preparations. The tent, tables, chairs and even the musicians' equipment had been scrutinized. Guests had been made to pass through a metal detector at the garden gate.

The laughter and chatter died down when Meles and his good-looking wife, Azeb, followed the bodyguards into the tent. All eyes were on the prime minister as he scanned the crowd. He beamed when he spied the newlyweds and crossed the floor to greet them.

"Congratulations, my friend." He threw his arms around Buddy. "You're really a member of the family now." He gave Hanna a triple cheek kiss.

Buddy had met Azeb before, and Hanna knew her from the war days. Her intelligent, angular face hinted at a forceful personality. She shook Buddy's hand, kissed Hanna and graciously wished them well.

Meles wanted to meet the bride's mother, so they led him and Azeb to where she sat with Fasika, Hanna's grandfather and other relatives. Torn between trepidation, bitterness over his anti-Amhara policies and gratitude for his rout of the monster who had murdered Hanna's father, they accepted Meles' cheek kisses with civil reserve. An awestruck Fasika shook hands. Hanna eyed Azeb's pricey couture dress.

"You know, you were supposed to ride over here on a horse," Meles joked to Buddy, referring to another old tradition. Hanna's mother translated this for the benefit of the other relatives at the table. Everyone chuckled politely.

The prime minister insisted he sit and be treated like everyone else. He and Azeb said goodbye to the elders with conspicuous courtesy and returned to their table. The party resumed.

Ethiopians like to feed each other. To perform *gursha* is a sign one cares. Buddy had prevailed on Hanna to dispense with the wedding gursha in which the guests watch the newlyweds feed each other the entire meal. The idea of eating while people stared at him made him self-conscious. They settled on a few token bites, the breach of custom raising a few eyebrows among the elders present.

The guests picked up their forks for the appetizer. The bodyguard who stood behind Meles cut a tiny portion off the prime minister's serving. He tasted it to make sure it was not poisoned.

The truncated gursha didn't mean Buddy was going to escape all embarrassment that night. For as soon as the meal ended, the Ethiopian music blared, and Hanna's family and friends broke out their eskista moves on the dance floor.

Buddy gamely tried to keep up. But there was no point trying to do it well—his role as a faranj was to entertain. Revitalized and emboldened by the food and champagne, he shed his inhibitions, and the evening became a blur of sweaty drinking and dancing interrupted only when Meles and Azeb, citing an emergency, took their leave.

In later years, Buddy could still recall scenes from that night. Hanna, angelic, yet ravishing, kicking off her shoes as they started to dance. The Gandel boogying with an old lady wearing a Habesha gown and 1950s-style pussycat eyeglasses. The little girl with elaborately-braided hair who challenged Buddy to dance with her and giggled at his valiant efforts. Steve doing a fierce tango with the big bridesmaid from that morning's melee. All three groomsmen, cigars in their mouths, drunkenly attempting some kind of Russian folk dance in time to the pulsing Ethiopian rhythms, falling on their backsides and roaring with laughter.

The party was still going strong when Buddy sat down at a table to catch his breath. The floral centerpiece's blood-red roses resembled the one he had given Hanna. Millions of them were grown on massive, foreign-owned commercial plantations the size of a small state, loaded onto jets and flown to the US and Europe every day for birthdays, anniversaries and Valentine bouquets.

Hanna had confided the government evicted thousands of Ethiopians from their ancestral lands to make way for these farms. It relocated them at gunpoint to isolated, unlivable zones where they could no longer survive. The proceeds from the sale of their land to the multinational European and Asian flower growers, she'd whispered, didn't go to the people who had lived on them. They went to the most senior TPLF veterans around Meles. The roses were Ethiopia's newest foreign exchange earner, topped only by coffee. But Meles' cronies used the money to buy upscale real estate, pay the generals and colonels to keep them loyal and hire retired US congressmen-turned-lobbyist to keep the aid flowing.

Buddy put the troublesome thought aside. He had guests to attend to.

On his honeymoon in the Maldives, Buddy read in the newspaper that Meles' emergency had been a protest at Addis Ababa University. Four thousand students had boycotted their classes. They'd demanded freedom of speech and the removal of bullying police and government agents from their campus.

As other universities and colleges around the country expressed support for the students' appeal, Ethiopian special forces had stormed the school and killed forty-one students and unemployed youth who had joined the protest. Another two hundred fifty young men and women had been sent to the hospital. Dormitory walls were blood-smeared and punctured by bullets.

Blue-uniformed Federal Police, called *Federalis*, in high-topped boots and armed with guns, shields and batons, had dragged students out of churches and mosques where they'd sought refuge and imprisoned them in a police training center outside the capital. They'd barged into the homes of workers near the university to beat women and children. Federalis had invaded the nearby Menelik Secondary School to break students' arms, legs and ribs.

That Tuesday and Wednesday, while Buddy and Hanna relaxed in the shade of graceful palms at their private villa on the Maldives' white sands, hundreds of frantic mothers and fathers traveled to the police training center to learn if their children were alive.

Addis Ababa looked like a city under siege. Mobs of youths fought violently with police. They ransacked shops in the Piazza and Mercato districts. Cars were destroyed and buses set on fire. Throughout Wednesday, gunshots and sirens were heard in the capital. Most businesses closed. Few residents ventured onto the streets.

Trucks full of Federalis rushed from one sector to another ready to quash any revolt.

The Red Cross put out an emergency call for blood donations.

Chapter Fourteen

BUDDY SCHWARTZ WAS busy after he returned to Los Angeles in the late spring of 2001 with meetings, press interviews and preparations for Hanna's arrival. He hired an immigration lawyer for her visa application. He bought a green Mercedes convertible, his wife's favorite color after years in parched lands, and scheduled driving lessons. An extra bedroom was cleared out and a decorator selected to follow her directives for turning it into an office when she arrived.

As spring changed to scorching summer, Buddy left his air-conditioned home for his air-conditioned office every weekday morning. Careful not to stay out in the 105-degree heat a second longer than necessary, he got in his air-conditioned Bentley for the exasperating, bumper-to-bumper drive to Burbank. Careers depended on stories here, and the breezy, Southern California architecture could dissolve in an earthquake. The monumental New York apartment houses of his youth had been anchored in granite.

He usually put in a good eight hours and ate lunch at his desk. Then he'd reverse the process and return to an empty house by six.

The evening news was nearly always devoid of any Ethiopian coverage. The temperature having dropped by then, he'd dine at the latest Hollywood watering hole with Alan or some other business associate. By ten p.m., he was back home where his cable television, correspondence and large, lonely bedroom awaited.

But on September 11, 2001, Buddy awoke to a different America.

While he was asleep, two jetliners had shattered New York's Twin Towers.

Buddy had friends at the news networks who, in the weeks that followed, shared with him over drinks or late-night bicoastal phone conversations details too excruciating even for the grief-stricken television reports of the disaster. The single bone fragment in a casket. The toddler asking where Mommy was.

He watched the video footage of people jumping from the towers' upper floors to escape the flames. Once, he played it back and forth on the digital console in his office as if repeated exposure to its horrors might inoculate him against his own fear.

Overnight, counterterrorism trumped all issues in Washington's relations with other countries. There were terrorists everywhere, it seemed, and Ethiopia's neighbors were infected. Yemen across the Red Sea. Sudan to the west. Kenya to the south.

The worst hot spot, Somalia, also bordered Ethiopia. That ungovernable state quickly became the focus of America's African strategy to deny extremists a safe haven from which to plan and launch more attacks on US interests abroad.

9/11 made America willing to play rough. The enraged superpower wanted foreign allies who knew how to play rough, too. Meles had proven he knew how. Any qualms Ethiopia's foreign friends had over his catastrophic Eritrean war and human rights abuses melted away like snow in a Los Angeles summer in the face of their urgent need for his help in the dirty war. Assistant Secretaries of Defense and State, seconded by the CIA station chief in Addis Ababa, pressed their local ally to send his large, but undisciplined, army into Somalia to wipe out the fundamentalists who had taken root in the collapsed, apocalyptic state.

Millions of dollars more poured into Ethiopian counterterror training, equipment, secret prisons, drones, technology, intelligence stations, vehicles and bribes. Like a flourishing plant watered with this torrent of money, Meles' military apparatus blossomed into a formidable regional proxy that kept America's own troops free for Afghanistan and, later, Iraq.

If he had already been important to Western security interests,

9/11 made Meles indispensable. Nobody cared if he used his burgeoning power to tamp down a little local opposition.

Nobody except the Ethiopians themselves.

For weeks, the terror attack on America delayed international travel. But, finally, the big day came, and Buddy waited outside the automated double doors of the customs area at Los Angeles International Airport for Hanna to re-enter his life. Sunshine streamed through the terminal's skylight.

Tingling with anticipation, he took one of her letters from his pocket. Creased from being refolded, he read it again.

"My darling husband, I send this through a friend because they are reading all the mail. Ethiopia has become a prison. Everybody is afraid to say what he thinks. It is like the days of Mengistu again. These past months, I think of you every hour. I wonder if you are real or were you a dream? When I feel your arms around me, I will know the answer—"

The doors opened with a mechanical clacking. First class travelers emerged with carts piled high with baggage. These days, most were Ethiopians connected to the regime.

Buddy searched each face. Not her, not her, not her.

The doors swung outward again. For a second, he didn't recognize Hanna with her hair in intricate cornrows.

Then they were in each other's arms.

"Are you tired?" Buddy asked a few minutes later as he turned the Bentley onto the Howard Hughes Parkway.

"I feel strange."

"Do you want to eat something?"

"I want to see the ocean."

"We'll see it on the way home. How was your flight?"

"Twenty boring hours." She checked out a large mall with shiny stores, movie theaters and parking lots as it went by. "The people who work in the airport are very friendly."

They merged onto I-405 North. "There are many cars," she observed. "And many people are fat."

The relationship had shifted. In Ethiopia, he was on her turf, the foreigner who needed to be taught. Now it was the other way around.

She surveyed the side of the highway. "There are no traders or poor people."

"We have some. But not like Ethiopia." They neared the Santa Monica exit. "You still want to see the ocean?"

She smiled eagerly.

A few minutes later, they cruised slowly down Ocean Park Boulevard. Glimpses of the sapphire Pacific flashed between the palm trees across the road. The Bentley glided past well-maintained, Art Deco apartment buildings. Buddy parked the car, took her hand and led her across the street.

Palisades Park crowned a tall bluff overlooking the ocean. The pleasant autumn weather had tamed the blistering summer. Tan, fit Californians in casual or athletic wear biked, skated and walked by them. He was glad her first sight of the city was on a good day.

They reached the fence at the cliff's edge, and the endless Pacific came into full view. Its curling fringe caressed the wide, beige beach. The shoreline was dotted with surfers, sunbathers and bodybuilders. Further up the coast rose the majestic Santa Monica Mountains.

For a minute, she gazed in awe at the ocean. "Can I touch it?"

He led her down a long, wooden ramp to the beach.

"Take your shoes off. We can leave them here."

"Will they be stolen?"

"I don't think so."

Bronzed beachgoers lounged on the sand or on brightly-colored plastic chairs. Others strolled by the water's edge.

"Everybody looks so healthy," she said.

"It's the gym," he joked.

She crouched by the foamy, shallow backwash and let the water run through her fingers.

"You're free here," he said.

150

She looked out to sea without reply.

They climbed back up to the street. A homeless man with an engaging manner confronted them. "Spare a dollar?"

"Sorry." Buddy steered her away. "We don't like to encourage them to panhandle here," he explained, afraid she might think him mean. "They have places they can go for help."

"Why did he want money?"

"He's a panhandler. A beggar."

"He looked like he eats enough." In Ethiopia, beggars often died from hunger.

They wandered over to the famous Santa Monica Pier with its Ferris wheel, rides and games. The tinkle of wind chimes and the smell of frying seafood filled the briny air. Quirky shops offered souvenirs, crystals, jewelry, shells, postcards and maps.

A glass booth held a robotic fortune-teller with a crystal ball. Dressed in a yellow tunic, black vest and gold turban, the bearded automaton sat under a sign announcing its name was Zoltar.

Hanna studied the disturbingly human-like machine.

"What is that?"

"It's a fortune-teller."

Buddy took a dollar out of his wallet and inserted it in a slot. There was a suspenseful moment. Zoltar's eyes lit up. Its hand moved over the crystal ball. Its mouth opened.

"Zoltar is here to give you the wisdom of the ages," said an electronic voice. "Do with it as you wish."

Hanna squinted curiously at the crystal ball.

"Some people say you can see the future in them," Buddy said.

"Oh. A *tanquay*," she said, using the Amhara word for witch doctor.

"Destiny is not a matter of chance," the machine said. "It is a matter of choice. It is not a thing to be waited for. It is a thing to be achieved."

A card slid out of another slot. Buddy picked it up. "Your wish has been granted," he read aloud.

She cast a suspicious look at the robot, and they continued along the pier. A magician performed a card trick for onlookers. A man played a steel drum. At an open-air trapeze school, teenagers swung back and forth over a net.

"They are training?"

"It's fun."

A sign in a souvenir shop celebrated Route 66 which officially ended on the pier.

She read the sign. "'Two thousand four hundred and fifty-one miles.' America is a big country."

"Yes, America is a big country."

They ambled down the beach some more then returned to the car and rode up Santa Monica Boulevard toward Beverly Hills. They passed industrial warehouses, car dealerships and Century City's glass office towers.

He interrupted her inspection of a Taco Bell restaurant sign to point out the West Hollywood Memorial Walk. "The names of movie stars are in the sidewalks over there."

"Why do they put them in the sidewalk?"

"It's just a tradition."

The shops grew more exclusive as they entered Beverly Hills. Luxury-filled windows promised an ideal world of beautiful possibilities. What would Hanna think when she learned one of those dresses would pay several years of most Ethiopians' wages? When she felt the lush materials while so many wore rags? Or saw the Pet and Pooch Lifestyle Center for animals that ate better than millions of her countrymen?

The homes on Santa Monica Boulevard became grander as it ran northward through Beverly Hills. The car entered the hilly part where the big mansions were. They rolled up Mulholland Drive. Finally, they turned onto Crestview.

Gravel crunched under the Bentley's wheels as Buddy turned into his driveway.

She stared in amazement at the immense house.

"You know," he said to put her at ease, "I never asked you, what does your name mean?"

"It is an Amharic word meaning, 'gift of God.'"

"Well, you're my gift of God."

"A buddy is a friend, yes?"

"Yep."

"That's a good name. My friend."

He opened the car trunk and removed her cheap, nylon suitcase. He unlocked the front door and led her into a tastefully decorated front hall.

"This is the burglar alarm."

"'Burglar'?"

"Thieves. You have to put in this code: four-nine-three-one. Are you hungry?"

She nodded, and he showed her the kitchen. The restaurant-size refrigerator was packed with fruits, vegetables, meat and snacks of every description including injera and other specialties he had ordered from an Ethiopian market downtown.

Hanna looked closely at the food. She went over to the sink, turned on the water and watched it run.

"May I please have a cup?"

Buddy opened a cabinet and gave her a cut crystal glass. Rainbow colors glinted in its facets. He sat at the kitchen table while she filled the glass and drank thirstily.

"I feel like Sheba in Solomon's palace," she declared.

"Hm?"

She recited the well-known legend. "Sheba went from Ethiopia to meet King Solomon in Jerusalem." She waved at the lavish furnishings. "In his beautiful palace."

Hanna sat on his lap and humorously batted her eyelashes. "Solomon wanted to make love to her."

Buddy tried to hold her, but she teasingly pulled away.

"The Queen said no." She picked up a salt shaker and pantomimed shaking some onto her hand. "But clever Solomon put spices in her food. And that night, Sheba was so thirsty—" Hanna mimicked dying of thirst. "She begged Solomon for water."

She slipped back on his lap. "But Solomon said she must make love with him first."

He couldn't remember the last time she looked so happy.

"And she agreed," she reminded him in a whisper.

He kissed her slender neck as she looked around the well-appointed room.

"I never want to leave this place," she said.

Buddy awoke to the sound of Oprah Winfrey's voice. Daylight flooded the room. Hanna sat at the end of the bed watching television. She was so pretty he wondered if he was dreaming. Then yesterday's events came back to him.

"Did I awaken you?" she asked.

"That's okay. How long have you been up?"

"A long time. I think I have jet lag."

On the television, Katie Couric interviewed Oprah.

"I made the decision," Oprah said, "in the midst of doing *Beloved*. I was doing some scenes—"

"I will grow my hair longer." Hanna touched her waist. "All the way to here."

"That will take years."

"*Beloved* is about an ex-slave and, during that process of doing that, I connected to really what slavery had meant—"

Hanna pointed at the television. "Who is that?"

"Her name is Oprah. Her show is very popular here."

"...And I realized that I had no right to quit, coming from a history of people who had no voice, who had no power—"

"Do you know her?"

"I've met her."

"And that I have been given this—this blessed opportunity to speak to people, to influence them in ways that could make a difference in their lives and to just use that."

"Your television is very nice."

God, she's lovely, he thought.

She caught his gaze, smiled a wonderful, Ethiopian smile, climbed back on the bed and nestled beside him.

He put his arm around her. "That story about Solomon and Sheba," he asked affectionately. "They lived together happily ever after?"

"No," Hanna said, her eyes on the television. "She went back to Ethiopia."

Chapter Fifteen

DESPITE THE SHADOW OF 9/11, 2002 AND 2003
passed agreeably. Managing the production company
and Help Ethiopia kept Buddy busy. Hanna settled into
her duties as the charity's director for public affairs and her new
life as an American.

She made friends in Los Angeles. Most of them were older
Ethiopian refugees from the Mengistu era. There was also a growing
number who had fled the Meles regime. They'd be taken in by a
friend or relative who had emigrated ahead of them and already had
a job and an apartment.

Nearly all joined one of the opposition groups that took
advantage of America's protections to criticize the government they'd
left behind. They read anti-Meles websites that were blocked back
home and raised money for those still inside the country who had
formed competing political parties.

The government tolerated these opposition parties to a limited
extent, so it could pretend to meet the donor nations' calls for
democracy. If they became too popular, their leaders, like Dr. Asrat,
could always be arrested on one contrived charge or another.

Political competitors and critical journalists were tortured
at the Maekelawi police station or some other detention facility,
convicted by the EPRDF's courts of "terrorism" or "fomenting
violent revolution" and given long sentences in the dreaded Kaliti
prison. Those who just needed to be taught a lesson could be cut
loose after only a couple of years in some of Africa's worst jails.

But Hanna had left with Meles' blessing. Pleased he had someone
in a position to keep a close watch on a prized asset like Buddy, he had
called when she put in her resignation, wished her good luck and only

instructed her to keep him informed of anything significant.

Los Angeles was a strange place. Americans talked so loudly. People asked how you were but didn't expect an answer. The food was bland and came in sickeningly large portions. So much of it was wasted along with water and electricity. There were monstrous traffic jams.

Little things were mystifying. A dime was smaller than the less valuable nickel. It didn't say "twenty-five cents" on a quarter. One tipped the waiter who brought you a cup of coffee but not the barista who made it. There were so many rich people.

The supermarket was particularly perplexing. Some foods were measured by the pound instead of the Ethiopian *medeb* which just meant a "heap." Others came in boxes instead of the *tassa*, a large serving can's worth. The cup measurement used in baking, at least, was similar to the *sini*, a ceramic cup used for coffee or spices. And the way fresh vegetables were wrapped with a wire twist resembled the *esir*, "bundle," for cabbage and khat. Here, sugar and coffee came in cans and bags instead of the wrap Ethiopians call a *tikil*. There were so many different brands and types of the same food. It was dizzying.

Inches, feet and miles instead of centimeters, meters and kilometers. Ounces, quarts and pounds instead of grams, liters and kilograms.

Still, there was lots to like. Hanna had experienced luxury at the Sheraton and on their honeymoon in the Maldives. Years earlier, Buddy had moved her from her mother's house to a building used by diplomats near the African Union. But she had never imagined daily life could be so pleasurable and convenient. Their well-built furniture. Her splendid, green convertible she had learned to drive. The way shop clerks, maître d's, her husband's business associates and his employees were so nice to her.

She loved to accompany Buddy to the beach, sit under an umbrella with a thermos of coffee and watch him surf. He and The Gandel had nicknamed her "Beach Bunny" although its meaning still puzzled her. She took swimming lessons in their own pool. Tennis lessons on their own court. Yoga classes. Parties. Lunches. Dinners.

Everyplace smelled so fresh and clean, even the bathrooms. There were garbage disposals. All-night drugstores. Fitness clubs. The free soda refills never failed to impress her. Credit cards.

And, of course, the shopping. The variety of fashion and shoes in the stores was astounding—and they took returns. She had a closet full of clothes as fine as Azeb's. The closet itself was the size of many Ethiopians' homes.

Their house was a refuge from a brutish world, a literal fortress. Push a button and, within minutes, an SUV filled with armed men would show up—not to beat, threaten or take you away but to defend you. Here, one didn't have to be afraid of the government. You could say what you wanted without fear of spies.

Most of all, there was the financial security of being married to a wealthy man. Buddy was so generous to her and her family. Her mother lived more comfortably now, unaware how aggrieved he still was about the circumcision. Fasika's university fees were covered.

But a secret hung over their affluent lives. The truth was, while Hanna made every effort to please her husband in the bedroom, they had never had what he considered real sex. It was too painful for her.

As Buddy had gotten to know her, he'd discovered she had suffered from genital pain and infections ever since the circumcision. One infection during the war had almost killed her. Several years after they became involved, he had paid for her to have reconstructive surgery at Addis Ababa's Black Lion Hospital that reopened the vaginal opening. But while the operation eased urination and menstruation, it failed to resolve the chronic pain caused by the scarring over the missing clitoris, dashing their hopes for normal penetration.

Before she'd moved to Los Angeles, the Internet had become commonplace, and Buddy had already searched for years on Google for any medical breakthrough that might help. At last, in 2004, Hanna's third year in America, he read of a clitoral repair technique pioneered by a French urologist. It removed the scar tissue, exposed the nerves hidden behind it and grafted on fresh tissue. The procedure promised to reduce the pain, restore some clitoral sensitivity and even make an orgasm possible.

This last point meant more to Buddy than he had ever admitted. His inability to satisfy his wife undermined his male pride.

Maybe that was the reason for the never discussed, but frustrating, distance he had always felt from her. Hanna tried hard to be a good wife. Yet some part of her was fenced off. A solid sex life might bring with it the deeper psychological connection he craved.

At first, she resisted the idea. The prospect of something sharp being taken again to such a sensitive place was frightening. But from the way Buddy kept mentioning it with a forced casualness that made her uneasy, it was clearly more important to him than he let on. Wanting to please her husband, she reluctantly agreed to his proposal. They made plans to fly to Paris for the procedure.

After the operation, Hanna appeared depressed. Buddy didn't want her subjected to the rigors of flying until she had begun to heal, so he took a suite at the Ritz for two weeks and pampered her in the hope it would lift her spirits.

From time to time, she flinched without apparent reason. When he asked if she was in pain, she denied it.

Buddy urged her to get into therapy when they returned to California. It was alien to Ethiopian culture to talk about one's traumatic or shameful experiences with a stranger, but she agreed to try it. He called The Gandel and asked him to help find an appropriate therapist, preferably Ethiopian.

His friend called back a few hours later to report he couldn't find either a specialist in female circumcision or an Ethiopian psychotherapist in Los Angeles. But he'd located an American one whose practice focused on refugee victims of torture he thought might do.

Hanna's mood improved after they arrived back in California. Yet four months later, she still hadn't recovered normal sexual sensation.

Finally, after repeated, patient efforts on both their parts, the response that meant so much to Buddy occurred now and then.

The therapy seemed to help, too. Twice a week, she got into her Mercedes and drove over to Brentwood for a forty-five-minute session. She liked her therapist, a sympathetic, older Jewish woman.

Hanna smiled and even laughed more often. But the intimacy Buddy anticipated the operation would deliver remained elusive.

There was still something about his wife he couldn't figure out. The lack of eye contact. The unemotional manner. A slight stiffness in her embrace.

Chapter Sixteen

IN THIS WAY, another year went by. Help Ethiopia continued to expand. Buddy and Hanna returned periodically to Ethiopia.

It was a different country to Hanna. In early 2005, Addis Ababa was tense. Hatred for the EPRDF was widespread. Behind the façade of a democracy, the ruling party reigned over nearly every aspect of life. The ordinary Ethiopian had better accept it if he or she wanted to farm, go to school, hold a job or even receive emergency food aid.

Open defiance was dangerous. Critics of the government were routinely followed, threatened, beaten and, every now and then, disappeared.

She and Buddy tried to avoid politics and get on with their work. They didn't see Meles much any more. When they did, everyone maintained an outward air of cordiality. There was still the infrequent lunch, its family-style informality a mark of favoritism, or khat and soft drinks in the prime minister's residence after a joint photo opportunity or press conference.

But there were many unasked questions. They had read the accounts by activists and journalists that described Meles' Ethiopia as an Orwellian surveillance state where neighbors spied on each another and every phone call and email was monitored by an army of intelligence agents evocative of the former East Germany.

In Ethiopia, they didn't discuss it for fear of eavesdropping devices. But at home in Los Angeles, the role of Help Ethiopia and other humanitarian organizations in propping up the Meles regime had become the subject of bickering and even argument.

Buddy was one of the most sought-after sources on Ethiopia

by international media. Many newspaper stories, magazine articles, blogs and television news pieces about its famines or economic development included a quote from him. Afraid of a government shutdown of his charity, he always portrayed Meles' government as an efficient and reliable partner in the war on poverty—the *sine qua non* of any Ethiopian administration's legitimacy.

It was true, on paper, Ethiopia's public health statistics proved Meles had reduced infant mortality, HIV transmission and malnutrition. Primary education and many other indices of good governance were reported as getting better. But the EPRDF lied about almost everything.

To Buddy, the lines at the feeding centers seemed longer. There were whispers of corruption, of billions secretly transferred out of the country. The brutality was undeniable.

But to delve further into the matter, let alone do anything about it, was pointless. That wasn't what he had come to Ethiopia for.

The donor nations' representatives regularly advised the prime minister that democracy would attract job-creating foreign investors. And Meles paid lip service to this notion. He even claimed he was implementing democracy in the face of great difficulties.

Yet every five years, when it came time for another election, opposition candidates were harassed, arrested on absurd charges, denied media coverage, roughed up, intimidated and, once in a while, murdered. The government coasted to victory on implausibly high vote counts.

Still, as the 2005 election approached, Ethiopians and the international community began to hope this poll might be less unfair. Meles was confident he had crippled his political opposition. To get those Western reporters and human rights activists off his back once and for all, he'd loosened some of the campaign restrictions on the hamstrung democracy movement, now coalesced into a broad coalition called *Kinijit*, meaning "Unity."

A few real debates were actually permitted on the government-controlled television and radio stations. Opposition publishers released some newspapers and magazines which described Kinijit's goal of an Ethiopia that respected human rights. The attacks and threats let up a little.

From the fields to the streets to the corridors of Western officialdom, the farmer, the beggar, the petty trader, the student, the teacher, the aid worker, the civil servant and the diplomat dared imagine the election scheduled for May 15 might introduce a new, genuinely democratic Ethiopia.

"Ethiopia held the freest and fairest election in its history today," the BBC commentator read.

At home on Crestview Drive, Buddy and Hanna sat on their bed, riveted to the television. The news showed impoverished Ethiopians in secondhand Western clothing trudging along dirt trails. "An amazing eighty-five percent of registered voters," the commentator continued, "walked and rode, sometimes for days, to get to a polling booth." In one clip, an old woman clapped her hands and danced because she'd voted for the first time. Behind her, others waited to cast ballots.

Then came words the couple could scarcely believe.

"Early reports indicate a defeat at the polls for the ruling party."

Like a bird startled into flight, an indescribable optimism arose in their hearts. After all the struggle and controversy, with Kinijit's electoral triumph, Ethiopia had emerged into the sunlight of freedom.

"Wow." All sorts of possibilities for the country would now open up. Democracy meant stability. Investment. Jobs. More foreign aid. Less misery and death for Ethiopia's long-suffering people.

"Make love to me," Hanna said.

Buddy pushed her back on the bed. Meles appeared to him in a new, more favorable, light—the first Ethiopian head of state to hold an honest election and hand over power peacefully.

Meles had become a hero.

Buddy already had an Addis Ababa press conference scheduled for later that year. After an internationally-respected election, the lame duck prime minister had figured, would be the perfect time for the Help Ethiopia executive director to encourage the donor community to give an emerging democracy more money.

This time, Buddy and Hanna were happy to do it. But before the event could take place, the regime issued an important statement.

Weeks had passed since the election. The time for the government-appointed National Election Board to certify the opposition's win had come and gone. To the consternation and anger of Ethiopia's voters, the election board had twice postponed the announcement. Ethiopia-watchers wondered what was going on.

As speculation and rumors about the delay rose to fever pitch, the international media was summoned to the palace. Bereket Simon, the government's press secretary, entered the banquet room with a sheet of paper. He stood behind the lectern decorated with the EPRDF's star and put on his reading glasses.

The room fell silent.

"After recounting the votes, the National Election Board confirms," the press secretary read in a deadpan voice, "the government has won with a decisive victory."

The room erupted in nervous, derisive laughter.

It was a blatant lie.

Meles' latest election theft embarrassed his foreign backers—the British prime minister was famously photographed sitting next to him at a meeting with obvious distaste. But Ethiopia's leader calculated, besides his anti-terror cooperation, foreign perceptions he had delivered economic progress would shield him from international pressure.

There was plenty to show off. By 2005, the physical look of Tigray, in the north, and Addis Ababa, in the country's center, had changed. Construction cranes punctuated expanding skylines. Fashionable restaurants and coffee bars that catered to foreign aid officials and families of the government's elite had sprung up. Half-constructed homes and apartment buildings seemed to be everywhere. A steady stream of government press releases publicized large agricultural, manufacturing and mining projects. The foreign media had moved on to disasters elsewhere with greater commercial appeal.

But the appearance of development was superficial. Despite the tall buildings, busy construction sites, foreign aid that now exceeded two billion dollars every year and the government's claims of economic and public health improvement, more Ethiopians than ever needed emergency food aid.

The regime blamed the weather and a lack of resources. Yet it had become apparent the EPRDF's economic policy didn't work.

Calling it "revolutionary democracy," the government owned all of Ethiopia's land. The plots the farmers plowed were not their own. Unable to borrow against them or bequeath them to their children, they abandoned their farms and moved to the cities when the rains didn't come and times got tough. This weakened even further the country's capacity to feed itself and increased its reliance on foreign handouts.

Centralized authority in the hands of a few TPLF insiders smothered entrepreneurship and innovation in a blizzard of corruption, red tape and inefficiency. There were no independent courts to reassure investors their money was safe. Such practices had been rife throughout Africa for the past half-century with disastrous results.

Ethiopia's foreign donors and analysts had called on Meles to loosen his grip on the economy. But Meles still pushed his discredited economic programs long after their disappointment had become evident.

This stubborn refusal to change in the face of mounting unemployment, hardship and criticism was hard to understand. Meles was an unusually intelligent man. Why wouldn't he listen to the experts? Why this willful blindness and denial when the evidence of failure was there for all to see?

An awful thought struck Buddy. Perhaps the whole system wasn't designed to raise up the poor but to control them. He tried to dismiss this disquieting possibility, but it just might account for Meles' baffling inflexibility. Tight control—dictatorship, in a word—justified as a "revolutionary" necessity gave Meles and his cronies life-and-death power over the population. Buddy had for years seen the unspoken reality on the ground. The villager in need of a meal, the farmer desperate for fertilizer or seeds, the businessman seeking a license, could have it on one condition— support the EPRDF and keep your mouth shut.

But why this need for such complete domination of the people Meles had liberated? The prime minister didn't seem especially egotistical. It made no sense.

Like a snake swallowed by a bigger snake, a possible answer to this second mystery, even more unpleasant to contemplate, came to mind. The corruption. Without mastery over a cowed people, how could their rulers get away with such tremendous corruption?

Maybe that was why Meles was so determined to maintain his bankrupt policy. Poor people would be too weak to stop the graft. They'd be too exhausted to think about abstractions like government accountability. There'd be no competition for the monopolies held by his family, loyalists and business partners.

Could the same government pledged to eradicate the country's overwhelming poverty secretly be encouraging it? Buddy couldn't believe Meles would knowingly keep Ethiopia destitute. But his actions made such a conclusion increasingly hard to deny.

The implications were staggering. By the fifteenth year of Meles' rule, maladministration had cost millions of lives. Hunger tormented those it did not kill outright. Life expectancy was not even the fifty-six years falsely claimed by the regime. Nearly half of Ethiopia's children grew up stunted, their brains permanently damaged from malnutrition. Parasites made everyday life hell. The anguish of loved ones drowned the land in heartbreak.

Their individual stories were lost in the fake statistics Ethiopia's economic and health ministries trumpeted to worldwide acclaim. The man dead at forty who might have lived to seventy had he been able to afford a doctor. The mother who buried four infants when, had the village's water been clean, she might have buried only two. The child intellectually disabled for life. The teen condemned to poverty because there was no jobholder in the family to pay for higher education.

They added up to countless human tragedies blamed on bad weather, swept under the carpet or simply ignored. In city hovels and on remote farms, orphans, beggars, unemployed youth, day laborers, sidewalk dwellers, prostitutes, farmers and their families were quietly suffering and dying in the poverty Meles had perpetuated while he and his comrades enriched themselves.

It was a crime on a scale that almost defied imagination.

It was mass murder hiding in plain sight.

Most Ethiopians saw the election fraud as just another tactic in their thieving government's war on them. But the poverty the stolen ballot prolonged left Help Ethiopia and the other aid organizations, despite their unhappiness with Meles, no alternative but to step up the fight against the growing starvation and sickness with more and more feeding centers, trucks, food, medicine and staff.

And in some kind of insane, yet inescapable, loop, that spelled more dependence on Meles. Dependence he could cash in for more foreign loans and grants.

By 2005, nearly twenty years after he'd met the rebel commander at his base camp in Tigray, Buddy felt like he was trying to drain the ocean with a leaky bucket. He didn't want to admit it, but he suspected Help Ethiopia was window dressing for the greatest wholesale killing and robbery since the Nazis had looted Europe.

Every good deed his charity performed helped a dictator who kept his people poor and hungry hang onto power.

And there was nothing he could do about it.

BOOK 3

Chapter Seventeen

AFTER THE DEFEAT of fascism, Haile Selassie turned to freeing Africa from colonialism. As the father of African independence, the emperor built Addis Ababa's modernist Africa Hall to house his and other African leaders' vision of a federated association that would steer the continent's development. A magnificent, stained-glass triptych, *The Total Liberation of Africa,* covered an entire wall with its depiction of African nations coming together to tackle poverty and disease.

In the decades that followed, Africa Hall was mostly used to legitimize corrupt dictators. But the location was impressive, and Meles had decided it would make a good backdrop for Buddy's press conference touting the EPRDF's achievements. There, the prime minister's celebrity defender would exhort the donor nations to overlook the hijacked election and approve a new, multi-billion-dollar aid package for the regime.

It was a dreary, November morning in 2005, six months after Meles' ballot scam, when a dyspeptic Buddy faced the international press in one of the wood-paneled, '60s-era conference rooms. A large banner strung behind him read, "Fighting Poverty Together— Approve the Aid Package!" He reminded himself to sound positive as he braced for yet another confrontation with the reporters. An equally cheerless Hanna handed out a glossy press release.

He'd heard that, a few blocks away, Kinijit supporters were protesting the stolen election. Maybe they hoped to attract some of the journalists from his event.

The demonstrators carried signs that read, "Development Needs Democracy," "Stop Election Fraud!" and "Where is the International

Community?" But while Buddy was giving his speech up the street, open-back trucks full of fearsome *Agazi* special forces drew up to the rally site. These were an elite commando unit of Tigrayan soldiers imported by Meles into the capital because they had few ties to the local population. Most of them didn't even speak Amharic.

The rangy Agazi, in their camouflage uniforms and red berets, dismounted. More trucks, packed with Federalis, appeared.

An Agazi commander picked up a megaphone and sternly warned the demonstrators to go home.

Their angry chants and slogans got louder.

A couple more warnings proved futile. The commander bellowed an order at his troops.

Gloved hands gripped batons.

Index fingers unlocked safety selectors on automatic rifles.

The commander coldly regarded the scene. He gave the megaphone to a subordinate and waved his hand above his head.

It took several seconds for the unarmed protesters to comprehend what was happening as flesh, blood and brains sprayed onto friends, the street and the sidewalk. People fell down.

Demonstrators, most in their teens and twenties, screamed and ran for shelter from the hail of 50-caliber rifle fire unleashed by unseen snipers.

Shrieks turned to gasps, groans and pleas for help as protesters struggled with their wounds. Some pressed shirts against spurting arteries. A few stumbled blindly and tried to wipe blood from their eyes. Many lay dead on the pavement. Scarlet cavities in their heads grinned like second mouths.

The commander gestured once more. The Agazi and Federalis advanced to clear the avenue. They shot, strangled and beat the remaining survivors like hunters finishing off their prey.

Ambulance sirens began to wail in the distance as word of the massacre spread.

Buddy's presentation had been interrupted a few times by what he assumed were jackhammers on some nearby construction site, but he finally concluded his remarks. "This year's aid package, if approved, will allow Ethiopia to turn the corner in its fight against hunger. And AIDS. And illiteracy. And underdevelopment." He paused for the light applause. "I'll take questions now."

A reporter stood up. "Since most experts agree democracy and economic development are connected, how do you relate that to the election fraud?"

"That's a political matter. I want to talk about feeding hungry people."

A commotion started at the back of the room.

"Can you really separate the two?" the reporter persisted.

Buddy sniffed the air. "You smell something burning?"

"Gunpowder," another reporter called out. "They're shooting demonstrators down the street."

"Shooting them?"

Everyone forgot the press conference and went outside. A few hundred meters away, Agazi and Federalis sauntered by cowering protesters. An occasional gunshot or short burst of automatic fire mixed with human cries.

Buddy stared, dumbstruck, at the carnage. His right arm hurt. Hanna was squeezing it.

"Fasika is there," she said anxiously.

"Fasika? What's Fasika doing there?"

Hanna's frightened expression answered his question.

"Jesus Christ."

Everyone was afraid to approach the violent scene. At last, the gunfire stopped. Taking courage in numbers, Buddy, Hanna and the reporters walked to the demonstration site.

Acrid smoke hung over slain demonstrators, discarded protest signs and scattered shoes. The wounded left bloody trails. Their moans made a chorus from hell.

Brakes squealed, sirens whooped and lights flared as ambulances arrived. Emergency medical technicians ran to help the fallen.

Buddy tried to slip through the police line with the medical

175

personnel. A Federali stopped him.

"I have to get in there!"

Behind the Federali, red and pink bits of human tissue were splattered across walls, faces and clothes. Pools of blood slowly widened around bodies in the street.

This can't be real. Gathering his wits, Buddy took out his cellphone and dialed Meles' office number. A rapid busy signal droned.

An American reporter from the press conference sidled up to him. "It's going on all over the city. They're taking a lot of people away in trucks."

"Your phone working?"

"They shut them off. Nice way to greet the press."

Hanna scanned the chaos for signs of Fasika.

"How does he have the nerve to do this with the foreign media and donors watching?" Buddy exclaimed.

"Meles is a fucking snake. But he's our big ally in the War on Terror."

Three swaggering Agazi knocked a scholarly-looking man in a suit down and kicked him in the stomach.

"Our tax dollars at work," the reporter added bitterly.

His remark gave Buddy an idea. He took out his roll of birr and pressed it into the policeman's hand. The Federali quickly looked around, pocketed the money and let him and Hanna pass.

They stepped over bodies and searched for Fasika. Emergency medical technicians triaged the injured. Buddy grabbed one by the sleeve.

"Where are you taking them?"

The man shook his head. He didn't speak English.

"Black Lion Hospital," another one said. "And the private clinics."

The hospital lobby was jammed with dead and wounded protesters. Some lay on the tiled floor and moaned repetitiously. Others, their skin grey and waxy and their eyes glassy and vacant, had stopped moving in a final humiliation. Frenzied friends and family tried to rouse them and attempted to summon help from the overwhelmed nurses.

Buddy and Hanna avoided the slippery, smelly blood congealing on the floor. They examined each body, dead or alive, that might be her brother's and joined those calling out the names of the missing.

The halls were lined with casualties. Every room was full. But there was no sign of Fasika.

They followed the sound of excited voices down a long, dank corridor to the morgue. The stench of formaldehyde was almost overpowering.

The morgue was stacked high with dead Ethiopians in blood-soaked clothes. Blood dripped from holes in their heads, backs and chests. Orderlies fended off hysterical relatives of the victims, pushed more leaking corpses on gurneys into the stinking room and left them on the heap.

Buddy looked around in confusion. "They should get ice trucks," he remarked stupidly.

Hanna gave him a startled look then checked the faces of the dead. Buddy pulled at limp arms and legs, so she could scrutinize those underneath. Satisfied that Fasika wasn't among them, they tottered out of the morgue and into a grassy vacant lot.

Many protesters who had accompanied the fatalities stood and sat on the ground in shock.

"Does anybody know Fasika Ashete?" Buddy hollered. "Fasika Ashete?"

Hanna repeated the plea in Amharic.

An Ethiopian woman in a bloodstained dress said something to her.

"He was arrested," Hanna told him.

"We've got to find Meles."

He had sent his driver to search the private medical clinics. But at the edge of the property, a cluster of pedestrians, food vendors and taxi drivers seemed oddly unaffected by the calamity going on a few hundred feet away.

The scene was dreamlike as Buddy neared it.

"Are you all right?" he heard Hanna ask.

"I'm okay."

He hailed a beat-up, blue-and-white Lada, a relic from the Soviet-aid era. The driver beckoned for them to get in.

"Menelik Palace." The driver gave him a blank look. "Menelik Palace!"

Hanna translated the request into Amharic—*Gebi*. The driver put the old car in gear. It lurched forward.

Sirens filled the air as the taxi crawled through a press of people and traffic going about their business as if it were a normal day. Pockets of violence continued on side streets where security forces had cornered fleeing protesters. An Agazi poked a screaming teenage girl in the eye with a long knife.

"Why didn't you tell me Fasika was involved with them?" Buddy furiously asked his wife.

"I didn't want to worry you," she replied in an apologetic tone.

The taxi came to a standstill in traffic. Two passing policemen with blood-spattered shirts peered in the taxi window and looked them up and down.

They left them alone and moved on.

Soldiers, tanks and rolls of barbed wire reinforced the palace's security perimeter. Hanna threw some bills at the taxi driver, and they got out. A shoeless man accosted Buddy and tried to sell him a handmade basket. Buddy brushed him aside and went up to a captain.

"Speak English?"

"A little."

"Tell the prime minister Buddy Schwartz needs to see him. It's urgent."

The captain unclipped a walkie-talkie from his belt, said a few Tigrinya words into it and listened.

"Go in."

The soldiers let Buddy and Hanna through the barricade. They crossed an empty section of the avenue deserted except for three armored personnel carriers. A sergeant waved them through a high steel gate fortified with more men and piles of sandbags.

The grounds of the royal compound were hushed as they walked uphill to the palace. Soldiers with automatic weapons, alerted to their presence, let them pass. A watchtower guard leaned on his tripod-mounted machine gun and eyed them carefully. They came to the Prime Minister's office building, were directed through a metal detector and went inside.

An atmosphere of barely restrained panic pervaded the entrance hall. Pale and shaken military aides came and went. Meles' wife, Azeb, and their eldest daughter tried to quiet two younger children. A soldier guarded a long row of suitcases.

Visibly aged, Meles nervously smoked a cigarette by a tall window. Barely glancing at Buddy, he shielded his eyes against the sun and tried to see what was happening beyond the security perimeter.

"I've got an armored column on its way to get us to the airport," he said as he surveyed the horizon. "You can come on our plane."

"Go with you?" Buddy sputtered. "You've got to stop the shooting! And Hanna's brother's been arrested!"

"Her brother?" Meles asked absently. "What is her brother doing with those troublemakers?"

"They're just demonstrating. And your soldiers are shooting them!"

"They are trying to make an illegal coup," the prime minister retorted. "We have the intel." He seemed to notice Hanna for the first time and said something to her in Tigrinya that sounded like a reprimand.

A military aide approached, saluted and briefly reported to Meles.

"They're getting it under control," Meles said. Clearly relieved, he gave an order to the aide, who saluted again and hurried away. Junior officers began to remove the luggage.

"Are you hungry?" he asked Buddy and Hanna as if they had dropped in for a friendly chat.

"Am I hungry?" Buddy cried incredulously. "You've got to make your soldiers stop shooting!"

Meles' mouth tightened with annoyance. "My men don't have America's resources, training or equipment," he replied testily. "You can't expect them to behave like the Washington police." He saw Buddy was distraught and softened. "It will be all right."

"I saw a child stabbed in the eye. How can it ever be all right?"

"I've got seventy-seven million poor people to feed," Meles explained with pained restraint. "I can't let a few opportunists stop that. Don't you see the logic of it?"

The aide returned, saluted and relayed another message.

"I have to see some people," Meles said.

As Buddy and Hanna stood there in astonishment, he summoned his family. Bodyguards surrounded them. They headed for an exit.

"Come see me on Sunday," Meles called over his shoulder. "I'm going to need your help with the press."

"What about Hanna's brother?"

"I'll see what I can do."

"Like with the school teacher?"

"Who?"

Buddy started after him. A bodyguard blocked his way.

Ethiopia's prime minister disappeared down a corridor.

For three agonizing days and nights, they waited with Hanna's mother at her house for news of Fasika. Buddy left eight messages for Meles but couldn't reach the beleaguered Ethiopian leader.

"Maybe you should not have yelled at him," Hanna said at one point during their long vigil.

"I was yelling?"

The state-controlled television news spun the massacre as a tragic necessity in the face of a violent coup attempt by terrorists. Straight-faced news anchors ignored the 193 murdered protesters and claimed six policemen had been killed by a wild mob. They played up this angle with scenes of the policemen's mourning families shown over and over.

Slowly, the dimensions of the crackdown became clear. In addition to the deaths, 763 Ethiopians had been wounded, many with stab wounds or blunt force trauma that smashed skulls and bones. The censored Ethiopian press didn't disclose it, but Buddy learned from calls to Los Angeles, where his staff had access to BBC and CNN broadcasts, an estimated forty thousand protesters, many of them children, were in concentration camps. The Kinijit opposition leaders, who had won the election and should have been preparing the transition of power to their new administration, had all been arrested.

Weeping could be heard throughout Arat Kilo. The situation felt so similar to the fate of Hanna's father twenty years earlier that she and her mother couldn't sleep or eat despite Buddy's efforts to comfort them. They drank uncounted cups of coffee brought by the distressed maid and scarcely spoke.

In the afternoon of the fourth day, there was a knock at the door. Hanna sprang up to open it.

A haggard Fasika stood there. His head was shaved bald and covered with fresh scabs. His clothes were filthy. There was a cast on his wrist.

His mother and the maid tearfully kissed him, but Hanna was strangely subdued. Fasika disengaged himself and asked for something to eat. A plate of stew was quickly brought. He wolfed it down as everyone stared at him in relief.

After he'd finished, he told them what had happened. He and his friends had been hanging out on the Addis Ababa University campus. There'd been a lot of talk among the students and some homeless youth about the stolen vote, what an embarrassment it was in front of the world, how Ethiopia had to join the ranks of civilized nations and how it needed good leadership. When word came that the opposition had called for everyone to protest at Meskel Square downtown, they had set out on foot.

There weren't any organized demonstrations yet. Drivers just honked their horns. But news soon spread that many workers had gone on strike.

Just as had happened near Africa Hall, Agazi and Federalis sealed off the area and attacked them. Fasika had been lucky to escape with a fractured wrist from a Federali's baton. One of his classmates had been shot through the side.

They had run for their lives but were trapped. Held for hours in the street, they couldn't eat, drink or go to the bathroom.

Trucks had pulled up. Federalis made them climb in.

His truck was part of a convoy hauling three or four hundred protesters. After a long ride, they wound up at a military camp ringed by guards and barbed wire. They were left in the open. There was only one spigot for water. People had to stand for hours to wait their turn.

That night was cold. The prisoners huddled together for warmth.

The next day, an Agazi captain showed up with an armed detachment. At gunpoint, he forced the prisoners to do calisthenics while he shouted insults and abuse. Some wept and collapsed from exhaustion.

Soldiers threw pieces of injera into the crowd. Convoys arrived with hundreds more prisoners.

There were no bathroom facilities. People had to relieve themselves in a corner of the camp. Without toilet tissue or containers for water, everyone became soiled. The air grew fetid.

The second night, a hyena got through the barbed wire and mauled three prisoners. A 14-year-old kid died. To keep the hyenas at bay, they made fires from garbage and branches that littered the camp. The animals' yellow eyes followed them from behind the fence.

Besides those bitten by hyenas, many prisoners, like Fasika, had serious injuries. They begged for a doctor, but none came.

In the morning, the captain returned and commanded them to crawl for hours on their knees over gravel. It was unbearable. Those who faltered or refused were hit with rifle butts or kicked.

The captain came back that afternoon. He made the prisoners form a long, single line. Two soldiers set up a table with a bucket of water, soap and a single razor. One at a time, each man, woman and child had his or her hair shaved off with the same rusty blade. The razor was completely dull before long. The soldiers hacked roughly at the remaining prisoners' heads and nearly scalped them. Because HIV was prevalent in Ethiopia, everyone feared contracting it from the shared razor.

More injera was tossed at them. Some prisoners broke psychologically and promised the guards they'd never demonstrate again if they would let them out. Fasika tried to tell the guards he was related to Buddy and Hanna and had met the prime minister. There was no response. Someone said the guards didn't speak Amharic.

The captain reappeared the next day. They were formed this time into rows. But before that day's torture began, the captain called Fasika's name and the names of two other prisoners. They were ordered to step forward.

To their bewilderment, they were taken away by jeep and delivered to a military hospital in the suburbs. Once brought inside, Fasika was left alone in an examination room, terrified he was about to be tortured. A military doctor entered without introducing himself and conducted a medical exam. He felt Fasika's injured wrist, asked some questions, left and came back after a few minutes with a splint and bandages. The doctor wrapped his wrist. A nurse led the youngster to a sink and told him to wash up.

Another jeep waited outside the hospital when he was released. The soldier behind the wheel told him in a friendly tone he would take him home. Fasika was scared he was being taken for execution, but he was driven right to his door and dropped off without incident.

His family listened to this account in amazement.

"It must have been Meles," Buddy said. Hanna nodded in agreement.

Fasika was itching to take a shower. His sister tied a plastic bag around the cast on his wrist, so he could bathe without getting it wet. He went into the bathroom. Everyone was too astonished to say much.

Ten minutes later, Fasika returned with his skin gleaming from the shower and a towel around his waist. He spoke to his mother and sister in Amharic. "I want to sleep," he explained to Buddy. Excusing himself politely, he went into one of the house's three bedrooms and closed the door behind him.

The others allowed themselves to eat something. They'd missed a lot of sleep, too. Buddy wanted to take Hanna back to the Sheraton, have a drink and get into that cushy bed.

Her mother had a heart condition, so first they made sure she was all right. Then they returned to the Sheraton and did exactly that.

That night's television news, perhaps to distract the public, repeatedly broadcast a local human-interest story about a twelve-year-old girl in the provincial capital of Bita Genet, about three hundred fifty miles southwest of Addis Ababa, who had been kidnapped and beaten by seven men trying to force her into a marriage with one of them. She'd been missing for a week before she was found being guarded by three lions which had apparently chased off her captors.

A nightmare about the Black Lion Hospital morgue woke Buddy. The sky was streaked with red, orange and violet. He didn't know if it was sunrise or sunset. His watch said six o'clock. Hanna read a newspaper on the balcony. The sight of her comforted him, and he forgot about the dream. He padded barefoot across the carpeted floor in his shorts and joined her.

Hanna held a government newspaper. The other papers' print runs had been confiscated. She put the newspaper down, took his hand and pressed it against her cheek.

"I want you to speak with Fasika," she said. "He must not involve himself in politics. I do not know what will come here, but conditions may become very dangerous. My mother will die if he is killed." She looked up at Buddy. "Will you talk with him?"

"Of course."

But this did not go as hoped. The next day, they sat down with Fasika at his mother's home. After coffee and solicitous inquiries about his wrist, Buddy got to the point. He spoke slowly and as simply as he could, so Hanna's brother, with his limited English, understood.

"We are family, Fasika, and I will speak to you very honestly. It looks like trouble is coming, and it is going to be too dangerous for you to go to the demonstrations again."

Fasika respectfully listened.

"You see how easy it is to get hurt. Or even killed. And your mother has already suffered enough."

To make sure the teenager got the point, Hanna repeated Buddy's words in Amharic.

"Your sister and I have important work here. If our family gets on the government's bad side, it could be a problem."

"Everybody must help to save Ethiopia," Fasika said.

"'Let somebody else save Ethiopia. You've got a mother to watch out for. Who will take care of her if something happens to you?"

Fasika thought for a moment. "You," he said.

"Is that fair?" Buddy asked him gently. "Is that fair to me and your sister?" He tried to catch Fasika's eye, but the young man, reluctant to confront an elder, looked away.

"Woyane," Fasika said softly, using Amhara slang for Tigrayans. "Kill Ethiopia. My grandfather fight Mussolini. I am same with my grandfather."

"You don't understand," Buddy chided. "We're Meles' friends. He got you released. He allows us to operate. I have to see him tomorrow. What am I supposed to tell him? That we're helping the people who want to overthrow his government?"

"If Woyane go," Fasika said. "Ethiopians could have many work. Help Ethiopia will feed some other country."

Before Buddy could respond, Hanna pushed back her chair and left the room.

He found her in the front yard looking upset. "What's the matter?"

"He is too foolish," she snapped.

But that night, as she lay next to Buddy and stared at the reflected light from the hotel grounds playing on the ceiling, she told Buddy the truth. Her younger brother's courage had made her ashamed.

They rested and listened to the doves coo on the balcony. His thoughts drifted to the girl who had been rescued by the lions.

He imagined her casually sitting on the ground between the great beasts, protected and unafraid.

Chapter Eighteen

BUDDY LOOKED DOWN at his plate. He had barely tasted his food.

They were dining with Joe Burke, one of the biggest talent agents in the business, and his wife, Lindsey, at the Beverly Hills Golf Club. Hanna had encouraged Buddy to join it after their return to Los Angeles in the winter of 2006. They socialized less and less these days, and she thought he worked too hard.

The club welcomed entertainment figures considered too *nouveau* for the more sedate establishments that catered to the finance tycoons and old money. The dress code—no jeans, T-shirts, leisure suits or turned-around hat brims—was irksome. But Buddy enjoyed the 1920s dining room with its sweeping view of the golf course and the skyscrapers of downtown Los Angeles.

Their waiter noticed his prominent guest's uneaten meal.

"Is everything all right, Mr. Schwartz?"

Buddy waved him away. "I'm not eating as much as I used to," he confided to Joe. "Don't seem to enjoy things any more."

With his bushy mustache and avuncular manner, Joe defied the stereotype of the slick Hollywood agent. "You should feel like you're on top of the world," he counseled.

"Yeah," Buddy said hollowly.

They finished their dinner and wine. The waiter brought over the dessert cart. He pointed to each sweet. "Apple tart. Chocolate mousse. Pecan squares. Key lime pie. Cheesecake."

While everybody ordered, Buddy eyed the cart's steel legs and rubber wheels. Their rattling reminded him of the gurneys carrying the dead into the Black Lion Hospital morgue.

"Anybody want a brandy?" he asked the others. Hanna gave

him a reproving look. More than two glasses of wine brought on the flashbacks, and he'd already had four.

"Come on," he urged Joe, ignoring her. "Have one with me."

The drinks came in large snifters. Buddy consumed half of his in one gulp.

"How about a movie?" Joe asked.

"What do you wanna see?"

"'Syriana?'" Joe suggested, referring to the latest political thriller.

"No. No violence."

"Maybe a comedy, then."

"People don't know what violence means," Buddy declared disjointedly. "Ah, nobody cares," he added in a disgusted tone. He stared into his brandy. "I gotta get out of this fucking business. I'm a TV producer who hates TV now."

"This 'fucking business' has been very good to us."

"Let me tell you something." Buddy gazed around the room full of entertainment executives and their families. "Twenty-five thousand kids died today from preventable disease. Another twenty-five thousand are gonna die tomorrow. Millions of them are sick, scared and hungry. We wanna make TV, how come that's not on the TV every fucking night?" He drained his glass of brandy. "You know my neighbor has a car collection worth ten million dollars? I'm sick of these people."

"So we're a bunch of selfish Philistines. Is that it? Nobody's doing anything except you?"

"That's what it feels like."

A hush fell over the table.

"I'm sorry," Hanna said to the Burkes.

"You don't have to apologize for me," Buddy drunkenly protested. "Waiter! Gimme a refill here."

Hanna shot him another look.

"Will ya leave me alone?"

Hanna drove them home in a windy rainstorm. They didn't speak during the ride except once when she said, "He was your friend."

When they got home, Buddy staggered up to the bedroom and flopped face down on the bed. Out of a black void, a slideshow of bodies, brain tissue and flesh on blood-smeared pavement began. The dripping corpses in the Black Lion morgue. The girl stabbed in the eye. The shrieking boy in the ditch at Shire.

His father, face down in the store.

A few minutes later, Hanna, dressed in her nightgown, got into bed beside him.

He snuggled up against her. Her hair smelled of shampoo.

"I'm sorry," he said.

"You must get some help."

"'Help?' I'm glad I'm depressed. At least I can understand a little what other people are suffering. I'm not forgetting them like everybody else in that goddamned room tonight."

"Sometimes it's good to talk to somebody."

"What's there to talk about? Life's a tragedy, and we don't understand anything."

She kissed his forehead. As he lay in her arms, he reflected on the irony of his often closed and secretive wife urging him to talk to somebody. The therapy's helped her, he realized.

The tree outside their bedroom scraped in the wind against the side of the house. Trees reminded him of the hanged Oromo boy. And there were trees everywhere.

"It makes me crazy that I'm doing so little."

Drifting into sleep, he imagined himself confronting Meles. Shouting angrily at him. Punching him in the face. He imagined them laughing and chewing khat together. Then fighting again.

"You're the only one who understands me," he said out loud.

Despite the incident at the country club, life went on in 2006. Buddy let The Gandel put him on an antidepressant. It reduced the flashbacks' frequency as long as he stayed away from alcohol, exercised and kept busy. But he soon gave up the pills.

"They're killing my sex drive," he complained to the doctor.

189

"It's a common side effect. Is it that bad?"

"Ever since Hanna had the operation, I need all the help I can get."

"Your symptoms will come back."

"I want to have a kid."

Chapter Nineteen

BUDDY AND HANNA now flew on a leased private jet when they visited her homeland. Public opinion in the capital was even more resentful of the government. Security was heavier. More topics were avoided in conversation with Meles and other Ethiopian officials.

The democracy movement that had so mortified him at the polls and had threatened to oust him the previous year now represented less of a threat to Meles. Its leaders, all practitioners of nonviolence, remained in Kaliti prison on trumped-up charges of terrorism or inciting armed rebellion. Their rigged trials were a Kafkaesque parody of justice meant to keep them preoccupied.

With their leaders in jail and the press muzzled, Kinijit's supporters grew disheartened and apathetic. Many gave up hope for Ethiopia's emergence from dictatorship and refocused their energies on the struggle for survival. To Buddy and Hanna's relief, Fasika seldom spoke of politics. His HIV test had been negative, and he'd resumed his engineering studies.

The international community cynically discouraged the democracy movement in the name of "maintaining stability." The American chargé d'affaires even advised the imprisoned leaders to accept the stolen election.

Thanks to Meles' well-connected lobbyists, Western governments continued to renew their financial aid. The vicious cycle of money, repression and death continued.

The regime was invincible.

The months went by with Buddy's work and marriage in the doldrums. Then the most unlikely of events changed his, Hanna's and Ethiopia's futures forever.

Hanna was a big fan of *Oprah* and frequently regaled him with what she'd seen on the popular show's latest episode. Lazing on the living room couch with the French doors open to the flower-scented desert air or with a cup of coffee in the kitchen, she watched it almost every day. But this program held her attention like no other she had seen before.

"This next guest's story affected me powerfully," Oprah announced. "Her story represents an issue that affects one hundred million women today—"

Buddy, just back from his golf game in a sweat-stained polo shirt, appeared in the living room doorway with a putter. "You should have come," he said proudly, toying with the golf club. "I took two strokes off."

Engrossed in the program, Hanna motioned for him to be quiet.

"The Embassy called," he informed her. "Meles wants me to do CNN for him."

"Look what they have on."

He slung the putter over his shoulder and, ignoring the effect of his spiked golf shoes on the carpet, perched on the back of the sofa. "You know, in the five years you've been here, I don't think you've ever missed a show."

On the television, a black woman with a courageous, yet anguished, expression materialized. "My name is Soraya," a female voice with a Somali accent intoned. "I knew what he was doing to me. I will always remember the sound of the scissors and the pain between my legs—"

There was a shot of four African women crouched in a huddle. A child's flailing arm flashed between them.

"To my husband, I was just property. Just a body without a head."

Buddy put the putter down.

"Now I understand," Hanna said, her gaze fixed on the television, "why you asked if I was angry."

He moved to comfort his wife but, absorbed by the show, she waved him off.

For a second, her eyes blazed with murderous rage.

Then she settled back to watch the rest of the program.

Chapter Twenty

A LOW-SPIRITED mood hung over them for weeks. They went through their daily routines of meetings, yoga, tennis, dinners and parties in an almost automatic manner. Neither could quite say what was behind this malaise, but the answer became increasingly clear as Buddy's CNN interview crept nearer to the top of his crowded calendar.

The day began as Hanna watched a make-up artist powder her husband's face. He sat in a salon chair, a large bib around his neck, in CNN's Los Angeles studio. Just down the hall awaited the cameras and millions of television viewers.

A production assistant poked his head in the room. "You're on in two."

"What the fuck am I supposed to say?" Buddy peevishly asked Hanna, their long-running disagreement breaking out again like a summer storm. "We've got to cut off all those hungry people because our friend over there's a little behind on democratic reform?"

"You must say something," she insisted, embarrassed by his demeanor in front of the makeup artist.

He lapsed into sullen silence. She'd been nagging him about his public support for Meles more than ever. His stomach burned, and he wanted to get an antacid, but there was no time.

"He is making millions of poor people die because he does not let them get any job," she reminded him. "Or he will not give them doctors or medicine. It is genocide." She checked if his shirt cuffs stuck out properly from his suit sleeves. He was gripping the chair's armrest so tightly his knuckles were white. "Our silence helps him. I cannot forgive myself for helping him get into power."

"Mr. Schwartz, you're on!" the production assistant called from the corridor.

The next thing Buddy knew, he was in the interview seat and halfway through his twenty-four-minute interview.

"So you feel the human rights picture in Ethiopia," the reporter demanded, "should not affect our relations? How do you respond to the critics who charge Meles has turned into a dictator?"

Buddy couldn't remember what he had just said. Focus, he told himself. "People are dying of hunger," he said emphatically. "This very minute. There's no time for theoretical political debate." He faced the camera. "That's why everyone must support the aid package. Write your senator and your congressman today."

Out of camera range, Hanna stood behind the reporter. Her face was a mask of disappointment.

"Thank you, Buddy Schwartz," he heard the reporter say.

"I don't understand what Meles is doing," Buddy blurted out. "He's a smart leader. He ought to know better."

Buddy slept well that night. When he awoke, he had nearly forgotten the previous evening's interview. But when he shuffled in his slippers down to the kitchen and skimmed the newspapers the housekeeper left every morning next to his glass of orange juice, there it was. The *New York Times* lacked any mention of the interview. But the *Los Angeles Times* had it on the first page of its World section: "Help Ethiopia Director Criticizes Ethiopian Leader Over Human Rights."

Dreading what he'd find, he opened the *New York Post*. The article on page four was worse. Captioned in the paper's trademark sensationalist style, it read, "Wise Up, Meles! Buddy Sez."

Over the next twenty-four hours, the articles were syndicated to hundreds of other newspapers and news websites worldwide. Buddy's interview was re-broadcast through CNN's global affiliates.

The BBC World Service, the Voice of America and Germany's Deutsche Welle picked it up, too.

Chapter Twenty-One

FEW PAVED ROADS connected Ethiopia to the outside world. The one that ran from Port Sudan, on the Red Sea, through coastal plains before it climbed Ethiopia's northern mountains was interrupted at the Ethiopian border by a tin shack customs station. The traffic waiting for clearance beside the rusted "Welcome to Ethiopia" sign made a captive market for the food sellers, petty traders and prostitutes who solicited the dusty container trucks, passenger buses with luggage tied to their roofs and overloaded, mule-drawn gari carts.

Business was good that day because the line had stalled. Nineteen Help Ethiopia truck drivers leaned out of their cabs to see what held it up.

Their lead driver was arguing with the Ethiopian customs agent.

"Fuck." In his bedroom at home, Buddy strained to hear over the bad phone connection what his country manager said. From what he could make out, the news was bad. "The trucks can't get through?"

"Twenty semis," the manager yelled into the phone. "Full of grain. Stopped at the border. The guards won't let them pass."

"Do they see they're our trucks?"

"They know, they know. Something is changed. They won't even take a bribe."

All that day and the next were spent trying to solve the problem by phone. "Hello, do you speak English? This is Buddy Schwartz. I want to speak to the minister of health...Hello? Is this the minister's office? I keep getting disconnected...Speak English? Who speaks English? Yes, English. Thank you...The minister is out? Who can I talk to? I have twenty food aid trucks stopped at the border. They said we need a new permit from the health ministry. I can't get anyone on the phone who knows about it…Try the social welfare ministry? But they said health! When will the minister be back? Next week? That's too late. I've got fifty thousand hungry people waiting for those trucks. Try the head of customs? I already tried him ten phone calls ago!"

Hanna entered as he paced back and forth with the phone in his hand. "This is Buddy Schwartz." He was almost pleading. "I need to speak with the prime minister. Right now, please. He's unavailable? I've got people who need that food, and they'll die if I don't talk to the prime minister immediately. Tell him Buddy Schwartz is trying to reach him. And it's important."

He slammed the receiver down so hard she feared it would break. "Meles isn't taking my calls. It must be the interview. Fucking media." A muscle in his cheek twitched. "I'll have to go see him."

"I heard he is going to London for a meeting with the PM," Hanna said. "He loves being received at Downing Street and all those fancy places."

"Ever since the Holocaust," Buddy said. "Everyone keeps saying 'never again.' But it is happening again. I'm not going to let these people down."

"I have some friends who want to meet you," Hanna suggested cautiously.

"About what?" he asked with a sigh.

"About Meles. They need your help."

He could guess what she meant. "No politics. I'm staying out of that." To his annoyance, that disappointed look crossed her face again.

"People are depending on me for their next meal," he reminded her in an aggrieved tone. "I can't put them in danger."

"The whole country is in danger."

Chapter Twenty-Two

"How do you like London?" Buddy asked. We're making polite conversation like strangers, he thought.

Hanna peered through the hired Rolls limousine's tinted window at bustling Piccadilly Circus. It was a raw, spring evening. The food convoy had been stuck at the border for a week.

"Many people are walking. And the buildings are strange."

Giant electric billboards cast the curious jumble of modern and Victorian architecture in garish, artificial daylight. The car's hermetic doors turned the jostling, beeping, exhaust-belching traffic into a soundless movie. Shoppers and tourists trooped silently past glass-fronted stores displaying the latest fashions, shoes and electronics. Signs promised discount prices.

"There's the Ritz." The hotel's dignified shopping arcade was busy with wealthy tourists. Buddy remembered good times there when he'd had another wife. "Like the one in Paris. But with a different owner."

He pointed to their left. "Buckingham Palace is down there. And there's Green Park." All she could make out was a black expanse dotted with soft white lights. "There's a park called St. James'. The birds are so tame, they fly up to you and eat out of your hand."

"There is a man in Harar, in the east, who feeds the hyenas. They are friendly with him."

They drove along the fringe of Hyde Park. Through its iron railing, old, great trees, mysterious in the dusky gloom, rustled in the March wind.

"They have a spot there called Speakers' Corner, where anybody can come and make a speech about anything."

"And nobody will bother the one who is speaking?"

They merged onto Kensington Road with its courtly shops, banks and hotels. Hanna gazed out the car's window with a melancholy air.

"What's wrong?"

She put her hand on his thigh but didn't answer. Their lovemaking that morning in their suite at the Savoy had been more passionate than ever. But as if sex had become her primary means of expression, outside the bedroom she was even quieter than usual.

A few minutes later, the Rolls turned left onto Wilton Place and entered the posh Belgravia district. Rows of regal, white stucco mansions housed elegant residences, foreign embassies and swanky hotels.

They rounded Belgrave Square and stopped at a palatial townhouse. A combined British and Ethiopian security detail stood out front. Buddy got out of the car and approached a burly ex-commando type with a crew-cut.

"Is he in?"

"Do you have an appointment?"

"Tell him Buddy Schwartz is here. I need to see him, and it's urgent."

The guard stared as if he were about to assault him then went inside. Hanna joined her husband, and they waited on the marble stoop.

The door opened. The bodyguard let them in.

A musty foyer decorated with English hunting prints opened onto a long, sepulchral hallway with Edwardian furnishings. A secretary, her footsteps clicking on the marble floor, appeared at one end of the hall.

"Mr. Schwartz? Come with me, please."

They were shown into a paneled study. An older, tired Meles sat on a long sofa and pored over a document.

"Oh, hello," he said nonchalantly as he read.

"I've got twenty trucks waiting at the border."

Meles put the document down. "You want my help after you embarrass me in the media? I ought to 'know better?' I should 'wise up?'"

"Well, you're hurting a lot of people."

"You've been misled by the terrorists." Meles spoke sharply to Hanna in Tigrinya. She replied tartly, and he glared at her.

"You should listen to me. I'm your friend," Buddy urged.

"Please. You should know by now, in Ethiopia nothing is at it appears." The prime minister's tone grew businesslike. "I want you at the African Union conference next month telling the media my government is winning the war on poverty. I'm getting a lot of static, and we need to put our best foot forward."

Buddy slumped on the sofa and gave him a frustrated look.

"I suggest," Meles said icily, observing his attitude, "you understand we have a mutual interest in cooperating. I make things happen in Ethiopia for everybody. Including you." He checked his watch impatiently. "Now, are you going to do it?"

"Just leave my trucks alone."

"I'm asking you again," Meles repeated. "Are you going to do the press conference?"

"I'll do it."

Meles regarded Buddy with undisguised exasperation. "You think it's easy running Ethiopia? You ought to come down and try it for a day. Then you'd see."

Neither Buddy nor Hanna talked much during the ride back to their hotel.

"Did you see that house?" she finally asked. "And the art and furniture?"

"I saw it. What was he saying to you?"

"He said I have to take you under control. I told him he is as bad as the dictator we overthrew."

They skirted Green Park. Dramatically floodlit, Buckingham Palace rose behind a big fountain topped by a golden statue.

"His wife is one of the richest women in Africa," Hanna said. "Anyone who protests is arrested for terrorism." She bit her lip in thought. "I must do something."

They rode in silence for a while. "Every time you help him get money," she resumed disapprovingly. "Or sit with him at some poverty conference, you make him more powerful. You are—what is the word? 'Legitimizing.' You are legitimizing a mass murderer."

"I need him as much as he needs me."

"Meles believes Western donors like you are fools he can manipulate. You have to be strong."

"I'm just a TV producer trying to feed a bunch of hungry people."

"You are not just a TV producer any more. You are a leader of public opinion. And what is the purpose to feed people if you support a dictator who kills them with his corruption and crazy policies?"

"Don't you think I know?" Buddy burst out bitterly. "Don't you think I'd like to put a bullet in his fucking head?" He looked startled as if he was surprised by his own words. "I'm getting killed in the press," he admitted glumly, referring to the smattering of critical coverage that had recently begun.

She gestured towards the driver. "Can he hear us?"

Buddy shook his head.

"My friends who want to meet you—"

He cut her off. "No. No way."

"Everybody says they want to help Ethiopia. But not to do what it needs."

"I'm not getting involved with politics."

The Rolls entered Whitehall, its grand government buildings monuments to the lost empire. Along Pall Mall, nineteenth-century private clubs sheltered aristocratic society and influence.

The commercial Strand was congested when they reached it. They passed a brightly lit theater. Its patrons were spilled into the street during intermission.

The light glinted in Hanna's moist eyes.

"Buddy, you are a good man," she said in a choked voice. "And you want to do good. But you live in a different world. Let me get out." She pressed the driver's intercom.

"Sir?" the chauffeur's voice came through the intercom.

"Come on," Buddy said to her irritably. "Don't give me a hard time."

"I want to get out," she told the driver.

"Will you stop it?" Buddy snapped.

The limo pulled over in front of a women's shoe shop closed for the night. A metal gate was drawn across its darkened plate glass window.

"My friends want me to take a leadership position with the opposition," she confessed. "It is a big propaganda coup if I join them."

Even in the shadows, Buddy seemed tired under his California tan. It had been a long time since she had heard him laugh.

"No way," he said.

She gripped the door handle.

"Hanna," he pleaded. "You're safe with me."

She got out and spoke to him through the open car door.

"I love you," she said. "And I tried to tell myself I loved my life in America. But Ethiopians cannot be Meles' property. I cannot stay quiet."

She took a pen and a little notebook from her bag. Tearing off a scrap of paper, she wrote something on it and handed it to him. "If you need to find me, use this address in Addis."

"What am I supposed to do? Drive off and leave you here?"

"Someday you will see there is no choice. We have to stop him."

"You're being ridiculous."

His eye fell on the expensive Cartier watch on her wrist. It was one of the wedding gifts that had been the source of so much levity during the pre-wedding ceremonies. Resentment at her ingratitude swept over him.

"Fine. Be an idiot." Glaring at her, he yanked the car door shut. "Go on," he ordered the driver. He curtly turned his face away as the Rolls drove off.

Buddy peered out the limo's back window. Hanna got smaller

and smaller as the car sped away. Unconsciously, he put his hand in his pocket and ran his thumb over the cross she had given him so many years ago in the mountains of Tigray. It was rubbed smooth from thousands of caresses.

Then she was gone, swallowed up by the crowd of pedestrians like a stone dropped in the sea.

Chapter Twenty-Three

FOR MONTHS AFTER his return to Los Angeles, Buddy reached for Hanna in bed at night only to remember she was no longer there. He understood her patriotism. But that she would choose her country over him and their life together was incomprehensible. How could she be so unappreciative of all he had done for her? All his expense and trouble to give her a good life in Beverly Hills—hadn't that meant anything? Bitterness, blame and self-recrimination tormented him like enraged birds of prey until they developed a dismal familiarity.

At least, he realized wryly, his new obsession was crowding out the flashbacks.

Simple tasks like shaving took effort. He became forgetful and paid less attention to what he wore. He spent a lot of time in bed. When he did muster the will to work, Alan sometimes saw him stare into space and move his lips as if in conversation.

A worn out and depressed Buddy turned to The Gandel.

"Can't you give me something?" he asked reproachfully. "You're not helping me." Floating in the Pacific, they sat on their boards with the tips pointed upward, so they could swivel when a good breaker came.

"I don't want to mask your symptoms. It's like a pimple. Let it come up to the surface. Then we'll take care of it."

A grommet wiped out under a crashing wave. The young surfer reappeared, retrieved his floating board and dragged himself back onto it.

"Some waves you can ride," the doctor said. "Some you let pass."

A seagull with a fish in its beak glided past them. The Gandel contemplated the sailing bird and the foam-flecked ocean, his thoughts lost in their rhythms.

"But don't try to fight `em head on, dude."

His own house, his car, eating and sleeping tortured Buddy with reminders of Hanna. Yet over the next year, his misery slowly subsided. To the relief of those close to him, he began to resemble his normal self again.

He let friends set him up on a few dates. They were unsatisfying, but he was able to forget his wife for a few hours.

With time, he came to accept she had to follow her conscience. He even felt a begrudging respect for her sacrifice.

But his instinctive reaching for her at night occurred less and less often.

Finally, it stopped.

Chapter Twenty-Four

IN ETHIOPIA, HANNA's speaking skill and experience had earned her a position as Kinijit's leading spokesperson. Several other high-ranking government officials had also defected. The minister of defense, one of the TPLF's founders and a national hero who had run the 1998 war against Eritrea, had fallen out with Meles, too. When he was subjected to the corruption charges that signified behind-the-scenes political infighting, a female judge named Birtukan Mideksa had defied government pressure and dismissed the case for lack of evidence. Another judge, ordered to whitewash the 2005 bloodbath, had instead fled to Europe. A former puppet president and a few other ministers had switched sides as well.

Meles was furious at these betrayals. More was at stake than mere friendship, the prestige of office, or even which policies would guide the nation. The former guerrilla had seized power shortly after the fall of the Soviet Union. Democracy revolutions had swept the globe and toppled dictators once thought unassailable in countries like Haiti, Indonesia, Panama, the Philippines, Poland, South Africa, the Ukraine and more. Strongmen who had commanded armies and security services, who could tax, reward and punish, were in exile, their immunity gone. Their teams of high-priced criminal defense attorneys battled lawsuits, media inquiries, forensic investigations, asset traces, human rights trials, residency challenges and criminal prosecutions.

A loss of control could mean arrest. Or worse.

Corruption within the inner circle had to be fostered to maintain loyalty. A despairing citizenry had to be stifled, at times violently.

All this took money. Foreign lobbyists and deception on a massive scale kept it coming in and the donor nations' focus off the human rights abuses.

And so the wheel went around and around with no way off the carousel for Meles except a coup or a bullet.

In the regime's early days, disloyalty like Hanna's could simply be dispatched with a hit squad. But the butchery of 2005 had at last aroused the international media. News coverage had grown harsher. Disapproving editorials had appeared in newspapers and magazines that for years had forgiven the EPRDF's excesses.

Ethiopia's leader knew the one thing American and European politicians feared was the media. Media drove public opinion. And public opinion meant votes.

In this new environment, getting rid of high-profile traitors required more subtle methods than the bullet, knife or club reserved for the less well-known. The defense minister, despite his acquittal, was re-arrested on other fake charges as he left the courthouse. The judge in his case, whose defiance had made her into a national heroine, was jailed for attempting to overthrow the constitutional order.

After he released a best-selling album of songs that criticized Meles and called for Ethiopia's freedom, the country's most popular singer, Teddy Afro, was arrested in Addis Ababa on a hit-and-run complaint in the death of a homeless man. At his trial, it turned out the accident had happened while Teddy was hiding out in the United States until things cooled down after the 2005 killings. That didn't stop the court from giving him six years. Even his lawyer got two months for good measure.

Besides sidelining bothersome critics and potential rivals, these show trials served a secondary purpose—to scare everyone else into submission.

When Hanna had joined Kinijit, the fact that she'd been associated with the prime minister raised public hopes the dictatorship's support was waning. This kind of popularity meant soon after she'd returned to Ethiopia, thrown in her lot with the tattered opposition and became a thorn in Meles' side, her phone was tapped with Chinese technology and her computer with British and Italian spyware. She was under surveillance by government agents and by those around her whom the regime had coerced with threats, money or blackmail.

A stone's throw from the palace at NISS, the National Intelligence and Security Service, ambitious men and women were assigned to figure out a credible, media-friendly way to destroy her.

Buddy saw her once on television. When he worked late in his bedroom with Alan, he liked to take a break and turn on the nightly BBC World News. And there she was in a story about Ethiopia's growing number of political prisoners.

Now in her mid-forties, Hanna stood outside an Ethiopian courthouse amid protesters with signs in Amharic and, astutely, in English for the foreign news viewers that read, "Let Them Go!" and "Democracy Means Development!"

"Here is opposition spokeswoman, Hanna Ashete," a reporter explained as the camera zoomed into a close-up.

Buddy hadn't spoken to his wife since that night in London two years earlier. But he was uncomfortably aware she had emerged as one of the most prominent of Meles' detractors. She had always seemed a little introverted. Yet her flair for articulating the movement's goals and her potential to rekindle the morale of those opposed to Meles' tyranny had become evident.

Alan heard her name and joined his partner before the television.

"In 2005, the world's poorest stood up," they watched her declare. "Our nonviolent campaign for democracy has overcome terror, torture and repression to demonstrate the desire of Ethiopians for a better tomorrow."

"She still looks good," Alan commented.

"Shut up."

Buddy scrutinized Hanna's image for clues to her welfare. He had seen photos of her on the Ethiopian opposition websites he now read daily with twinges of guilt while hoping his laptop wasn't monitored with NISS' European spyware. But it felt like ages since he had actually heard her speak.

They gave her thirty seconds.

"Ethiopia is the shame of the world. We are a beggar country yet also one of the most corrupt."

"They'll kill her for this." It was mortifying to see her risk her safety while he was comfortable in Beverly Hills.

"When a government is not accountable to the people, it allows them to be hungry and poor because it is not afraid of losing its power. That is why Ethiopia must have democracy to feed itself and develop the capability to solve its own problems."

With admiration, he noticed how expertly she stressed the right English words and stood at a studied angle for the cameras.

"Recently a man," she recounted, "who I am certain was paid by the government, approached me on the street. He slapped my face and called me a whore. He said I could get hurt. But that is all right."

Buddy had already heard this story through the grapevine, but the reminder sent his blood pressure soaring. Meles had claimed to know nothing about it.

"I also received visits from the police who asked many times why I was doing this. The government sent me warnings I could avoid the same fate as our imprisoned leadership if I resigned from Kinijit. Or if I would secretly work as a spy against my friends. Or if I would return to the United States. But I am part of a movement that has the salvation of Ethiopia as its purpose, and my life is dedicated to Ethiopia. My colleagues and I had a crisis meeting, and we decided to go on with our work."

The interview ended. It's a big world, and there was other news.

Buddy tried to guess when they would air the segment again. Something she had once told him came to mind—how, when she was a girl, she and her friends, singing "Abeba-ye-hoy," the New Year's celebration song, would go house-to-house to give out yellow flowers they'd collected in the meadow.

He missed her terribly.

He was in his Burbank office when the call came. From the caller ID, he knew it was the palace. It was Meles himself without the usual secretary to confirm the other party was on the line before making the transfer. They exchanged pleasantries then Ethiopia's prime minister got down to business.

"I want to talk to you about Hanna."

"We're separated," Buddy reminded him.

"Oh," Meles replied. "Right."

There was silence on both sides, and Buddy could almost hear the complicated gears in that brilliant mind turn.

"If you're separated," Meles finally suggested, uncharacteristically tentative, "I assume you don't condone what she is doing?"

"I don't get much news of her these days."

"You're not in communication with her?"

"I'm not. What's the problem?"

"She's mixed-up with the wrong people. I don't know what's gotten into her."

"I know she was upset about 2005. You know her brother was caught up in it."

"I thought we took care of that." There was another silence. Sounding as if he had just read from a file, Meles added, "He is a student at the university. He is fine."

"What's Hanna doing exactly?"

"They think they're going to turn this place into another Rwanda."

"I can't imagine Hanna wants to turn Ethiopia into another Rwanda."

"We won that election, you know," the prime minister declared although Buddy hadn't asked. "Hey," he continued incongruously. "If they want to make a revolution, let them go into the bush like we did. And good luck to them." Another long pause followed. "I hope this won't affect our relationship," he said ominously.

"I didn't want her getting involved with politics."

"I'm glad to hear that. Very glad."

With that, he hung up. Buddy dumbly held the receiver and tried to imagine what he had just done. Or failed to do. Why hadn't he defended his wife more vigorously? What signal had he unwittingly given Meles?

He and Hanna had never discussed their new status.

What were her thoughts were on that subject?

Chapter Twenty-Five

THE PALE ORANGE sun broke over the Pacific and slowly bathed the sleeping Malibu coast in warm light. Songbirds greeted it with joyful arias. A few surfers waited for a good wave.

Buddy and The Gandel squatted on the beach and waxed their boards, enjoying the Zen-like exercise and ocean breeze.

"I've been having this weird dream," Buddy confided.

"Speak to me, dude."

"I'm in this shoe store, and Meles Zenawi comes out of a back room. Like a storeroom. He's holding a shoebox. And I'm worried I can't afford what's in it."

"Then what happens?"

"I wake up. I've had it a few times."

The Gandel mulled this over. "Meles...we've never talked about this. Deep down, how do you really feel about him?"

"I don't know. He's like a partner. Someone I have to work with. We don't see each other much lately."

"And how do you feel when you see him in the dream?"

"Kind of anxious, I guess."

"Well, he represents some negative emotion you're not in touch with. The storeroom—do you see it in the dream? Do you go inside it?"

"No, you can't see it. It's behind a curtain."

The Gandel looked out to sea. "The brain models itself in dreams," he explained. "When you see a divider of some kind—a fence, a border, in your case a curtain—it often represents the divide between the conscious and the unconscious." He touched up a spot on his board with the waxy rag. "I'm not sure what it is—fear, maybe anger. But you've pushed it back into some hidden part of your mind because it's too scary or inconvenient to think about."

The doctor's brow furrowed with concentration. "Try this," he finally offered. "One of the Native American tribes—I forget which one—has this thing they believe about your 'dream enemy.' They say, when you meet your enemy in a dream, make him give you a gift."

A pod of dolphins cavorted in the water by the pier.

"Meles isn't my enemy."

"People you see in dreams usually represent some part of yourself."

The dolphins splashed and vanished.

"Before you go to sleep," The Gandel advised, "remind yourself to be aware you're dreaming when the dream starts. With a little practice, you can do it and even control what happens in the dream. If you get that dream again, try to control it and make Meles give you a gift."

He smiled. "And let's see what he gives you, dude."

Chapter Twenty-Six

IN 2007, HOPING to blunt foreign criticism of the 2005 election fraud and its grisly aftermath, Meles released from jail the best known of the ballot's winners after he'd humiliated them one last time by forcing them to sign forged confessions and beg for pardon. The horrific conditions in which they'd been held left some broken in spirit and many in health as well. Divisions and disagreements, some self-inflicted, others craftily instigated by NISS, the intelligence service, arose within the opposition. What was left of Kinijit split into those who adhered to the coalition's nonviolent ways and those who'd decided armed resistance had become necessary.

The release of Kinijit's top leaders was clever public relations on Meles' part. It provided the diplomatic fig leaf his international allies needed to maintain his financial and military assistance. But the cunning prime minister didn't take any chances. To keep the democracy movement off-balance, he harassed its less-visible middle and lower ranks, especially their most talented members.

Usually, NISS would monitor these up-and-coming political competitors or the more outspoken critics among the media and allow them to function until they became popular enough to pose a genuine threat. Then some pretext would be engineered to remove them from the scene. Their backgrounds would be analyzed for the slightest infraction which would be distorted and prosecuted by those whose monstrous crimes were officially covered up. Often, as in Dr. Asrat's case, their words or writings would be twisted or invented to imply some sinister conspiracy deserving the most severe punishment.

Those in the democracy movement who clung to nonviolence knew they had to walk on eggshells. They did everything they could to prove by their words and deeds their dedication to peaceful principles. But even when no evidence of violent intent could be found, the government had a ready supply of compromised wretches forced to give false testimony in the bogus indictments that had become its hallmark.

As a Kinijit rising star who could so convincingly make the case for Meles' removal, Hanna fell into this category of possibly dangerous challengers. Meles' phone conversation with Buddy had convinced him the influential American neither would, nor could, do much about her fate. Her dossier revealed she had not yet received her US citizenship. The US Embassy would care little about her, either.

But like a cat playing with a mouse, Ethiopia's leader could afford to watch Hanna and bide his time. His former press aide was tolerated for several more years while she carried out her duties. She gave speeches that attacked the regime for which she had once fought and laid out a vision of a free and prosperous Ethiopia in which human rights were respected. She helped organize political meetings. Worst of all, she gave interviews to the foreign media.

Under the microscope of the ever-watchful NISS, every word and action was painstakingly recorded and examined.

Satisfied that Buddy and Help Ethiopia were truly apolitical and didn't provide any support to the opposition, Meles permitted the charity's license to be renewed. He still saw Buddy once or twice a year. For the sake of their shared interest in feeding hungry Ethiopians— at least those Meles wanted fed—they went through the motions of friendship and ate, joked, drank and chewed khat together.

Buddy had long grown indifferent to the global acclaim. And Meles' treatment of Hanna and her fellow citizens infuriated him. But hundreds of thousands of lives depended on his playing the diplomat. After the lesson he'd learned in London, he made sure always to praise Meles in the media and avoid any further hint of criticism.

The positive press helped Meles rake in the foreign aid and made Ethiopia's dictatorship stronger than ever.

Chapter Twenty-Seven

DURING THESE YEARS, Buddy tried The Gandel's advice without success. Each night before he fell asleep with flashbacks, Hanna, Meles and Ethiopian poverty's terrible mathematics flitting like ghosts through his mind, he firmly reminded himself to be aware he was dreaming when a dream occurred.

He didn't use drugs and was a light drinker, so his dreams tended to be vivid. But he couldn't master the technique. Morning after morning, he woke only to recall after a few groggy moments his task.

At last there was a small breakthrough. But the dream wasn't about Meles. He found himself in the London Ritz's shopping arcade. Displayed in one swanky shop window was the photograph of a teenage Ethiopian prince who had been captured by the British in 1868 and taken as a prisoner to England. Buddy had seen the picture online because the Ethiopian government had recently requested the return of his remains.

In the famous portrait of the unhappy royal youth before being packed off to England with other booty, he was posed by his captors, in a long shamma and silver necklace, seated beside a shield and a strip of animal hide to remind viewers of his exoticism.

Buddy took another look. The prince had been replaced by a topless Hanna in the same pose. She gave him a lascivious smile, and he knew he was dreaming.

"This isn't real," he told himself, simultaneously asleep and awake.

He awoke intrigued by the strange experience.

This modest success encouraged him, and he continued to practice. The shoe store dream reoccurred, but he was unable to remember the technique in time.

He had a couple more dreams during that period in which he could briefly manipulate their events. Once, he even willed himself to fly and delightedly soared around his bedroom. This journey into his own mind was so absorbing he almost forgot its original purpose.

But one night, when he didn't expect it, everything came together.

"I had the dream where I was in the shoe store," Buddy informed The Gandel. Astride their boards, their legs dangled in the cold Pacific as the two friends rose and dropped with the glassy, blue swells and watched for a big wave. "Meles came in from the storeroom." As he spoke, he realized the store in his dream had been the shop on the Strand where Hanna had left him. "He was holding the shoebox and, like always happens, I was worried how I was going to pay for it. Then I remembered I was dreaming and what you'd said about the Native Americans making your dream enemy give you a gift. So I told him to give me the box. And he gave it to me."

The Gandel listened to his friend with interest.

"I opened it, and there was nothing inside except this little rainbow just hanging in the air inside the box. Its colors were glowing like...very intense. It was beautiful."

"Then what happened?"

"That's all I can remember."

In the distance, a jet ski skimmed by with a hum. A Rolling Stones song faintly played somewhere.

"A rainbow," The Gandel mused. "Do you have any associations with rainbows? What's the first thing you think of when somebody says the word, "rainbow?"

Buddy pondered the question.

"Hope?" The Gandel prompted.

"The Rastas call Haile Selassie's throne the 'Rainbow Throne.'"

"Haile Selassie, eh?"

"Yeah."

The Gandel jerked his chin, and Buddy knew he'd spotted a promising swell. With practiced motions, they turned in the water, lay flat on their boards and got ready.

White foam broke the towering wave's crest. They paddled quickly with their hands. Rushing water lifted them. The Gandel skillfully leapt up into a crouch. Buddy did the same. His knee ached. I'll soon be too old for this, he thought.

Their feet adroitly angled the boards to stay on the liquid wall. All else was forgotten in their exhilaration as they rode it in.

When they'd finished, both men stood knee deep in the tugging tide with their boards under their arms and contemplated the ocean. The sun was up, and the air was balmy. A snowy egret hunted water bugs in the shallows.

"I'm thinking about this Haile Selassie thing," The Gandel said. "The vessel of Solomonic wisdom, handed down through the millennia. I think there's something about him that holds meaning for you, dude."

"I don't know," Buddy said.

"Just wait and be open to it," The Gandel said. "Like a good wave. It will come."

Chapter Twenty-Eight

BUDDY TRIED NOT to let the sauerkraut on his hot dog fall out of the bun. It was a rainy Fourth of July 2011—five years since he'd split with Hanna—and he was at the US Embassy's annual Independence Day reception at the Addis Ababa Sheraton.

The crowded event played an essentially unhelpful role in American diplomacy. Although the Embassy had a close working relationship with Meles, US policy was to maintain contacts, public and covert, with opposition figures as well. One never knew which dark horse could one day wind up on top in revolution-prone countries like Ethiopia.

For this reason, the Embassy traditionally invited, along with the diplomatic corps and prominent local Americans like Buddy, a mix of Ethiopian government officials and the regime's nonviolent opponents. The ever-hopeful Americans, who sincerely wished to see their ally democratize—so long as their own interests were not put at risk—tried to use the affair to build dialogue and reconciliation between the various factions.

EPRDF officials pretended to cooperate so they could appear to be democratically-minded. Opposition politicians used the opportunity to urge their powerful host to switch its support to the popular and moral choice they represented. All they got were thanks for their views. American altruism had its limits. The United States usually stuck with whoever had more guns.

Nonetheless, the party presented a rare moment in which the country's political enemies were at least in physical proximity. They shared the room with feigned cordiality.

Since Buddy was in town that Fourth and stayed at the Sheraton, he'd decided to attend. The reception was in the hotel's Lalibela

Room, transformed for the occasion with red, white and blue paper bunting and flags. The celebration featured American regional cuisine and atmosphere. It would be a respite from Ethiopia's spicy fare and relentless dysfunctionality. And there were always a few things to discuss with the ambassador and his guests.

The ceremony opened with a presentation of colors by the embassy's marine security guard detachment. The daughter of an embassy official sang "The Star-Spangled Banner," and an Ethiopian guest sang the post-Derg Ethiopian national anthem, "March Forward, Dear Mother Ethiopia." Young Ethiopian graduates of the Mekane Yesus Jazz School creditably performed "America the Beautiful," Duke Ellington's "Take the A Train" and George Gershwin's "Summertime."

Buddy sat at a table with executives from a few of the other charities that operated in the country, the embassy's commercial attaché and the Federal Police Commissioner General. The conversation ranged from the guerrilla insurgency in the Ogaden to the weather and agricultural projections.

Something moved at the edge of his peripheral vision.

Suddenly, Hanna stood over him.

"Buddy?" she greeted him enthusiastically as if she'd encountered an old college friend.

He rose in surprise and stood there passively while she threw her arms around him and kissed him three times in the Ethiopian way.

"How are you?" he stammered. He sensed the police commissioner staring at them and drew her aside, so they could speak privately.

"I am happy to see you," she said effusively. She was thinner, and her cheeks were sunken. "I think of you often."

"Charitably, I hope," he awkwardly joked.

"Yes, of course."

As they chatted, it was clear they'd gotten over their previous anger. But both of them had changed. To speak with his politically charged wife—under the police commissioner's gaze, no less— made Buddy nervous. Hanna assumed the room was bugged and cautiously parsed her words to avoid the slightest turn of phrase that could be misinterpreted as encouraging violent political change.

She did not display the burning zeal one would expect in a revolutionary. Her life was difficult. She had lost her government pension, and he'd been afraid to send her money. The regime controlled the banks, the transaction would be flagged by NISS, and he'd be tied to opposition activities. Yet her stubborn undertaking to save her country had apparently imbued in her the ability to withstand the struggle's hardship and humiliation.

He wanted to give her some cash then and there but was afraid to do so in the presence of the Ethiopian officials. She'd probably just pass it on to her beloved democracy campaign, anyway. Her Cartier watch was missing from her wrist.

"How long are you staying?" she asked excitedly.

"Not long."

Hanna looked at her husband eagerly, but her smile faded at his stony expression. He was not without sympathy for the decision she had made. But how would Meles interpret it when the intelligence report of their meeting inevitably wound up on his desk? Appearing too friendly with an enemy of the regime, even here at the embassy party, could have unpredictable consequences.

"I'm not sure it's a good idea to get together," he heard himself say.

"No?" Her manner turned cool. "I should go." She squared her shoulders and walked away.

"Hanna!" he impulsively called after her.

She twirled to face him with a hopeful look.

"I wish you good luck," he said lamely. "From the bottom of my heart."

She stared at him for a second, turned and marched off.

He sat down and shrugged at the police commissioner's quizzical look. The discussion had shifted to the problem of rural migration to the cities, but his thoughts were elsewhere.

Hanna joined some other opposition leaders across the room. One laughed—at what, Buddy couldn't tell. Had she taken a lover?

He tried to analyze the body language of the men closest to her.

She left the party a short while later without looking his way again.

For weeks afterward, he obsessed over their conversation. Her friendliness unsettled him. Was she lonely for him? Had it been to impress the police commissioner with her important connection? Something in the way she had straightened her back when she'd walked away hinted at even greater reserves of inner strength than he had known. Ashamed of his impotence in the face of her evident danger, he berated himself. He could have shown more understanding of what had happened between them. He could have urged her to abandon her mission and return to him. What had made him push her away like that?

It was fear. Fear of Meles. Fear of NISS. Fear of the police commissioner.

There'd been something else, too, a feeling that had emerged fleetingly from the shadows before it scuttled away like a rat in a tunnel. But not before he'd recognized it.

He was afraid of Hanna.

Chapter Twenty-Nine

THE DELICATE BALANCING act went on for another year. Meles and his clique of TPLF political and security officials grew richer and more domineering. The illusion of Ethiopia's economic progress became more widely accepted around the world. Ordinary Ethiopians' secret torment increased each day. Hanna was still allowed to attend her meetings and give her speeches. But despite their strenuous efforts, she and her colleagues failed to reunite the divided opposition coalition or help the public overcome the paralyzing despair 2005 had created.

So no one understood why, in the summer of 2012, Meles, although long confident Buddy would not be a problem, finally pounced. Perhaps it was his usual practice of mowing the political grass, allowing the opposition to grow just enough to be able to point to it as evidence of his democratic credentials but never letting it flourish. Maybe it was a long-simmering desire for revenge for Hanna's disloyalty.

Some speculated it was somehow linked to the most recent phony election, rubber-stamped with the regime's ludicrous claim of a ninety-five percent victory. Or maybe Hanna was just one of many names on a list he'd approved without much thought while distracted by other matters or crashing after a khat high.

Maybe all these reasons had something to do with it.

It was eight a.m., and Buddy was still asleep at home in Beverly Hills when his private line rang. The US Ambassador, as a courtesy, was calling to give him the news personally. The facts were scant. Hanna had been taken the day before from the apartment she had lately shared with two other Kinijit members. A journalist had been seized the same day. The arrests followed a wide sweep of Oromos a week earlier in which two hundred accused OLF members had been detained.

The charges that she planned attacks in Ethiopia and conspired with the militant opposition were so stunningly similar to other indictments as to suggest complacency on the part of the prosecutors. Or, as was frequently the case with Ethiopia's bureaucracy, mere incompetence.

"It's a terrorism charge, so there won't be bail," the ambassador explained. "Of course, we've made our dissatisfaction known. But it's their country and their laws."

"C'mon. They wouldn't last a day without our money."

"Most of our funding goes for food, health and education." The ambassador's reminder echoed an argument Buddy knew all too well. "If we cut that off, who suffers? It won't be Meles."

"What about military funding? I don't think his generals will be too happy if that's taken away."

"Let's say we cut that," the ambassador replied. "Meles withdraws from Somalia, where he's carrying our water for us. Who's going to go in there? US troops? When we're already stretched thin in Afghanistan, Iraq and Korea?"

"Something's got to be done," Buddy persisted angrily. "She's no terrorist. It's ridiculous."

"We'll raise it at our next meeting," the ambassador promised. Buddy knew he meant it. He also knew that Meles would brush it off, and the ambassador would simply move on to the next item on the agenda.

The news was not completely unexpected. Because of the EPRDF circles in which he moved and the sporadic Western coverage of Ethiopia's human rights troubles, little information about the democracy movement used to reach Buddy. But ever since he had surreptitiously begun to follow some of the anti-Meles websites, he had learned the stories of other heroic victims of the dictatorship. People like the journalist Eskinder Nega, sentenced to a long prison term for his investigative journalism into the 2005 massacre. Hailu Shawel, the Kinijit chairman who had willingly traded a lucrative business career for Kaliti's horror chambers. Merera Gudina and Bekele Gerba, the Oromo nonviolence leaders. Andualem Arage, a former Kinijit spokesman who suffered head injuries when authorities put him in a cell with a violent criminal. Birtukan Mideksa, the brave judge who had resumed speaking out after her first release from jail and had been re-arrested. Berhanu Nega, the economics professor who had fled abroad to mobilize armed resistance. And thousands more.

"Here's what I don't get," Buddy told the ambassador. "Meles is helping us fight terror. I get that. But 9/11 killed three thousand people. Maybe another attack will kill a few thousand more. We lose more people than that every month from car accidents. And meanwhile, with the help we're giving him to stay in power, millions of Ethiopians are dying. Okay, maybe it's just from malnutrition, or from not having a doctor or medicine, and it's not dramatic enough to make the evening news. But it's a horrible way to die, and I don't understand how we can justify our complicity in a crime of that magnitude on the off chance it will save a few thousand of our own people. It just doesn't make any moral sense."

"That's above my pay grade," the ambassador said. "I'm paid to protect Americans."

"He's not even doing a good job for us in Somalia. Things are getting worse there. And what are he and his buddies stealing while their people are starving? A few billion every year?"

No answer came. A faint sigh was heard.

After he hung up, Buddy called Meles' office and left a message for the prime minister to call him back on an urgent basis. His next call was to The Gandel. Fortunately, the doctor was between patients and answered.

"Hanna's been arrested."

"I'm so sorry. Can we help her?"

"I'm waiting for a call from Meles. I don't know what to do."

The line went quiet. "Did you ever think any more about that Haile Selassie thing?" The Gandel finally asked.

"I can't figure it out."

"I'm not that familiar with his biography, but you must have picked up quite a bit on him during your trips there. What does his story say to you?"

"He's best known for what he did in World War Two, I guess."

"You've got plenty of experience breaking down a story. Pretend it's a script. What are the themes?"

"Let's see…finding courage when the odds are against you. Collective security." Outside his bedroom window, the California sky was a perfect turquoise. "And there's a detail about him most people don't know that's kind of interesting. When the fascists invaded, he led his army in the final battle. He was even personally fighting. But they were beat. The country was lost. Everything was falling apart. He was in danger of being captured. So you'd think he'd get on a plane and get the hell out of Dodge, right? Or maybe organize what's left for guerrilla warfare. But he didn't do any of that. No, he took this long, dangerous trip all the way up north, in the middle of all this chaos with the enemy everywhere, to Lalibela. And you know why? To pray. He left everything behind and went all the way up to this old church carved into the rocks to pray."

"I'm not a big fan of prayer, dude. God doesn't need us telling it what to do. We're better off shutting up and listening."

"I don't know if he prayed or listened or what. But he went up to the church. That's all I know."

"Do you see any relevance to your own problem?"

"I don't know. Maybe."

"I gotta go. I got a patient waiting."

"He's not really a bad guy."

"Who's not a bad guy?"

"Meles."

"Meles is a Surf Nazi, dude."

Buddy put down the phone. His expression grew thoughtful. As if he had heard something interesting.

Meles called back just before lunch. "I want Hanna out of jail," Buddy demanded peremptorily. He had never used this tone with the prime minister before.

For several moments, neither man said anything.

"The legal process has to take its course," Meles finally replied.

"Please," Buddy said sarcastically. "You control the courts, and you know it."

"I wish," Meles dryly responded.

"You can do it, and I want you to get her out."

"And then what? Let her go back to plotting her next terrorist attack?"

"She's no terrorist, Meles. It's bullshit."

"I thought you were separated," Meles complained. "Why is her fate of such concern to you all of a sudden?"

"She's still my wife."

"You want an Ethiopian woman? We have forty million others you can choose from. And there's another forty million in all the countries around us that look like Ethiopian women if that's your taste."

Buddy felt his bile rising.

"Sorry," Meles hastily added, sensing he'd overstepped. "We're more casual about divorce here than in your country."

"I want you to make this happen for me. I've done a lot for you, and now it's time for you to do something for me."

"And she has that brother. The two of them are no good."

There was a long pause. Buddy could picture Meles in his palace office figuring out the situation's angles.

"I'll tell you what," Meles said. "Can you be here next Monday?"

"What?"

"I have a press conference next Tuesday, and they're on my back. Be here, charm them a little and tell them what a good job we're doing on poverty. Come in Monday, and we'll figure out what you're going to say."

"Not with Hanna in jail."

"I'll see what I can do."

"Thank you."

"We need each other." The reminder sounded like a warning.

"I want her out," Buddy repeated.

The line was dead.

Meles had apologized for his wisecrack, but it was too late. Buddy had long suspected the man was a sociopath, but there had always been some way to rationalize or overlook what he'd observed. This time, he'd gotten a glimpse inside the room before the door had been quickly shut.

He took a minute to meditate—twenty slow, deep breaths while he visualized the beautiful, white sand and aquamarine waters of the Maldives. When he felt calmer, he opened a drawer in the nightstand beside his bed. Beneath Hanna's letters was his datebook. He opened it to where he had copied down the address she had given him the night they parted in London.

The address of her contact in the opposition.

Chapter Thirty

Two DAYS LATER, on a crisp, Addis Ababa evening, Buddy knocked on the door of a house in Arat Kilo. Not far from Hanna's, constructed of stone and cement, it was a nice home by local standards. A dirt yard contained a child's tricycle. An illegal satellite dish peeked out of a window. They probably watched banned opposition broadcasts from the States.

Someone inside answered in Amharic.

"It's Hanna's husband," Buddy said.

The door opened, and a bookish, worried-looking young man, perhaps a teacher or an office worker, stood there. Buddy recognized him from the Embassy's Fourth of July party.

"Come in," he said in good English. He motioned for Buddy to enter.

The home was simply furnished. Children's toys—a plastic soldier, a yellow metal truck and a Caucasian baby doll—lay on a sofa. The doll's open eyes reminded Buddy of the massacre victims in Black Lion Hospital.

With an apologetic smile, his host pushed the toys aside and invited his guest to sit. His wife, her hair unkempt, held her dressing gown closed with one hand and peered into the room.

"*Buna*," he said to indicate she should make coffee.

Within an hour, three more opposition members had joined them. They shared the coffee and uneasily made small talk. Once the coffee was finished, the homeowner pointed to a back door. No explanation was needed. They all stepped outside where any hidden microphone couldn't pick up their words.

It was a moonless night, and the yard was dark. A homeless

family the owner allowed to camp there lay on the ground under a tarp. It was a common practice in the capital.

"They don't speak English," the homeowner reassured Buddy. The Ethiopians fell silent. What did the American want?

"We've got to stop the killing," Buddy said. It was a relief to speak freely for once. He noticed the indescribable beauty of the stars, and a thought struck him. Asrat was right. And we stood by while they murdered him.

"Meles is very difficult to get close to," the homeowner said. "He rarely leaves the palace. There are circles and circles of security. But a big foreigner like you he trusts. You can get close to him."

It took Buddy a moment to grasp what he meant. "I thought you guys were nonviolent," he protested, disturbed by the direction the conversation had taken.

"They won't let us operate peacefully," another opposition member explained. "Some of us have decided to try a different way."

"I save lives. I don't take them."

The Ethiopians regarded the faranj with polite contempt.

"Look, I'm just a TV producer," Buddy added defensively. "But I'm seeing him Monday. I'll take you with me. We'll warn him there's going to be a civil war if he doesn't stop."

"He's not going to stop," the homeowner said patiently as if explaining things to a child.

There was a brief discussion in Amharic between the Ethiopians. They appeared to come to some sort of agreement.

The homeowner's tone grew more serious. "Before you see Meles, we will give you two bunches of khat. One will have its stems tied together with a brown string. The other will be tied with a blue string. You must give him the khat with the blue string. Understand?"

"It is very important you give him the correct bunch," another Ethiopian interjected. "And not chew any of those leaves yourself." He studied Buddy carefully. "You're known as his apologist. You must go on defending him exactly the same afterward. If you give any hint of what was done, we will all be killed."

"I'll make him see," Buddy insisted. "You've got to let me try."

"Maybe you think this is a big TV show," a third Ethiopian said. "How many more must die while you're trying?"

Buddy didn't answer.

"If you decide to help us," the homeowner said, "mark the 'Do Not Disturb' sign in your hotel room with an X and hang it outside your door. We will know."

The Ethiopians looked Buddy over.

"Sometimes writing a check is not enough," one of them said.

A personal message from the Federal Attorney General awaited Buddy at the Sheraton.

It informed him Hanna would be released the next day.

Chapter Thirty-One

At six a.m. on a chilly Friday morning, Buddy waited in the Mercedes with his driver outside the main gate of Kaliti Prison. He wished he had a coffee and was about to send the driver in search of one when the gate opened. A guard let Hanna out.

She stopped short at the sight of the car. Then she walked to it rapidly, opened the door and got in.

Her head was shaved and scratched. She was even scrawnier than the last time he'd seen her. It was the first time he'd ever looked at her without the slightest sexual interest.

"Are you all right?" he asked, shocked at her appearance.

Without reply, she pulled down the rear seat vanity mirror and examined herself in it.

"Did they hurt you in there?"

She stared into the mirror and ran her hand over her shaved head.

"Do you want to eat something?"

"Take me to the hotel," she said. "Let me get cleaned up and get my passport. Get us on a plane going out of here. I don't care where it is going. Take me out of this country."

That early in the morning, the drive back to the Sheraton didn't take long. Forty minutes later, Buddy slouched in an easy chair in his hotel room. Through the bathroom door came the muffled sounds of the shower running and Hanna sobbing.

He eyed the "Do Not Disturb" sign on the other door's handle. Finally, he rose and entered the bathroom without knocking.

Under the running water, Hanna hunched against the shower wall. She was an unrecognizable stranger. In her wretched expression were a pain and grief he had never seen before. Like some ancient ember stirred, that image of the crucified Christ he had seen decades ago in Italy flickered in his mind once more.

Getting soaked, he took his gaunt wife in his arms. They clutched each other and wept like children.

"I understand you," he cried. "Now I understand you."

Later, washed and naked, they lay together in bed without passion.

Buddy remembered the "Do Not Disturb" sign. He looked at it then eased himself off the bed. He put on his trousers.

Gently, he slid the sign off the door handle.

He sat at the writing desk, pushed aside the sightseeing brochures, took a pen and marked the sign with a large X. He went over it again to make sure it was dark enough.

Sign in hand, Buddy opened the door. The hotel corridor was empty. He hung the sign on the outer handle. For a few seconds, he watched it dangle. He closed the door quietly and walked out onto the balcony.

He gripped the balcony rail in the weak sunlight, the wind cool against his bare chest. On the surrounding hills, white and ochre-colored apartment buildings rose haphazardly like a Cubist painting under an overcast sky. It was a peaceful scene. But he knew beyond those hills, across Ethiopia's cities and vast countryside, millions of people were in a desperate struggle for survival. People just like him with fears, hopes, dreams and disappointments.

People in unimaginable pain.

He thought of his mother, her aged vulnerability, the softness of her cheek when he kissed it. And Steve. It was great they'd been able to get together. He pictured his home in Beverly Hills. The flowers on his patio in the heavenly Southern California sunshine. The thrilling Pacific and the breaking waves.

Would he see any of them again?

Chapter Thirty-Two

IT WAS MONDAY morning. No one had contacted Buddy since he'd left the sign on the door to his room. At a loss for what else to do, he put on a suit and tie, got in his car and rode to his appointment with Meles.

Addis Ababa's streets glided past the Mercedes' window. Favorite moments with Hanna from long ago replayed in his mind.

His cell phone rang.

"Human Rights Watch called last week," Alan announced, his raspy Bronx accent breaking up over the satellite channel. "They wanted you to sign an open letter about the political prisoners."

"It's too late."

The car slowed down in traffic. Ragged boys ran up to the car, offered packets of Kleenex and shouted, "faranji, faranji, money, money!" Buddy ignored them as they pressed their faces against the car's tinted window and tried to see inside.

"What was that?" Alan asked.

"Kids trying to sell stuff." He was about to hang up. "Alan?"

"Yeah?"

"You've been a great friend."

There was a long silence at the other end. Alan knew his old partner's moods like a mariner knows the tides.

"What's going on?"

"Nothing," Buddy replied. "I just wanted to say that."

His finger hesitated then pushed the phone's red button.

Soldiers blocked the road ahead. One of them waved the car away.

"They closed the Mercato," the driver explained as he took another street. "They say the terrorists put a bomb on a bus there this morning."

"I know who put the bomb there."

The royal compound's fenced-in hill, where the palace hid behind eucalyptus trees, came into view.

The Mercedes headed for the entrance's steel gate and joined a line of vehicles awaiting clearance to enter the compound. Buddy checked his phone to see if he'd missed any messages. There were none. With relief, he assumed the plan had been canceled.

A teenage khat-seller girl approached the Mercedes. Feral-looking, her hair was matted and her fourth-hand Western dress was gray with dirt. She held two small bunches of khat up to the window and barked something at Buddy in Amharic.

He lowered the window. She dropped both bundles onto the seat beside him. He gazed uncertainly at them then up at the girl.

She exclaimed something in a demanding tone. He fumbled in his pocket and gave her his roll of birr. She took his hand and kissed it. Usually, the touch of her filthy fingers would have made him uncomfortable. This time, they did not.

The string around one bunch was brown. The other was blue.

He looked up. The girl was gone.

Buddy stared at the two bundles of khat. Finally, he tucked one into the left inside breast pocket of his suit and the other into his right inside pocket.

After what felt like an interminable delay, his car slowly rolled up to the gatehouse. A guard bent down to see who was in the car.

"I have an appointment with the prime minister," Buddy said.

The guard picked up a phone and called for authorization. He pointed to another security post inside the gate.

At the checkpoint, a soldier sat on a folding chair with a leashed German shepherd at his feet. The soldier rose and followed the excited, sniffing animal around the car.

Another soldier held a pole topped by a mirror. He instructed the driver to open the trunk. The soldier looked inside and passed the mirror back and forth under the sedan. Satisfied, he directed them to a parking lot near the prime minister's office.

The driver found a parking space.

"Stay with the car," Buddy said.

His heart pounded as he strolled through the manicured grounds. Look relaxed, he told himself.

Just inside the entrance, another security team made him walk through a metal detector. One guard patted him down.

A neatly attired protocol officer waited for him. "Mr. Schwartz? Welcome. Please come with me."

They proceeded down the long corridor where Buddy had watched Meles and his entourage slip away that November day in 2005 after the demonstrations had been suppressed.

His palms were soaking. With Meles' sharp instincts, a sweaty handshake could arouse his suspicions. Panicked, he tried to remember if Meles shook hands when they met or if they merely hugged.

"The prime minister is looking forward to your visit," the protocol officer said pleasantly.

Down another hall, they entered a comfortable waiting room. A secretary behind a desk was on the phone.

"One moment, please." The protocol officer stepped into an office. Buddy sat on a sofa. The secretary nodded hello. He realized he was grinning like an idiot. She was distracted by her phone call, and he furtively wiped his palms on a cushion. They immediately grew wet again.

The protocol officer ushered a Sudanese delegation out the door then turned to him.

"Please come in."

Meles sat behind his desk. With a friendly chuckle at the sight of him, he rose, came around the desk and stuck out his hand. Buddy cupped his own hand firmly for the handshake, so their palms wouldn't touch.

The prime minister appeared not to notice anything amiss. He let go of Buddy's hand and embraced him.

"It is good to see you," he said. "Have you had lunch?"

"Thanks, I'm not hungry."

"How is Hanna?"

239

"You made her sign a paper confessing to treason and begging for a pardon?"

"She had no business getting involved with those troublemakers," Meles declared regretfully. He returned to the white and gold chair behind his desk. "Believe me, there were plenty of people who were dead set against her ever being released."

"What about the others? You've got thousands of democracy activists in concentration camps. And a lot of them are being tortured."

"The courts will deal with them."

Buddy gave him a skeptical look.

"We've held on to power," Meles said bluntly. "And that keeps us saving lives. You've got to admit, there's a certain logic to it."

"Yeah, but the lives being saved are mostly Tigrayans. What about everybody else?"

"We're one of the fastest-growing economies in the world. Ethiopia is a big success story."

"It's a 'big success' mainly for you and your friends. I came here to feed hungry people. Not help polish your image while you kill them."

"That's just propaganda," Meles protested indignantly. "We're a democratic government of laws now. We're not murderers."

"I've seen the burned villages in Oromia. I've seen the demonstrators with bullet holes in their heads. Do you think I don't hear about you keeping food and medicine from people? The Amhara forced sterilizations?"

With an impatient *tsk*, Meles went over to a map on the wall and jabbed his finger against it.

"Ethiopia. One of the poorest countries in the world. But here, Oromia. Gold. Rich farmland. Here, Ogaden. Oil. Gas."

He looked plaintively at Buddy. "We could feed the country with this. But we've got a few narrow-minded people who only care about their own asses. While I've got ninety-two million people to take care of."

Seeing Buddy was unconvinced, Meles wagged his finger.

"You're a good friend to us," he said. "But you're a nice, middle class American boy who's probably never even held a gun. You're not in California here. This is a different world." He sat down and leaned forward earnestly. "For centuries, the Amhara kept their boot on our necks while they took everything. Now it's our turn."

"But how are you ever going to move forward," Buddy exclaimed, "if you keep going around like that? With each tribe kicking the crap out of the other while everybody starves, and the country goes down the toilet?" He contemplated Meles. "But it doesn't matter, does it? 'Cause you and your friends have your twenty or thirty billion, or whatever the fuck it is, in some bank overseas where you can always retire when it's time for musical chairs again. Isn't that what all our public appearances and all our donations and all our aid really go for?"

Meles gave Buddy a pained look. "Do you realize how many terrorists we've killed for you?"

"I'm sure you've killed some terrorists. And that's great. Great. But most of them aren't terrorists at all, just people who are opposed to you destroying what little's left of their country. So doesn't that make you the terrorist?"

The Ethiopian jumped up, startling Buddy. He pointed to his empty chair.

"Come and sit here," he demanded.

"What?"

"Do you have any idea what I have to do," Meles asked heatedly, not bothering to hide his irritation, "to keep this place from coming apart at the seams? What I have to do to keep Egypt, Eritrea, Sudan, the foreign intelligence agencies, the generals, the warlords, the tribal chiefs, the sultans, the pirates, the bandits, the greedy businessmen and all the other bloody-minded morons from completely blowing up this fucking country?"

He pointed at the chair again. "Come and sit in this fucking chair for just one day. You sit here and see what it's like to run Ethiopia."

Buddy didn't move.

241

"All right," Meles said, relenting. "Why don't you leave such matters to the politicians? Let's talk about helping each other." He took a newspaper clipping off his desk and studied it. "You didn't sign the letter. That was smart."

The former guerrilla leader put the clipping down. Its caption read, "Mr. Meles, Let Them Go!" It was the open letter Alan had mentioned.

Buddy regarded the prime minister. "Yeah," he said at last. "Forget it." He took the khat tied with the brown string out of his pocket, pulled off a few leaves, pushed them in his mouth and returned the bunch to his pocket.

Meles' face lit up with amusement. "I say, you really have gone native."

Buddy smiled, removed from his other pocket the bunch with the blue string, tore off a sprig and handed it to Meles.

The prime minister sat on the edge of his desk and munched on it. He tried to gauge the American's mood. "Extreme problems require extreme remedies," he explained between bites.

"There's a certain logic to it," Buddy replied.

Meles' eyes gleamed with contentment.

Chapter Thirty-Three

"WOULD YOU LIKE more coffee?" Hanna's voice surprised Buddy. It took him a moment to remember where he was. But there were the familiar paintings on his living room wall. The view of the tennis court through the window. The clink of fine china as Colonel Kabede held out his cup to Hanna for a refill.

"*Yekenyeley*," Kabede thanked her while she poured it.

Buddy shook his head sadly. "A blood infection," he repeated. "That's terrible."

Hanna rejoined him and took his hand.

"Yes," Colonel Kabede agreed. "Terrible in such a young man." He paused. "There was one odd detail. Much of his eyebrows and his mustache...fell off."

The colonel gave them a searching look.

They stared back impassively.

All sipped their coffee.

"We're at the funeral," the BBC reporter said into his microphone, "of Ethiopian Prime Minister Meles Zenawi, who died three months ago, following hospitalization for an undisclosed illness, at only fifty-seven."

The funeral procession, the largest Addis Ababa had seen in a century, passed the reviewing stand on Meskel Square where Buddy and Hanna sat with the other VIPs. Hanna had regained some weight. Her hair had begun to grow back.

The great boulevard had been swept. The city's walls were plastered with posters of Meles' face, the edges already frayed. Hundreds of buses had delivered thousands of Ethiopians, some loyal, some paid and others coerced, to stand along the funeral route and, with cries and trilling, mourn—or pretend to.

Dozens of brilliantly-robed priests with colorful parasols marched in dignified unison. A black SUV went by. A liveryman in a red jacket and black top hat like an English fox hunter's drove the horse-drawn, black-canopied hearse. The coffin was draped with Meles' version of the flag and large bouquets of white roses. A framed photograph of the prime minister as a long-haired student rebel was mounted at its foot.

Horsemen, also in red jackets and top hats, and an honor guard of officers with rifles over their shoulders surrounded the hearse. Behind them, column after column of uniformed soldiers stepped smartly in formation. Plain clothes agents in black walked alongside and pensively surveyed the crowd.

The BBC reporter, spiffy in a tan safari suit, darted with a microphone among the guests. A sloppily-dressed cameraman struggled to keep up with him.

"The controversial leader ruled this famine-plagued nation since the victory of his rebel forces in Ethiopia's civil war twenty-one years ago," the reporter continued. "Here is Buddy Schwartz, director of the Help Ethiopia organization that raised millions for famine relief and a good friend of the late prime minister."

The reporter thrust the microphone into Buddy's face. The cameraman crouched and began to film.

"Buddy Schwartz. You're known as a staunch supporter of Prime Minister Meles. What would you like to say on this historic occasion?"

Hanna gave her husband a frightened glance.

"He developed the economy and fought poverty," Buddy said.

"So you still defend him?" the reporter pressed.

The cortege trudged by. A large Ethiopian cross carried by a gloomy priest reminded Buddy of the condolence call they'd made earlier that day. After completing their new daughter's adoption, they'd stopped by the royal chapel to view the open casket and shake hands with a shattered, black-robed Azeb and her tearful children. The cross affixed to the white silk lining above Meles' embalmed face had been a simple, silver cross without Ethiopian Orthodoxy's traditional latticed edges. Maybe someone had noticed God's mercy wasn't so endless after all. Another addition to the goddamned flashbacks, he thought morosely.

"Collective," he murmured, more to himself than to the reporter.

"Excuse me?"

Buddy watched the funeral procession. "He was a great man," he said unconvincingly.

"That was Buddy Schwartz, director of Help Ethiopia," the reporter said. "Here is the American ambassador—"

The reporter brushed past them to the next guest. Buddy put his arm around Hanna. Together, they watched the funeral procession disappear down the broad avenue.

Slowly, the drums, wails and howling grew softer.

Until everything was a small blur in the distance.

An Invitation to the Reader

Money, Blood and Conscience is a work of fiction, but it was written to call attention to an important truth. Meles is dead, but his TPLF, the cause of so much human tragedy, remains, like a wounded animal, a dangerous and destabilizing force.

In April 2018, the beleaguered dictatorship offered up a new prime minister, Abiy Ahmed, who's made many important reforms. Birtukan Mideksa, the former judge and opposition leader, now heads the National Election Board. Repressive laws have been lifted. Some abusive officials have been fired and even arrested. Many political prisoners have been freed. The general atmosphere has improved.

But as of this writing, these hard-won gains are imperiled. Ethiopians, who need and deserve a say in their own affairs as urgently as any people on earth, have not yet had a free and fair election. The TPLF continues to siphon hundreds of millions of dollars out of the economy that are desperately needed to save lives. Plotting a return to power by sowing chaos, it promotes ethnic conflict that's made millions homeless and puts the country in danger of race war.

There's been no accountability for the genocide, politicide (mass murder based on political affiliation) and democide (killing by gross incompetence and neglect) of the Amhara, Oromo, Somali, Anuak, Konso, and other tribes by the TPLF. Punishment of the perpetrators is important if other African mass murderers are to be deterred.

After the Second World War, the West vowed that "never again" would such evil be allowed to occur. Yet it has happened again in Cambodia, Rwanda, Bosnia, Congo, Sudan, Myanmar, and elsewhere. Ethiopia must be added to this list so that its long- ignored story may be preserved for future generations.

You, the reader, can be part of this historic fight for justice. Please follow events not only in Ethiopia but everywhere despotism and poverty afflict the innocent. Support democracy promotion organizations. Tell your elected representatives the poor urgently need empowerment and government that's accountable to them.

It's their fight, but we can stand with Ethiopia and the rest of the world's starving and oppressed.

Let today be the start of a new era in human history when we heed history's lessons.

When "never again" turned from words to action.

David Steinman
April 2019

Acknowledgments

This project would not have been the same without the Taproot Foundation whose wonderful volunteers generously contributed their time and talents. Ilene Goldman, Lori Duin Kelly, Sam Lamont, Andy Mather, Beth Pollak, Kristen Simons and Caera Thornton provided invaluable editorial feedback.

Thanks are due to María Spitaleri and Paul O'Connor for graphic design, Sam Rong for video production, Eugenia Halsey for voiceover services, Chang Liu for strategy and Nishank Chandradhara for technical advice in connection with the book's promotion. Jonathan Lin Davis and Haitham Abdo ably coordinated digital market research. Andrew Chapman of Social Motion Publishing provided suggestions of inestimable worth. Molly Tullis, Colin Raunig and Neha Saraiya coordinated smart and effective public relations. Chandana Gangadhar, Ann Mary Mathew and Molly Flanagan are dedicated social media managers for Operation Conscience, a social campaign to educate the public about Ethiopia's secret holocaust.

Thanks to Bridget Kelly of PIIPA for securing legal assistance and for her moral support.

I must express my appreciation to Abebe Gellaw and Anteneh Merid Emeru for their wide-ranging help and to artist Amanuel Gebre for the map of Ethiopia.

Project managers Andrew Prestage and Nicole Memoly steered the ship with great skill and professionalism through many shoals.

And particular thanks to H.I.H. Prince Ermias Sahle-Selassie Haile-Selassie and H.I.H. Princess Gelila Fesseha Gebre-Selassie, whose patriotism and foresight inspired my first steps on this long journey.

A Special Note

The West cannot make a foreign country free. Only that country's own people can do that.

But we can do more to help them.

Democracy has proven to build international peace and prosperity. And nonviolence—civil resistance that removes a tyrant's support—has proven to be a more humane and cost-effective way to secure democracy than war.

Unfortunately, most people trapped inside dictatorships don't yet know how to use nonviolence for self-liberation. Repression and censorship prevent them from learning how to use it.

The author is pleased to be affiliated with World Liberation Radio, a project to test a novel solution to this problem—using radio to teach nonviolence to oppressed populations on a global basis.

If the pilot project proves successful, World Liberation Radio aims to empower disenfranchised and marginalized people everywhere with nonviolence instruction.

Mass education in nonviolence is important because the planet is once again sinking into authoritarianism. We must act now to avoid an Orwellian future.

Readers interested in learning more about World Liberation Radio and contributing to its crowd funding campaign may visit WorldLiberationRadio.org for more information.

CPSIA information can be obtained
at www.ICGtesting.com
Printed in the USA
LVHW112333271119
638724LV00007B/128/P